Cold Storage, Alaska

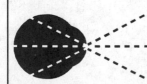

This Large Print Book carries the
Seal of Approval of N.A.V.H.

COLD STORAGE, ALASKA

JOHN STRALEY

THORNDIKE PRESS

A part of Gale, Cengage Learning

GALE
CENGAGE Learning·

Farmington Hills, Mich • San Francisco • New York • Waterville, Maine
Meriden, Conn • Mason, Ohio • Chicago

GALE
CENGAGE Learning®

Copyright © 2014 by John Straley.
Thorndike Press, a part of Gale, Cengage Learning.

ALL RIGHTS RESERVED
Thorndike Press® Large Print Reviewers' Choice.
The text of this Large Print edition is unabridged.
Other aspects of the book may vary from the original edition.
Set in 16 pt. Plantin.

LIBRARY OF CONGRESS CATALOGING-IN-PUBLICATION DATA

Straley, John, 1953–
    Cold Storage, Alaska / by John Straley. — Large print edition.
        pages ; cm. — (Thorndike Press large print reviewers' choice)
    ISBN 978-1-4104-7018-8 (hardcover) — ISBN 1-4104-7018-0 (hardcover)
    1. Ex-convicts—Fiction. 2. Small cities—Alaska—Fiction. 3. Alaska—Fiction.
    4. Large type books. 5. Domestic fiction. I. Title.
    PS3569.T687C65 2014b
    813'.54—dc23   2014008192

Published in 2014 by arrangement with Soho Press, Inc.

Printed in the United States of America
1 2 3 4 5 6 7 18 17 16 15 14

For Sophie Rosen

CHAPTER ONE

Annabelle had put the tea kettle on just moments ago. Now it was whistling, yet she didn't get up to attend to it. Recently the past had become a hallucination constantly intruding into the present moment, so she wasn't certain what really needed doing.

She had been thinking about Franklin Roosevelt: the grinning man with the cigarette holder who was never photographed in his frailty. But now it was early spring in the last year of Bill Clinton's presidency, and all the news was about the president's failings. Flawed men kept ruling the world, and the radio in the corner with the long antennae squealed on and on about it. Not that the news mattered much to Annabelle now. It was raining hard, and all of the events of her life — past, present, and possibly future — were taking on the quality of a slightly malevolent screwball comedy.

She sat in her chair looking out the window. She had been distracted by so many things lately: presidents, family members, and lost animals all swirling around her. The glass on the door rattled, and she looked up expecting to see her uncle, Slippery Wilson, walk in slapping his wet leather gloves against his pants, even though Slippery Wilson had been dead for more than three decades. She found herself listening for crying from the crib, even though both her boys were grown men. The younger one, Miles, was down at the senior center cooking dinner, and Clive was getting out of prison.

"Never matter," Annabelle said aloud to herself. She got up and turned off the radio in the corner.

Throughout the afternoon, she had been trying to remember the joke she had heard the day before. It was good, she remembered, and she thought that it would have been good to tell Miles. But the joke eluded her in its detail.

Out her window, the hillside fell away to the inlet. Alder trees grew quickly on the disturbed ground where the boys had built her house. A gust of wind came, and she thought she saw some darting color. A flash of yellow, she couldn't be sure, but it seemed like a match head exploding. Yellow with red sparks flaring in the trees. She slid her glasses up her nose and was almost certain that she saw the bird fluttering up and away.

"Buddy?" she said aloud, as the kettle boiled over and doused the flame.

On that same day in April 2000, Clive McCahon, Annabelle's oldest son, was released from prison. He was thinking about his plan to get home.

He had hated living in Alaska as a kid. His father had assumed he would become a fisherman. His mother had assumed that no matter how he made his living, it would be made right there in Cold Storage. Only his grandma Ellie had told him not to listen and to dream his own dreams. Having grown up on an island in the North Pacific, Clive had longed for the great American highway. He dreamed of cars and deserts and long, straight roads. Ellie had always given him books about cars for every birthday and Christmas. Cars and guitars, he dreamed of, bands he heard on the radio and beautiful girls who didn't know everything about him. Ellie had understood his itch to move on. Only she seemed to understand that living in Cold Storage, Alaska, was like being born into a small maze where everyone constantly bumped into one another. As soon as his father died in the Thanksgiving Day storm, Clive had left. He had flown north to Haines, bought a car without ever owning a license, without ever learning to drive, and took off. He was fifteen. Ellie's ashes had been scattered at sea and his father's body had never been found, so he didn't consider that he had anything holding him to his cloistered island town.

Clive was thirty-five now. It was early April, and the clouds were clearing away after a morning rain. The air was so clean it almost burned his lungs. Clive had served seven out of his ten-year sentence in McNeil Island Penitentiary, and he was wearing his old court clothes: a dark blue suit his mother had bought him on one of his few visits home as an adult, now far too tight in his shoulders and upper arms. Feeling the sun cut through the trees, he set his cardboard box on the ground, slipped off the coat, folded it neatly, and placed it on top of the box. He had called ahead to order a cab.

There were only a few people getting off the prison boat, mostly staff members carrying lunch boxes and rain gear. There was one other inmate, a skinny white kid with red hair who walked down the dock to meet an old man waiting beside a sputtering Ford LTD. The convict approached, the man opened the passenger side door, and a woman in a blue house dress got out and threw her arms around the boy before he could put down his gear. She cried and snuffled into his neck, while the old man rubbed the back of his shoulders.

Clive shifted from one foot to another, waiting for his ride. A yellow minivan finally rolled up.

"You Stilton Cheesewright?"

Clive was still watching the kid being greeted by the old couple. He wondered if he had seen the kid inside but didn't recognize him. He hadn't recognized the false name the cabbie was saying, either.

"You're Stilton Cheesewright, yeah?" the driver said again. He reached behind and opened the back door of the van.

"Absolutely." Clive didn't know why he'd given the cab company a false name; it was simply the first name that popped into his head and had nothing at all to do with the plan. He set his box of personal effects in the back seat, slammed the door, and walked around to sit in the front passenger seat.

"You want to go to a grocery store?" He

11

squinted at his run sheet.

"That's right," Clive said. "If it's not too much trouble."

"No problem, Mr. Cheesewright. Would you like me to wait while you shop?"

"Naw . . . just drop me. I might be a while," Clive said, but then added, "You know a place with really fresh lettuce?"

The driver smiled. "I think if you want the really fresh stuff you should go over to the Farmfresh store down Sixth. It's good, you know. They really do buy it from the farmers and everything. It's a couple of miles out of town, but it's worth it."

"Perfect," said Clive. The driver punched the meter and wheeled to his left, down the road away from the prison.

Clive watched the fence posts stutter by. He watched the sunlight filter through the evergreen trees, and he watched a cow eating in a green field, a rusty bell hung from her neck. She lifted her head as the cab sped past, and Clive could imagine the soft clonking of her bell. Clive asked to stop for a moment; the driver put on the turn signal and eased the van to the gravelly edge of the road. Clive thanked him, leaned back in the cab's mildewed seat, and smiled. He sat that way for a few moments, smiling and listening for the cow's bell.

12

"You do a long stretch?" the driver asked.

Clive nodded, his eyes closed. "Yes," he said. "It's time to go home, I guess."

"You want me to get going?" the driver asked.

Clive nodded again, his eyes still closed.

"Let's go get you some lettuce then," the driver said, and pulled the blinker all the way down, rolling the cab back onto the road.

Clive was both happy and nervous. He had looked forward to this day with an urgency that few people who haven't been in prison could know. But just as it was happening he felt a kind of raw anxiety. He could not go back to crime, and although he had scrubbed his mind clean, he knew that in this world of free men he understood little else besides crime. Crime was now, in his new state of mind, too chaotic, too unpredictable. Clive wanted to be rooted to something as certain as the rising of the sun.

McNeil was an old federal prison that had been remodeled as a medium security jail when it was turned over to the state of Washington. The Birdman of Alcatraz had actually done most of his time at McNeil. The main building had the original feel of the place: thick iron doors, WPA-style murals on the walls of the mess hall. It could have been a large public library in some small Midwestern town if it weren't for all the sex offenders.

In jail, Clive had been known as the "Milkman," for that's what the newspapers had dubbed him. He had been a semifamous drug dealer when he had been caught — famous for his method of delivering his drugs and famous for never snitching on his customers or his partners.

He had seen arterial blood spurting and painting the shower floor red. He had seen the black holes that handmade knives leave in young white skin. He had heard all the swearing that there was in the world and the blubbery threats made through spit-stuffed lips. All he wanted now was peace. No grittiness. He was done with it. He would always be a sinner, he knew that, but he could at least try not to sin as much. He had thought that even if he could cut back on his sinning by ten percent, that would still leave him plenty of room, while giving him a shot at some minor redemption at least.

In the last three years, he had purposely kept himself in segregation. He told the jailers he was going to be killed and that was the truth of it, but that was not what mattered. He wanted the quiet of the stone slice of ten by ten, the only noise a basketball bouncing on echoing concrete in the exercise yard where they let the segregated inmates out, one at a time, an hour and fifteen minutes every day.

All he took into segregation with him was a Bible and a pencil. He kept his journal in the margins.

It wasn't until the beginning of his third year in segregation that he started listening to bugs. A blue fly landed on the edge of the Bible page, which was open to Numbers. The fly twitched what he imagined to be its filthy legs. The spidery printing of the first word was almost the size of the fly itself:

How can I curse whom God has not
    cursed?
How can I denounce whom the Lord has
    not denounced?
For from the top of the crags I see him,
From the hills I behold him;
Behold a people dwelling alone,
And not counting itself among the nations.

"What?" Clive said aloud, leaning even farther toward the book. "What was that?" But the fly had not said anything.

■ ■ ■ ■

There were two picnic tables beside the store where Clive was going to eat his salad. Cigarette butts fanned out on the pavement. An overflowing garbage can sat next to a bike rack. Clive brought his packages out and set them down carefully. He had asked the produce manager to wash all of the vegetables. He had bought a plastic bowl, a cutting board, a knife, and some bottled oil and vinegar dressing. He reached inside his bag and took the knife and the cutting board out first. A kid, riding a trick bike in the parking lot, stopped long enough to stare at the skinny man in the dark suit smelling a tomato, then hopped the bike onto the rack, skidded down the top pipe on his cranks, landed, and wheeled away.

The spring weather in western Washington was strangely warm. Clive sat and slowly cut the vine-ripened hothouse tomatoes. He washed all the vegetables under the outside spigot once again, just to be certain. He peeled the carrots and sliced them into thin strips. He had two kinds of lettuce, one red pepper, a bottle of artichoke hearts, and one fresh avocado. He spoke to no one, but chopped and sliced with great deliberation.

After all the vegetables were laid out in his bowl, he stared at them and licked a bit of ripe avocado off his fingers. He added the fresh Dungeness crab meat to the salad. He opened a bottle of white wine and poured himself a glass. He said a short prayer, swore that he would never eat canned spaghetti or unidentifiable meat ever again, and ate his first meal in the free world.

The bottle of wine was three-quarters empty by the time the cabdriver came back to check on Clive. He was sitting at the picnic table with his back against the building; long shadows from the poplar trees next door played out across the parking lot. The salad was gone, and Clive had the wine bottle stuck down between his legs and a plastic fork in his mouth.

The cab rolled up on the crunching gravel and came to a stop. The driver lowered his window.

"You got a place for tonight, Stilton?"

"No, I guess not." Clive pulled the fork out of his mouth.

"You got a plan?" He fished out his smokes.

"Oh yes, I have a plan." He looked back at the cabdriver. "Foolproof."

It was only then that Clive noticed that the driver had brought a little dog back with him. The corgi stood now on the driver's lap, sniffing the damp air through the open window.

"What's your dog's name?" Clive asked.

"Bandit," the driver replied, and the dog wiggled up and put his whole head out the window.

"You haven't got a plan," the dog said.

"Excuse me?" Clive said, a little distressed, for never before had he heard an animal speak so clearly. But then again it had been a while since he had seen such a large non-human animal.

"You got a place to go?" the driver asked.

"Sort of. I'm going to pick up my dog." Clive offered the driver the bottle of wine. "Then I'm going back to Alaska."

"It's a long way to Alaska," the driver said, and took a drink from the bottle. "You're going to need some money for that."

"Well, that's what the plan's about," Clive said. "I've got my money the same place where my dog is."

Bandit sniffed the air again and shot his ears straight forward. "You don't have a plan," the corgi said again. Which distressed Clive all the more. The dog was telling the truth.

"I got a little travel trailer out back of my place. You can spend the night there if you want," the driver said as he stroked the little dog's head.

"No. I'll be all right," Clive insisted.

"Get in," Bandit said, and Clive gathered his things.

CHAPTER TWO

The joke went like this: The doctor comes back into the waiting room and tells his patient, "I'm sorry, Mr. Smith, but I have some bad news. It appears you have only eleven minutes to live." The horrified patient beseeches him, "Please, doctor, isn't there something you can do for me?" The doctor looks around the room and at his watch and says, "Well, I suppose I could boil you an egg."

The joke was everywhere on the boardwalk. It seemed to Miles McCahon that it had infected the residents of Cold Storage like a flu virus. He heard it everywhere, and he was beginning to wonder why.

Maybe it was the darkness or the rain. Maybe it was the fact that almost everyone in Cold Storage was either clinically depressed or drunk most of the time. But they *loved* that joke, and Miles was beginning to take it personally.

Miles had spent most of his life in Cold Storage. There had been trips out for a few years in college and his years in the Army Rangers. When his brother had gone to jail in 1993, Miles had been in Mogadishu as a medic with his delta team and had mustered out soon after that well-publicized mess. He had told himself he was never again going to leave the quiet of Cold Storage, but now he was beginning to wonder.

Miles was the medical technician and physician's assistant in a village without a doctor. He splinted broken bones and stopped bleeding. He stitched up severe cuts and treated people for shock. He monitored medications and researched medical issues for the 150 residents of this failing fishing village on the outer coast of southeastern Alaska. He was the closest thing to a doctor they had, and maybe it was for this reason he didn't get the same amount of glee from the joke as everybody else obviously did.

Miles was cooking Sunday dinner at the community center. He had used some of the money left over from a health and prevention education grant the previous PA had written. That PA had tried to hold classes on heart disease and diabetes; he had started "Healthwise" informational gatherings to which only a few people came,

21

but none of those people were the ones who really needed the information. The principal of the school and the secretary came to the first two classes, the city administrator and her husband came to a few more, and then nobody came. The PA left town after six months.

But the money had to be spent because the administrators in Sitka could not show unspent money in their program at the end of the fiscal year. They phoned Miles and told him to do whatever he could to clear the account. The administrators had kissed a lot of ass in Washington to get these funds, and it would be an insult to leave them unspent. So Miles started hosting dinner parties on Sundays. He tried to cook reasonably healthy food, but health concerns couldn't get in the way of turnout. This Sunday he was cooking three meat loaves, each roughly the size of a carry-on luggage bag.

"I don't see why you can't buy us some beer," complained Ellen from her wheelchair next to the Jell-O molds.

"Ellen, I can't buy alcohol with the health education and prevention money. We've been through this. I'm already on thin ice for the cheesecakes and heavy cream."

"That's just like government thinking,"

the old woman wheezed. "I mean, what if — I'm saying *what if* — I'm going back to my place for a beer and I slip and break my hip? What the hell kind of health education is that?"

Bob Gleason piped up, "You're not going to break a hip. You always drink someone else's beer." Here he nodded toward Miles. "Besides, you ride that frigging wheelchair everywhere you go, even though there's not a frigging thing wrong with your legs."

Ellen didn't give even a hint she'd heard Bob's comments. "Miles, you could at least buy us some beer," she insisted, "if you were really serious about doing a good job."

"Listen, Ellen, next week I could maybe include some non-alcoholic beer in the order."

Ellen stared up at him with strange, squinting eyes as if he had suddenly started speaking Japanese. "Non-alcoholic beer?" she asked feebly. She reached a claw-like hand for something to hang on to, accidentally landing it in a bowl of raspberry Jell-O with bananas hovering at the top.

"Somebody better get her medication," came a wheezing voice from over by the furnace.

"Take more than near-beer to kill her. Better men than us have tried." Bob levered a shingle-sized slice of meat loaf onto his plate, set it next to the pond of gravy in the potatoes. "Goddamn, this looks good, Miles. Don't have any boiled turnips, do you?" He held out his plate.

As luck would have it, Miles did, and he ladled them out quickly. Bob's hand wavered, and hot water slopped against the side of the old man's thumb.

"Christ, Miles, watch what you're doing, would ya?"

"I'm sorry." Miles handed him a napkin. "I'm just kind of in a hurry."

"I heard." Bob nodded knowingly, staring down at his plate of food. "There's a cop here to talk to you." He reached onto his plate, fingered a slice of turnip up into his mouth. "It's about your brother."

Miles wiped his hands on a dishcloth and took off his apron. He walked out the door without saying a word to anyone.

The police officer, Ray Brown, had sent word to Miles that he was in town as soon as he'd gotten off the floatplane. Miles had been in the middle of getting the giant meat loaves ready and so had arranged to meet with the trooper at the clinic later in the day, just before Brown's plane took off for Juneau. That way, he thought, he could talk with the officer and then walk him back to the hall to check on the community dinner. It might be a good thing to have a police officer with him when he returned, in case any fights broke out in his absence.

Miles wasn't eager to show that police officer around. No matter where they were from, visitors always wanted to ask questions. They started with history: why is this place here? To this Miles would usually answer, "Fish . . . mostly." He longed to tell the whole story but the truth was people didn't really want to know.

What they really wanted to ask was, "Why in the hell would anyone live here?"

But to truly understand, it helped to know the whole story. Just walking around town you wouldn't feel the history of the place, wouldn't know its old jokes or see the ghosts who still roamed around in everyone's memory.

Cold Storage, Alaska, was first settled by white men in 1934. These white men were a group of Norwegian fishermen looking for a place to ride out the storms on the outer coast. They drove a few pilings and ran a boardwalk along the edge of a steep-sided fjord. They chose it because of the good anchorage with protection from all four directions of the compass. But as one of the Norsky fishermen put it, "She's hell for

25

snug except when it's coming straight down."

Cold Storage got approximately 200 inches of rain a year; the exact number was subject to debate. That rain led to the second reason the old Norskies chose to build on this particular spot: a natural hot spring just off the beach where the thermally heated water dribbled out between the rocks. The old fishermen cribbed up some walls and a roof and made a quite passable tub where they could lounge in the warm water while watching their wooden boats ride at anchor out in the bay.

In 1935, the town got an infusion of energy when a battered logger, a woman Wobbly, and her little girl with glasses fled the mine strike in Juneau in a leaky dory and made the place their home. The logger was named Slippery Wilson. The woman was named Ellie Hobbes. She was a pilot and a committed anarchist. The little girl with the thick glasses was Annabelle. When Slip and Ellie built the first store, the old fishermen complained that the town was growing too fast. But when Ellie turned the store into a bar a few years later, the complaining stopped.

No one in his family had been fond of the police. It wasn't an active antagonism, it was more of a wary indifference bolstered by living in a town some ninety air miles from a police station. There had been the old man who ran the supply boat who had been some kind of detective in Seattle. But that was long ago, and he had never done any policing in Cold Storage. The old Seattle detective was dead now, and only a few of the older people remembered the stories about him.

Miles stopped at the door of the clinic and put his hand on the cold metal knob. He didn't want to go in, but as he considered going back to his meat loaf, the door jerked open, and Ray Brown stood before him in an immaculate blue state trooper uniform. He was pressed and tidy. His round, brimmed, Mountie-style hat had gold braid laid out against the blue. He was imposing, like a patriotic monument of some sort. It made Miles feel a little like Jeanette Mac-Donald.

"McCahon!" Brown barked, as if giving Miles permission to have the name. He jutted out his hand. "Ray Brown. How are ya?"

"I'm doing well, thanks," Miles began. He was about to mention the fine weather for flying and maybe add something about going fishing if there was time.

"Two things," Brown lumbered on. "First,

a little bit of shop and then some personal business."

"Personal business?" Miles walked around the big trooper to pick up the coffee pot sitting on a table in a corner of the waiting room. The coffee had been reheating for weeks as far as Miles knew. He just turned the same coffee on and off every day and evening. It didn't matter because no one ever drank it. He kept it there only to chase people out of the clinic.

"That's second. The first thing has to do with Harold Miller. Do you know him?"

"Coffee?" Miles held out the pot.

"No, I'm topped off." Brown patted his flat stomach. "Harold Miller?"

"I know a Mouse Miller." Miles put the pot back into the plastic coffee maker.

Brown unsnapped the breast pocket of his shirt, took out a small notebook and flipped through the pages. "I think that's him. Fisherman." Then Brown rattled off a social security number.

Miles looked for any trace of humor, any sign that the trooper was going to relax. It didn't seem likely. "I don't know Mouse's Social Security number, but the date sounds like it matches his age. How can I help you, officer?" Miles sat down on a chair next to the coffee pot.

Brown remained standing, and for a second Miles worried he was going to click his heels together.

"Harold Miller has been reported missing. I'd like to get some information together."

"I haven't seen Mouse around. Have you been down to his boat?"

Brown had started writing in his notebook, didn't answer the question. After a long silence, he lowered the notebook and asked, "When was the last time you think you saw him?"

"Geez . . . I don't know, couple of weeks ago. I don't know if he even has family here in town. I think I heard he was going to fly in to Juneau for some change of scenery for his drinking."

"Ex-wife," Brown said to the notebook, "he had an ex-wife."

"Really? I didn't know Mouse was married." And then in a bright voice, a bit curious, "Who's his ex?"

The trooper was writing again. He looked up with a vaguely thoughtful expression on his face. "So, would you say it was two weeks ago that you saw him last?"

Miles leaned back and scanned the paint on the ceiling. "I don't remember exactly." If Trooper Brown had shown any trace of

29

humor or humility, Miles might have offered to look at his calendar to see if there were any notations, but he didn't.

"Okay." Brown stabbed a period emphatically onto a page. "It's just a formality. He's probably sleeping it off somewhere." He clicked his ballpoint pen as if unchambering a round, put the pen and notebook back into his front shirt pocket, and pulled another chair away from the wall and around to face Miles. He sat down, knee to knee with the PA. Miles sat up straight and put his coffee cup down.

"Now, two," Brown said. "I believe you have a family member who is incarcerated?"

Miles waited, wondering if that was the final form the question was going to take. "Actually, if you include my extended family, I have several relations who might still be serving time. Maybe you could be a little bit more specific."

"So, that's the way it's going to be." Brown stared down at Miles for several long moments.

"Excuse me, Trooper Brown, is there some reason that you're being rude?" Miles smiled and tried again to be friendly.

Trooper Brown didn't hesitate and didn't smile. "I don't like drugs, and I don't like Satan worshipers."

Miles looked perplexed. "Wow! No. I mean, who does? Well, drugs . . . I assume you are not opposed to penicillin, unless you are a Christian Scientist?"

The Trooper waved him off. "Your brother worked for a major drug dealer in Seattle. I don't want him moving his business into Alaska."

"First thing, Trooper, I haven't heard from Clive in years. I have no reason to think that he's going to come to Alaska after his release. Frankly, I doubt it, and even if he does, I have absolutely no reason to believe that he will be engaged in any illegal activity. This is not exactly a promising spot to go into the drug trade. Unless you had some blood pressure meds or fiber supplements you wanted to move."

"You are a veteran . . . Army Rangers, is that right?" Brown said.

"That's right," he said patiently.

"*You* were the guy in that photograph?" This was neither a question nor a conversation starter; it sounded more like an accusation.

"I know the one." Miles's flat voice did not invite further comment.

"That was some shit, huh?"

"Yes, it was some shit, all right."

"But that doesn't mean I want your

31

brother up here selling drugs."

Miles was beginning to wonder if Trooper Brown had some kind of neurological damage or perhaps a kind of Tourette's syndrome that manifested itself in non sequiturs. "Trooper Brown, does this somehow tie back around to Satan worship? If not, I'll keep my eyes open for Mouse Miller and if I find out anything, I'll be sure to let you know. And if my brother shows up and is involved in any illegal activity, I'll let you know that, too."

Brown leaned forward. "I've heard things. I've heard things about a Weasel character and about drugs off shore and about his sick movies and about his gatherings of men. Listen, I don't care if you are some kind of war hero. If I get one whiff that you're allowing some Satanists to use drugs or that your brother is back in business, if he gets one strange package, if he makes one phone call to his old associates back in the Seattle area, I'll have him and anyone who helps him" — Trooper Brown paused and stared at Miles for emphasis — "back in jail so fast it will make their head swim."

A swimming head, Miles thought to himself. What does that really mean anyway? "Look, we've gotten off to a bad start." Miles tried to brighten the tone of his voice.

"You've never been here before, have you? Let me show you around town. I'll give you the whole tour. It will help you get to know the place. We can ask around about Mouse."

"Thanks for the offer." Brown's smile was icy. "But I can do my own legwork. I was born in Alaska, you know."

"Ah!" Miles said, as if long-term residency explained and forgave everything. He walked over to the door of the clinic and opened it.

"Let me explain something to you." Brown loomed over Miles. "Your brother has an old associate named Jake Shoemaker. He's a smart guy, he has a lot of holdings in Seattle, and a lot of money. Your brother never gave up this Jake Shoemaker, and let's say Jake owes him now."

"All right, let's say that," Miles said, smiling to the scowling face of the trooper.

"We have reason to believe that right now your brother is looking to reestablish contact with Jake Shoemaker. I also have reason to know that law enforcement in Washington is very interested in taking Jake Shoemaker down. So if you hear from Clive, you tell him to talk to me right now. You understand? If he sells one ounce of product in this state, he's going away for much longer than the seven-year bid he just did. But if he helps us put Jake away, he can breathe easy for a long time. You understand me, Miles?"

"I understand, Trooper, but this is all theoretical as far as I'm concerned. I have not heard from my brother, and I honestly doubt that I ever will."

"Really!" the Trooper boomed. "Well, we know that there are people right now bringing drugs in off the coast of this town. Right this second."

"This second? Wow. You better get to arresting somebody then!"

The Trooper put his hand on the doorknob to leave. "Your mother's name is Annabelle. Isn't that right?" asked Brown, as if he knew every thought Miles had ever had.

"That's right, it's Annabelle. You know, that's a great idea. You should go talk to her."

Not expecting this answer, Brown squinted at him.

Miles walked over and tapped the big blue policeman on the chest hard enough that they could both feel the bulletproof vest underneath the uniform. "But I'd be sitting on this if you're going to talk shit about Clive to Annabelle." Miles raised his eyebrows, faintly nodded. "And while you're at it why don't you ask her about Satan worship?"

Brown turned and walked out the door.

"I've got to get out of this town," Miles sighed to himself. The only thing keeping him from walking down to the boat dock right now and striking out was the possibility of being there when Annabelle gave Trooper Brown a monumental ass chewing.

Annabelle lived alone in a damp frame house near the end of the boardwalk and up a set of stairs into the hillside. She had not been feeling well for the last three months, and Miles had tried to talk her into going to the hospital in Sitka. She had chronic heart disease and diabetes, but lately she'd been losing weight and her color was not good. Miles suspected she had something new, something more serious going on, but he didn't know. Neither did Annabelle. Miles wanted to find out, but Annabelle did not.

Miles thought about that as he watched Brown's lumbering figure barrel down the boardwalk. Miles had tried to talk his mother into moving to Arizona where the hospitals were clean and warm, where they could sort out what was going on with her health, where she could eat avocado sandwiches and watch the Mariners on TV.

"I don't even like avocados. What in the heck are you talking about?" She'd shaken her head bitterly. "Besides Arizona? What do I look like? A cactus?" She shook her head again and looked out the window, closing the book on the subject.

Miles knew it wasn't Arizona that was the problem. Annabelle didn't want to leave Cold Storage because she was waiting for Clive. She imagined seeing her older son, tall and rangy, walking in the door of her house. He would have some outrageous story to tell about who he had met on the road and what adventures they had gotten him involved in. Miles was a good boy, but Clive made her laugh. Clive would lift her off her feet and swing her around the kitchen while Miles fretted about what might get broken.

Recently, Annabelle had been considering the possibility that she might not be alive by the time Clive walked through her door again. Still, she did not want to leave Cold Storage. She suspected the weight loss and the weakness was cancer, but it didn't matter that much to her. She liked the taste of the meals Miles cooked. She liked to watch the tapes of old movies she had flown out from town. She liked to do needlepoint in the late afternoon while the tea kettle rumbled on the oil stove, and she liked listening to the rain. Death was no big deal, she told herself. At least she was under her own tin roof and not in some concrete jail.

Miles waited a few minutes before walking back up the boardwalk. As far as Satan went, there were only two signs of the Dark Lord in Cold Storage. One was a band that two kids had tried to start called the Boomerang Bombers, which had caused quite a stir in the school about six years ago. The boys, Ajax and Billy, painted pentagrams on the school district's drumheads and had to write a letter of apology and work at the school for two weeks during spring break. As far as Miles knew, the Boomerang Bombers had never played a public performance, but out of solidarity for the only death metal band along the coast, the man named Weasel had the band's name and a pentagram tattooed to his shoulder, fostering the rumor that Weasel was some kind of Satanist mentor to the boys. Which was dismissed as far too ambitious for Weasel by anyone who knew him.

By the time he got within sight of the community center, Miles could tell Trooper Brown was ready to leave. A loud screeching voice was issuing from the windows like smoke. Miles couldn't make out the words, but old people were steadily streaming out of the front door. Some were using their canes, a couple had walkers, but they were making remarkably good time. They moved as if flames licked their heels.

Miles reached the door just as Trooper Brown hurried out. His face was scarlet, almost as if he'd been burned, and he was trying to put his notebook into his pocket but seemed to be having trouble finding the front of his shirt. Miles didn't say a word. The trooper looked at him momentarily, averted his eyes, took two steps away from the community center.

"Did you find Mom? I think she's in here," Miles said evenly, without sarcasm.

But Trooper Brown was in some sort of preverbal state of rage or perhaps shock. He had never before been tongue-lashed by an old lady in a wheelchair. Annabelle was probably lucky he hadn't pepper-sprayed her.

"D . . . D . . . D . . ." the trooper tried to say.

"Don't leave town?" Miles offered. "Don't worry, we'll be here. We'll keep an eye out for Mouse. Have a safe flight." Miles waved, turned, and walked into the community center.

Bob Gleason was standing by the door,

eager to greet Miles. "By God! You missed it, Miles. She unloaded both barrels on him. I'm telling you, I've worked in logging camps some thirty years and I've never heard the likes." He grinned.

Miles looked over to where Annabelle sat by herself, tears rolling down her cheeks. He walked over and handed her a paper napkin. "Got something on your chin." He didn't look at her, didn't draw attention to anything in particular.

"You're a doll," the old woman said. She took the paper napkin and held his hand for a moment, took several deep breaths as if shaking off some great exertion or bad dream. "That wasn't really a cop, was it?" she asked.

"State trooper. I guess he found you, huh?"

"Oh my God, Miles." Annabelle smiled up at the younger of her two sons. "You know what your father would have called someone like that?"

"Well, there are several names I think he might have used." He smiled back, remembering.

"He would have used some choice King's English on him," sniffed Annabelle.

"Yes, I suppose he would have." Miles laughed.

"My God," she huffed. "You remember Uncle George?"

"Dimly," Miles said. "I was just tiny when he died."

"Well, he was a good man, and he had been a cop. I told you about how he didn't arrest Slip and Ellie, haven't I?"

"Yes, you have, Mom." Her son smiled and stroked her thin arm.

"If that flibbertigibet of a cop thinks I'm going to drop a dime on Clive before he's even done anything wrong, then . . . well, then . . . I just don't know."

Miles smiled at her. His mother had always peppered her speech with crime jargon she had gotten mostly from Travis McGee novels. But he noticed she used more of it after Clive had gone to jail. Miles thought it was her way of showing loyalty to her wildest son.

She sat smoking her cigarette, remarkably tranquil for a woman who had apparently used some choice King's English on an officer of the law.

"You really think Clive will be here soon?" She stared out into the swirls of smoke surrounding her head.

"I don't know, Ma."

She looked around the room at the dishes of uneaten food sitting right where people had left them before fleeing: meat loaf and cooked cabbage, potato salad, and gelatin. She smiled.

"Say, Miles?" Annabelle looked up at her son. "Can you do something for me?" She snubbed out her cigarette and slid her glasses up her nose.

"Sure, Ma." They both knew he worried about her. "What did you have in mind?"

"Could you boil me an egg?"

Bob Gleason broke into applause.

After the dust settled, diners started creeping back into the community hall; they hadn't forgotten their free dinners. Miles sat by himself in a corner, listening to people talk, eating some of his own meat loaf and mashed turnips. Bob and a friend from Juneau were doing the dishes, laughing, joking, calling out to people in the hall. When they were done, Miles made himself an extra sandwich and wrapped it up. He waited until he heard the trooper's float-plane take off, stuffed the sandwich into his wool coat, and walked down to the floating dock where his skiff was tied.

It had been years since Miles had caught a king salmon. He had spent hours in his boat dragging a line through the water. He used the right gear, fished at the right depth,

41

trolled at the right speed, and still he had been denied. He had a subsistence permit and had dipnetted enough sockeye salmon to smoke up for the winter. He had brought in coho salmon and chums when they were running. But there was nothing quite like catching a king salmon. The electric tug and the zing of line spooling off into the deep green. It had been so long since he had had that feeling. He longed for it like an old man longing for youth.

Tonight as he scanned the sky and checked the wind fluttering through the pennants in the rigging of the few boats left in the harbor, he was — despite all odds — flush with optimism.

He walked down the boardwalk, noticing the soft spots in the planking. Rot was creeping up from the water through the pilings and in around the edges of the entire town. He could smell mildew, sooty diesel stoves venting out of broken stacks, a whiff of fish slime, and the egginess of the thermal water trapped in the old, concrete bathing tub.

It was early spring; he would have enough daylight for fishing. The herring had been spawning late on the outer coast, and he had heard people were catching king salmon out at the mouth of the bay. He was determined to bring one home.

Miles had an aluminum skiff with a temperamental outboard motor. He had fought the engine, sworn at it, even threatened it with violence. Only in the last three months had Miles's relationship with the cranky piece of equipment changed; he now tried to think of it as a kind of teacher, one with the temperament of a wild animal. If you wanted something from an outboard such as this, you had to display the virtues of understanding and patience. If you rushed up to it and started jerking on the starter cord, the soul of the machine would immediately fly out into the cold air and what would be left on the stern was an inert pile of metal. You could pull on that cord until your knuckles bled. You could change plugs and clean the fuel filters. It would not matter. The engine was no longer of this earth. It was as if the outboard were watching him from the trees as he pulled and swore and pulled and swore until steam rose from his sweater and sweat stung his eyes.

Miles arranged everything in the skiff carefully; the trooper had put him in a bad mood. He took a deep breath and slowly let it out before speaking softly and gently to all the equipment.

"Well, old girl, I've heard there are fish

out there. What do you say to going out there with me?" He patted the machine, checked the mixture of the fuel. Whenever he could, he'd add some of the fresh gas stored in a sealed jug under the hatch. He pumped the bulb on the fuel line and pulled the choke halfway out. He pulled three times until the engine sputtered.

Closing off the choke, he opened the throttle halfway, then paused to say a few words he had settled on months ago and never changed. In a perfectly serious voice, free of irony, he spoke: "I want to thank you for all the hard work you've done in your life. I promise I'll treat you well today."

The sun hung behind thin and ragged clouds. Across the bay, Miles saw a raven watching him, sitting all by itself, shrugging and ruffling its feathers in the wind. Lonely, Miles thought. Lonely for the irascible soul of the outboard engine.

The light at the head of the bay was silver grey now above the dark green sea. Beyond the few islands to the west lay only the Gulf and distant Kamchatka in Asia. To the east, mountains rose up two thousand feet on both sides of the inlet and eased back against the more fractured and eroded slopes of the outer coast. Here the sky widened, and the wind freshened. Here the

44

swells were larger, and the breeze carried the smell of waves broken apart on the shore. As he ran up and over the smooth swells coming in off the coast, Miles passed through occasional warm pools of air; they carried the scent of cedar trees from the outer islands.

Just ahead, gulls circled a tight ring of water, and Miles began to slow the motor. He saw dark squalls rolling in toward the coast from the north, but to the south, clouds floated almost white, threaded with blue. The gulls were diving on some tiny silver fish. Herring, Miles guessed, although he couldn't see them clearly enough to tell for sure.

He quickly rigged his salmon pole and lowered the throttle on the skiff's engine as far as it would go. He picked up a green hoochie, a small plastic squid surrounding a hook that danced behind the twisting motion of a silver flasher. Miles watched the progress of the dark squalls to the north; he didn't want to be caught in the rain. He let the flasher drag out perhaps thirty-five feet behind him, snapped his line onto a downrigger with a small cannonball attached to a wire cable pulled by a hand crank, and adjusted his reel's drag, keeping his thumb on the spool of monofilament line. He lowered the cannonball to sixty feet beneath the boat, played out the line from his reel; the tip of his pole bent over from the weight of the rigging.

Miles put his rod into the pole holder and navigated a course through the circle of feeding birds. If a fish didn't bite, he would move, change depths, change gear. For now, though, he let out a long breath, eased back against the plastic seat bolted onto the hard wooden bench built into the skiff.

Miles loved this kind of slow fishing. Since returning to Cold Storage, he had rediscovered his respect for the uneventful life.

Miles had served in the first Gulf War. All it had left him with was an almost unquenchable thirst and a sliver of metal in his shoulder. There had been a photograph of him in a national news magazine, the one to which the trooper had referred. The image of Miles helping another bleeding man into a helicopter had spun its way around the world. The image meant nothing to him now. He could not, nor did he want to, recognize himself in the photo.

Miles's father had been a good fisherman who had disappeared off the coast in a storm while Miles was a small boy. But he didn't dwell on grief. He had been satisfied with where he was. Even as a fatherless boy,

Miles had loved the little cabin on the water and the thousands of acres of ancient forest just up the hill. In this he was like his old Uncle Slip, who had loved every unchanging stone and tree of the place. Though Slippery Wilson was good with tools and hard work, he was uninterested in catching fish, and Miles was beginning to think he might have inherited some of the old man's bad luck.

Somewhere near his skiff, a loud exhalation of breath woke Miles from his thoughts. Miles fussed with the drag on his reel. First he tightened it, and then he loosened it back up. He unscrewed the top of his water jug and drank about half of it down.

He heard the loud breath again and scanned the waves. The western sky glowed with a pink haze above the wavering line of the horizon; the view of the outer coast was blocked by islands, their humps glowing with silver and tipped with red as the sun washed over the curve of the ocean.

Underneath his boat, a cloud of silver fish roiled in the green. He could hear them boiling up on the surface. He reached over and turned off the motor. The sea was thick with herring pushing their quicksilver bodies into the air and slapping them down on the surface. The air smelled cold, oily.

Down below, he could see large slices of silver shoot under his hull.

Miles, twitching with energy, lifted his pole from the holder. The drag was rolling, and he tightened it down slowly. A large salmon leaped into the air a hundred feet from the boat, a rail of pure lightning coming up out of the darkness of the water. Miles pulled back hard, felt a sudden and heavy jerk; his fish was gone.

The water was quiet. The cloud of silver had moved on. But he heard the breath again, and he held tightly to the side of his skiff, half expecting to be nudged by an orca whale chasing the school of fish.

He looked in all directions, even peering into the sky, until he caught sight of a sea lion some twenty feet behind him, its head steady above the water, seemingly impervious to the motion of the waves. Its eyes glowed milky brown with sympathy and from its mouth drooped a king salmon, graceful as flowing mercury.

"Goddamn it!" Miles shouted.

The sea lion looked at him for a long moment, shook itself, huffed a short breath, then dove under the waves.

"You son of a bitch!" Miles yelled out over the cowling of the outboard to the ripple of water left on the surface. "Bring me back that fish."

But the sea lion was gone, and Miles was left with the food in his freezer. Muttering about bad luck, he tied off the loose end of his line, lay his pole down on the floor of the boat, and jerked on the starter cord. No response. He pulled again. Silence.

He shouldn't have been swearing. Miles knew that. And now he knew he might as well get used to the idea of sitting out in the bay for a long time. He would sit and take some deep breaths, try to get his mind right so he could coax the soul of the cranky machine back into the boat.

CHAPTER THREE

Lester Frank was the only Tlingit Indian living full-time in Cold Storage. There were traditional native villages elsewhere in the area: Hoonah, Sitka, Juneau, Angoon; even Pelican had native communities. Cold Storage had Lester Frank, a contemporary artist who lived next door to the clinic. Miles had asked him once why he had moved to Cold Storage, and Lester had given his characteristic answer: "I study white people."

Lester carved wood and silver. He painted in acrylic and even sculpted in stone. He said he was writing a book about white people called *Circling the Wagons,* but no one had ever seen even a scrap of a manuscript.

Lester's house was one large, square room with a smoky wood stove sunk down three steps in the center. His bed was high up in one corner, a kitchen was in another corner, and everything else was desk, bookshelves, and studio space. As Miles walked up the boardwalk from the dock, Lester stuck his head out the shoreside window and yelled down, "Oy, Doc! Where's all the fish?"

"In the sea where they belong." His voice was barely loud enough to carry.

"I got tacos. Plenty of them and good tomatoes, too. You come up and eat." He shut his window without waiting for a reply.

Miles went into the clinic and checked the bulletin board for messages. He looked at the answering machine to see if anyone had called. The relay towers up on the ridges were always being blown over and phone service was sketchy; there would be weeks in the winter without any telephone contact at all. Tonight there was a fine, strong dial tone but no messages.

The sky was almost dark, and the air thick with moisture as Miles walked up the stairs to his apartment. He hung his wool coat in front of the oil heater, reached into his refrigerator to grab a bottle of sparkling apple cider, and went back next door for dinner. He could barely see Lester standing at the far end of the room, laying a warm flour tortilla on a plate.

"Just in time. I got venison. I got cheese."

"I'm not too hungry. I ate at the center before I went fishing."

51

"You never eat your own cooking. I know that. Eat a taco, for Pete's sake."

Miles took the plate and ate the taco. Arguing with Lester was like arguing with the weather.

"I saw you, you know. I saw you in your skiff before you went fishing." Lester walked down three steps to a seat in front of his cast iron stove.

"You saw me doing what?" Miles tried to flatten his voice.

"I saw you praying to that piece of junk engine." Lester shook his head, held up an empty glass.

Miles walked down and poured sparkling cider into the cup. "It's not a prayer exactly."

"It's some goofy new age prayer." Lester snorted into the mouth of his glass. "I'm telling you, man, you are going to be a whole chapter in my book about white people: the man who makes devotions to recreational equipment." Lester smiled.

"It's not recreational equipment," Miles mumbled from his seat on a round of wood next to the woodbox. "It's a thinking thing."

Lester rolled his eyes, slapped his friend on the shoulder. "A thinking thing? I don't know about that. That engine was owned by an Indian. It just doesn't care for white people is all."

"Why not? What did white people ever do to that engine?"

"How should I know?" Lester said. "Do I look white?"

They sat silently while the fire inside the cast iron box popped, sucked air through the draft. Lester was comfortable without words spoken every second, which suited Miles; he sat and ate his venison taco.

They finished and started eating cookies that Lester had had flown in from Juneau. He probably could have afforded the most expensive cookies on the market, but he preferred cheap, off-brand things bought in bulk. At first they appeared to be brand cookies you could recognize, but once you bit into them you were reminded that you were in bush Alaska and a long way from the centers of culture where people probably ate a better class of cookie.

Miles washed the dry crumbs down with juice. Lester took a bite and stared at the grate on the front of the stove. The fire rumbled, and a gust of wind pushed against the sides of the old frame house.

"So, you going to the movies tonight?" Lester asked.

"What're they showing?" Miles held little hope of surprise.

"*The Bad Lieutenant.*"

"Ah, Christ, isn't that the third time?" He picked up a stick of wood to feed the fire.

"I think it might be the fifth time in, like, six months. It's Weasel. He loves it. I think it makes him happy or something." Lester opened the door to the stove, and Miles threw a piece of wood on the fire. "I think Weasel wishes he were Harvey Keitel," Lester added, shutting the door. "Harvey Keitel lets ugly white men think they're still sexy."

The Cold Storage Film Society was made up entirely of men. After a truly horrendous argument about *Reservoir Dogs,* the women had splintered off into their own film group and had "Movie Tuesdays" instead. Now an insurrection was starting up again in the men's group.

"Naw, I'm not going," Miles said. "Are you going?"

"I might."

The two men sat for several minutes, listened to the fire hiss and suck at the grating; the new stick of wood was damp. A gust of wind slapped against the house, and Miles looked toward the dark windows to see the reflection of a tiny light above Lester's workbench.

"Have you seen Mouse lately?" asked Lester.

"No." Miles didn't look away from the window. "Didn't he fly to Juneau?"

"I don't think so. I went down to his boat a couple of days ago, and his stuff was all there like he had just walked out."

"You tell that to the cop?"

"Hell no. Mouse doesn't need to be found by a trooper." They both sat looking into the fire box for a few more moments before he added, "He wasn't looking so good when I saw him last."

"Not so good . . . like how?" Miles turned his face away from the window.

"Not so good like drunk, pale, thin, and about ready to fall over."

"That doesn't really distinguish him from many people around here."

Both men let the silence sit between them again while wind pounded against the window.

"I didn't even know you had a brother, let alone a high-ranking crime boss brother," Lester said.

"Yeah, well, you learn something new every day."

"Your brother going to come here?"

"I have no idea."

"I hope he does." Lester looked over at him.

"You do?" Miles kept his eyes on the floor. "Why?"

"You know, for my book." He laughed, stood up, and slapped Miles on the back. "I better get after it." Over at the bench where his jeweler's vise held a thin strip of silver, he picked up a tool and started working. He sold his work in two galleries — one in Seattle and one in New York — and a shipping deadline was coming up for each one.

Miles rinsed off his plate, dried it, and placed it back in the cupboard. He walked out of the house.

So sure was Clive that he had money waiting for him at this last stop, he gave fifty dollars to the driver for the ride. He scratched the corgi's head as he was getting out, but the dog seemed to be ignoring him now.

Clive's dog, Samson, was the kind of golden retriever who got progressively wider and wider. Eventually, he could have been used as an animate end table. Samson was sweet-natured and loyal beyond all reason. Clive remembered Samson lying on the rug, watching baseball on TV. Any time Clive made the slightest move, the dog would lift his head and stare, sometimes worried, sometimes excited, but always with the knowledge that something good was going to happen and it would start with Clive. Samson was an optimist.

During the early years in prison, Clive had not dared to think about him. He'd left Samson with Oscar because there was no one else; he'd told himself that Oscar could be trusted and that he loved dogs. But during those early years the goal was clear: everything good on the outside had to be buried away and hidden from the life inside, the life that circled the concrete hole of protective segregation.

Oscar worked for Jake Shoemaker, though it would take a lot of digging to figure that out. The warehouse where Oscar was the manager was called Little Switzerland. It sat in the Never-Never Land of warehouses and sketchy motels and iron-barred bodegas in the neighborhood you get lost in when you miss the turnoff for the Seattle-Tacoma airport. Stunted pine trees were planted in a border around the edge of the paved parking lot, and Oscar sat in a windowless office inside the first door of the building, the one closest to the chain-link fence. He was a short man with a full moon face and a thin covering of mouse brown hair swept back over a bald spot.

He sat back in his chair, flicking a butter-

fly knife back and forth with a quick clicking sound. His feet rested on an open desk
drawer, and the light made him look even
whiter than Clive had remembered.

"Hey, man, your dog's dead." Oscar made
it sound as if they were in the middle of an
argument.

"What do you mean, dead?" Clive reached
over, grabbed the front of his shirt, pulled
him to his feet.

"Don't put your fucking hands on me."
Oscar's teeth were clenched, and he held
the knife blade up to Clive's ear awkwardly.

"Just tell me what happened." Clive didn't
pay attention to the knife. He was looking
at the pudgy man's mouth instead, noticing
the missing tooth.

"What can I tell you, man? He was old,
and I got a ton of fucking vet bills. If you
want to get snotty about it, I suppose I
could let you pay me back for them. I mean,
you were the model of a concerned pet
owner. Fuck!" Oscar threw the knife on top
of the desk, and Clive eased him down into
the seat. "Just don't touch me again. All
right?" Oscar added, reminding himself that
he wasn't a man to be messed with.

"Did you want me to break out of Mc-
Neil, swim across the Sound, and take him
to the vet?" Clive sat down on an overturned

wastebasket in a corner, his body sagged, and tears came to his eyes.

Clive hadn't cried when he was arrested or when he was sentenced. He hadn't cried on the DOC bus that drove him out to McNeil. He hadn't cried that first night in the dorms when men rustled around his bunk like bears at the dump. He hadn't even cried the first time he was assaulted in the sign shop and had spent those weeks in the infirmary.

But now he was out of jail, Samson was dead, and he was going to cry like a baby. "He was a good dog," he said in a thickening voice.

"Yeah, he was." Oscar pretended to read some invoices. He didn't want to watch Clive cry; he didn't like to witness any kind of weakness. He waited a second. "I got another dog. You want him?"

Clive didn't say anything for quite a while. He was thinking about Samson, curled up those last few months on the blanket of his cell. He was thinking about the look in the golden retriever's eyes and thinking that even then Samson was probably already dead. He looked around the messy office, covered with old cardboard cups and circle-stained copies of *Soldier of Fortune* magazine; he was amazed that he had ever thought this life of crime was anything but pathetic.

"What kind of dog?" Clive wiped his eyes.

"He's an ugly son of a bitch." Oscar looked at Clive. "A guy left him here in trade on a bad debt. He said he was a fighting dog. He said he'd be a good guard dog for the warehouse. I mean, the fucking dog is ugly and scary enough to chase anybody off, but he don't listen to a goddamn thing anybody says." Oscar got up and grabbed a large ring of keys off the desk. "Let's go look at him. You can have him if you want."

Outside, Oscar opened up a chain-link gate with barbed wire coiling along the top. Clive's stomach tightened.

Oscar laughed. "Hey, dude, we got the keys. No worries. I'm not locking you up." He jingled the keys and laughed again.

"I got to get into the locker, Oscar," explained Clive. "Can you arrange that for me?"

"Is it cool with Jake?"

"Of course it is. I did his time, didn't I? I should think it is very cool with Jake. Call him if you want."

"I don't know. There's nothing much in there anymore. But still, Jake would take my nuts if I let you in."

"Oscar, man, it's all my stuff. Jake's just

been paying the storage bill."

Oscar stopped, jingled his keys again, shifted his weight from foot to foot. "So," he asked, "you aren't going to mind sharing whatever's in there?"

"Sharing? What, like the United Fund or something?"

"I thought you'd want to cover the vet bills I fronted. Shit. You know, I don't have to let you in that locker." He looked Clive in the eye.

"We'll work something out." He put his hand on Oscar's shoulder and turned him back in the direction they'd been walking. "Let's go take a look at that dog." Gently, he put a little pressure on the small man's back.

"Don't fucking touch me," said Oscar with enough bluff to maintain his dignity.

They came to another fenced area. Inside was a shack and tied to it was a strange gangbanger mix of rottweiler, pit bull, and wolf, a brindle-dun carnivore without an ounce of extra fat and with chewed-off ears.

"Lord have mercy," Clive said under his breath.

The dog was 120 pounds of head, jaw muscles, and shoulders. His eyes scanned the yard and stopped on the men. Slowly, he walked forward with the off-kilter stare of a Mexican street dog charged up on a jolt of methamphetamine. He did not look anything like Clive's golden retriever. He looked like something that fed on golden retrievers.

"What's his name?" There was a degree of awe in Clive's voice.

"Well, his father was supposed to be a real good fighting dog. That dog was called Big Brother, and I guess he made a ton of money for the guy. When he dropped this dog off, he said his name was Little Brother, but it doesn't matter. He won't come to anything."

"Does he bite?" Clive walked around the fence; the dog's dark eyes followed him.

"I don't give him the chance," said Oscar. "When I want him out, I open the gate to his pen. He wanders around inside the fence. When I want him back in the morning, I carry this and he goes back in." He reached over and picked up a wand with a battery pack on the end. "It's a cattle prod. They use 'em for loading bulls into trucks."

"Then how do you get the chain on him?"

"I put this on." Oscar picked up a single sleeve attached to a thick glove that looked like a piece of hockey equipment. "Got this from a guy who trains attack dogs. I put it on and clip the chain to his collar. This dog's never actually bitten me, but shit, I mean look at him."

"What do you mean, 'actually' bitten you?" Clive inched closer to the fencing.

"He's never bitten me, man, but I know he really wants to." He touched the switch and there was a metallic buzzing sound; the dog cowered in a corner. Oscar walked closer and jabbed the end of the probe through the fence; the dog started snarling, thick saliva falling through its teeth. Oscar kept pushing the probe further until it hit the dog; there was a sharp yelp and the animal fell to the concrete.

Clive put his hand on Oscar's elbow and pulled him back.

"I said don't fucking touch me, man!" He swung around and glared at him. Clive recognized that look: Oscar both did and didn't want to kill someone right now. Clive hoped Oscar never went to jail, for prison was the place where cowards learned to kill.

Clive slowly took the prod away. "It's okay." He smiled. "I'll take the dog."

As he got closer to the fence, the dog got to his feet, sniffed the air in front of him as if there were a frightened cow being lowered into the pen. Clive saw deep scars around his throat and shoulders; his back leg had a crook to it like one that had been seriously broken and badly set.

"Little Brother . . . That your name?"

The dog's expression didn't change. He said nothing. Clive leaned in to listen carefully.

Nothing. Silence like looking down a well.

"Well, I guess I'll take you with me, dog." Then he turned to the ugly man and fished his wallet out of his pocket.

"Here's fifty bucks for nothing, and there is nothing more. Now open my locker."

Oscar snorted, grabbed the bill and backed slowly away, keeping his eyes on the big boulder-headed dog, who watched him like raw meat.

The next morning, Miles walked down the boardwalk from the café to his clinic. Several appointments were penciled in that day, but the calendar didn't really matter because most of the people in Cold Storage couldn't be bothered with making and keeping appointments. Most of the patients simply showed up any time their aches or pains occurred. Miles turned a corner to find Billy Cox sitting in the doorway. Billy was squatting, eating an apple. His large green poncho spread over his shoulders and hung to the ground like a tent. Billy was a fisherman now but had once been the lead vocalist and percussionist for the short-lived death metal duo Boomerang Bombers.

"Hey, Billy!" Miles greeted him and reached into his pocket for the keys.

Billy didn't speak at first. He was eating his apple with such concentration it seemed that if he turned his attention away, even for one moment, the apple might disappear.

"Miles, have you ever gotten a really, really good apple when you were expecting a crummy one?" Billy finally asked just as Miles opened the door.

"Yeah, I have." He wanted to get to the point. "How are you doing today, Billy?"

"I mean, you bite into a series of soft mushy things and you kind of get used to them, but then you get a really good one." He stood up, his poncho rolling water off onto the deck. "And it makes you both kind of happy and sad." He put the last of the core into his mouth.

"Come on in, Billy." Miles switched on the lights inside. "Sit down a second and I'll get things going here. You want to make the coffee?" He was already tipping water into the coffee maker.

The entire clinic was about twenty feet by thirty. It was built on pilings out over the inlet, on the water side of the boardwalk. Miles had a small office, a storeroom, a drug locker, a very small meeting room in the back corner with space for four people, a waiting room with a coffee pot, and an examining room. The clinic was clean and decorated; health posters and framed wildlife photos hung on the freshly painted walls.

After the incident with the trooper, Miles had decided to make a fresh pot of coffee. The thick liquid burbled down through the grounds, and its tropical steam rose up into the room. Billy took off his poncho.

Miles turned on his new computer in the office, checked to see if the fax machine had spit out any indecipherable messages. He did a quick walk-around to make sure nothing had been disturbed and double-checked the fastenings on the red metal drug locker holding the sedatives and narcotic pain killers. There weren't many. Miles didn't like the responsibility of keeping a large supply, but there were some people in the fishing fleet who thought of Miles's red drug locker as a kind of cornucopia of pleasure, and he'd once been asked to donate a tour of his drug locker as a prize for a local fundraiser. Not samples, just a simple look inside. Miles declined.

"How's the coffee coming, Billy?" Miles scrolled down through the emails, mostly tasteless jokes or boring drafts of policies

66

that didn't apply to his practice, pausing only long enough to read the headings and hit the delete icon.

"I'm making up some Colombian. That okay with you, Miles?" Billy called. "Looks like you're out of the Deadman's Reach."

"I got more on the way from Ketchikan. Why don't you pour us both a cup, and I'll meet you in the exam room?"

Going through the stack of mail, Miles's eyes stopped on the return address of one envelope. It came from the probation office of McNeil Island Correctional Facility in Washington state. It read:

The Probation Department is sending this message to inform you that you have a family member by the name of Clive J. McCahon, who has stated his intention of residing with you upon his release. Please review all information below concerning the mentioned inmate. If you cannot, for any reason, abide by all the listed conditions of probation for your family member, please contact this Department immediately. If you are willing to assist the Department in the supervising of this inmate you must provide your name, Social Security number, and physical address by return mail. This is your responsibility and the Department will take no further action.

Beneath this message was a list of data: Clive's birth date, his Social Security number, and his record of conviction. At the end, like a fishhook, was the release date. He saw it and looked at his cartoon desk calendar; Clive's release date had already passed three days ago.

"Miles, you're out of sugar. You want me to run down to the boat and get some for you?"

Miles stared at his desk calendar.

"Miles, it don't matter to me, man. I don't do sugar in coffee, you know, but if you want some, I got some down on the boat. It's probably hard as a brick, but I could break you off a chunk."

Miles shook his head as if waking up from a dream. "Naw, that's okay, Clive."

There was a long silence in the waiting room. "Huh? Whatchya call me?"

"I'm sorry, Billy." Miles clicked out of his email and left the office. "I was thinking of somebody else."

"Hey, Miles?"

"What?"

"Did you know that trooper was asking everybody in town about your brother?"

"Yeah, I know."

"He even said there'd probably be some kind of reward if we turned him in."

"I don't think that's true, Billy," Miles said sadly.

"Miles?" Billy asked again. The coffee machine gurgled.

"Yeah?"

"Your brother doesn't sound all that bad to me."

"He's not a bad guy." Miles smiled. "You know, for a career criminal."

Miles put away the letter from the Washington Department of Probation. He decided there was nothing he could do about Clive at the moment but there might be something he could do for Billy, but even that was uncertain for many of Billy's problems were metaphysical.

Billy had been born in El Cajon, California, but had come to Alaska with his parents when his dad went fishing. His pop earned money by fishing for salmon from his own small wooden boat and by fishing for halibut and black cod with a couple other guys who had more expensive permits. When his father grew sick of it, he left for California. When Billy's mom grew sick of the rain, she did, too. Billy was sixteen. The transition wasn't as hard as people from the outside would expect. Billy just stayed on the boat. Guys from the fleet gave him a hand with chores he couldn't do alone. He finished high school and worked hard maybe sixteen weeks a year and spent the rest of the wet months reading and volunteering in the school. His health insurance was covered by the local tribe in Sitka because his mother had been a tribal member from California. A good thing, because his new religious interests had caused him to come into the clinic more often.

Billy was twenty-four now and had decided he was a Tibetan Buddhist. The little library didn't have many books on Tibetan Buddhism, so he settled for a few books about the Dalai Lama and the movie version of *Seven Years in Tibet.*

After seeing pictures of the Dalai Lama smiling, Billy asked the librarian at the school in Cold Storage to find out how his name was written in the Tibetan language. She surfed around on the Internet, printed out a copy of the script, and gave it to Billy the next day; she told him the Dalai Lama's name translated into something like "Ocean of Wisdom." Billy painted the Tibetan symbols onto the blades of his kayak paddle and believed that each time he dipped his paddle into the sea, he was in effect saying

70

a prayer.

It was this new form of prayer that had been causing Billy to come to the clinic. Billy was paddling more than anyone could remember. He was off for days at a time; sometimes he would take off at the height of the worst storms of the season. When he came back to the docks in Cold Storage, he was soaked; apparently he never got out of his boat to rest.

Miles flattened Billy's palms to examine the ulcerated blisters that covered his hands. "Billy, why don't you wrap your hands or wear some kind of gloves?"

"Gloves get wet, then they rip and make it worse. I just need to toughen the skin a little more."

"You could at least get some better kind of seat in that thing. These sores on your tailbone aren't healing. I'm telling you, why don't you find another way of getting around and let your skin heal a bit? Is your shoulder still bothering you?"

Billy shook his head; he wasn't even listening. He really came to talk to the only person in Cold Storage who seemed interested in him.

"I've decided," said Billy. "I'm going to do it." He rubbed some ointment into his hands.

"Do what?" Miles was hopeful. "Give up paddling for a bit?"

"No," he replied. "I'm going to take my kayak to Seattle."

"You mean on the ferry?"

"No." Billy sounded serious. "I'm going to paddle to Seattle."

"Really?" Miles said, trying his best to keep a sarcastic tone out of his voice.

"His Holiness is going to be there. In Seattle. He's going to make an appearance at the Opera House or something. He's going to give a talk, and I'm going to be there." Billy's eyes, wide and unwavering, looked straight into Miles's.

"Why do you have to paddle?" Miles motioned him up so he could look at the infected sores on his tailbone.

"I'm going to raise money to free Tibet. You know, like a walk-a-thon or something, but paddling. I'll get people to pledge money for each mile if I can make it all the way."

"You'll get folks from Cold Storage to pledge?" He tried to hide the note of skepticism starting to sour his voice. "Christ, Billy, I don't know . . ."

"Listen, Miles, they only have to pay if I make it, right? It's about eight hundred miles. Nobody will think I'm going to get there, right? I mean, make it in time to see the Dalai Lama in four months. They'll sign up. I get just five or six of them to sign up and that makes a few grand to give to His Holiness."

Miles looked at him, trying to form an objection to this plan, but the battered young man continued. "The money's not the main thing. I'll be praying the entire way. By the time I get there, I'll be ready. I'll have some dough to give him, and I'll probably have a shot at getting to meet him." He stopped to breathe. "He's a good guy, Miles. He'll meet me if I come all that way."

Billy lay on the examining table, his butt in the air, and Miles cleaned the infected ulcer on his tailbone. He didn't say one word while he washed the wound with water and alcohol and wiped the blood away from the edges of the sores.

"What do you think, Miles?"

"I think you ought to stick around and meet my brother."

Miles washed his hands and checked his watch; he had to walk from the clinic down to his mother's house. The boardwalk ran about a quarter of a mile south along the coastline from Cold Storage; there the wooden ramp ended and a gravel trail wound through the woods to an estuary of a little stream. The school was built on the flat area to the north of the stream, and a hundred yards back to the north, just before the boardwalk ended, sat what was left of Ellie's Bar. The tin roof was sunk down in the back corner, and the front windows were broken with a few torn tarps nailed over the openings. Even though the bar was closed, it was still the preferred residence of several of the outer coast's most dedicated drinkers.

Mouse Miller had a small wooden troller and slept in the bar whenever he was in town. He was a tiny man, fitting for the size of boat he ran. He had a long beard and wore one shirt for most of a year. He had loved one of the last barmaids who had served drinks in Ellie's, had loved her with an ardor that was unmatched up and down the coast. The majority of bills tacked to the dripping ceiling of the fallen bar were his.

When he was in town, Mouse would often drink to the point of blackout. He would light candles and kerosene lanterns in the bar, and drink brandy that he'd brought up from the boat. He would drink and carry on conversations with the dead barmaid off and on for days; he would moan and bang on the bar, and he would pin more money up on the ceiling. Miles thought about Mouse and knew he should ask around town, but then he had plenty of walk-in traffic at the clinic; he didn't have to go hunting up a drunken fisherman.

The wind blew a squall of light rain, and the steep hill on the other side of the boardwalk moaned, sizzled as the wind pushed through the trees. Miles put up his collar and walked up the stairs toward his mother's house.

The faint smell of mildew and boiled cabbage filled the kitchen. In a corner sat a diesel stove, a large square metal box with chrome grillwork that could have come off a '49 Ford coupe. On top of the grillwork sat a copper tea kettle, and above the stove, dishtowels hung drying over metal rods hinged to the wall. The edges of the dishtowels swung slightly in the rippling heat.

Beside the electric range, an electric percolator bubbled quietly.

"Get yourself a cup of coffee," Annabelle called from the other room. "Then come in here and sit with me."

Miles poured himself a cup, carried it into the living room.

Annabelle lay back in a recliner. She wore a sweater over her nightgown and housecoat

75

and heavy wool socks and strange-looking slippers that had the heads of two cartoon mice jutting out of the toes.

"Hi, honey! What's going on with you?" Her voice creaked.

"Not a lot, Mom." He took a straight-backed chair from the card table, set it close to the old woman's feet, and sat down. He looked at the stuffed mice slippers for a long moment, caught himself staring at them, and didn't know what to say.

"I've never seen you wearing mice on your feet before," he managed.

Annabelle wiggled them from side to side. "Oh, I know they're ugly as sin, but they go on easy over my socks. I been feeling a little chilly in the mornings."

"Uh, Mom . . ." he started. "I really think you should go into Sitka and see the doctor. I mean, you know, it might be something simple. Might be a couple of pills. I really wish you would let me get you in to see your doctor." He took a sip of his coffee; his tone was easy. This was as hard a sell as he was going to make.

"Yeah, and I wish I had a million bucks. I'm not going to spend that money flying into Sitka." She reached over and touched Miles's hand as if to reassure him, but then her small frame shook and pumped with coughing, frighteningly deep and strong coughing, and Miles thought she could break a rib coughing this way.

"You know, I can arrange to have the clinic pay for the flight," he said. He put down the coffee cup and handed her a tissue from the little box with a crocheted cover standing on the nightstand next to her chair.

Annabelle spat into the tissue, quickly covered it and threw it in a wastebasket near her feet.

Miles reached into his pocket and felt the message from the probation department, the news about Clive getting out of prison. He knew he should tell his mother the news. He even felt his hand starting to bring the paper out of his pocket, but he stopped.

"Mom," he stammered, "I'm sorry, but I get the idea you don't want to go to Sitka because you are just waiting for Clive, and if that's the case . . ."

She held up her hand to stop him. "I saw the darnedest thing. Just the other day. I'm certain I saw that old bird of mine. I saw Buddy in the trees. That can't be right, can it?"

"No. I don't think so," Miles thumbed the letter in his pocket. He didn't tell her about Clive. He was not sure why. He told himself it was to protect her, but truthfully, he wasn't sure.

The water continued to rattle against the sides of the pot, and he could hear the greasy flame flutter down in the oil stove. Out in the inlet, a trolling boat was working its way out toward the coast. Miles could hear the old engine labor away, and he could almost hear the gulls crying out as they wheeled over the stern. Up on the mountains, the wind wheezed through trees that had been there for eight hundred years; some had blown over and were rotting back into the ground. Everything was old up on the hillsides, but the rain was older than all of that and it was falling again, as it always had, as it always would.

They said nothing. The wind blew, and a limb kept ticking against the window.

"You don't know anything about him coming back, do you?" she said suddenly.

"Who?" he said with a start.

"Buddy," the old woman said, and looked up at him through her thick lenses. "They can't live that long, can they?"

She sat forward, started coughing so hard that he leaned her even farther forward, causing her thick glasses to fall into her lap. He rubbed her back between her shoulder blades until the coughing subsided. He got

78

her some water to drink, and after putting on her glasses, she looked up into his eyes as tired as he had ever seen her.

"Just get me some pills," she spat out, "or some heavy-duty cough syrup."

"Okay, Ma." He stood up.

"Do me another favor, would you, pal?" Her voice was weak.

"I'm not going to boil you an egg, in case you are going to ask."

"No." She smiled. "Pop in that movie there. I was watching it last night and fell asleep."

Miles wheeled the television closer to the recliner, straightened out the cords, turned on the TV, and pushed the button on the VCR. The dusty screen on the TV flickered and glowed silver. There was Bedford Falls, and there was Jimmy Stewart, madly looking for the eight thousand dollars Uncle Billy had let slip out of his hands. There was Uncle Billy's raven hopping on the counter of the failing Building and Loan.

Annabelle waved at her son as he walked toward the door, and he waved back; neither said anything.

Miles walked down the boardwalk toward the clinic, thinking about his brother's return, knowing that, despite what the probation department said, there was still less than a fifty percent chance that his brother would actually show up. At least he could always hope.

A light rain was falling, and the sun was beginning to rise above the ridgeline to the southeast. Shafts of light cut a silver highway across the water. Gulls chattered as they sat near the pilings of the fish plant built in the 1950s on the site of what had once been the Norwegian fishermen's bathhouse. Miles felt deep down in his bones with a kind of mortal finality that he was home from the war.

He would open up the clinic, but nothing much would happen today. He'd call the hospital in Sitka, and a few people would come by the clinic with their simple and sociable complaints. Nothing would happen today, and nothing much would happen tomorrow. Even if his brother were to come to town, there was not enough to keep Clive busy. Clive would have to bring his own excitement to Cold Storage, which might be exactly what the trooper was concerned about.

CHAPTER FOUR

"I'm sorry," Jake Shoemaker simpered in an uncommonly polite voice. "I know this must be inconvenient for you." Oscar sat on the couch, his hands tied behind his back. "I mean, it's more than just inconvenient; this is frightening, I'm sure."

Oscar's mouth was covered with a strip of silver tape, his skin was white, his eyes wide open and red-rimmed. Spattered across his yellow polo shirt was his own blood.

Jake didn't like this kind of scene. He knew that when it came to violence, he was being blown forward by some old fear. It was probably as simple as a fear of failure, but he didn't want to think about that very deeply.

Jake's father had been a logger in the eastern Cascades. He had wanted to leave the woods, but he never did. Sometimes after work he would gather Jake and the gear into the truck and head up to a green lake

81

surrounded by dusty hills. The wooden rowboat they pulled up into the weeds had more than a little rot around the oarlocks. Jake would sit in the stern while his father gingerly pulled on the oars, not wanting to rip the locks out of the boat.

Jake remembered his father wearing an oil-soaked hickory shirt opened down to show a chest burned mahogany red from the sun. He remembered his father opening a beer, making his first and only cast, leaning back and saying the exact same words every single day: "Hey boys, chow!" Jake couldn't understand what in the hell he and his father were doing there. They never caught any fish, and it made him angry.

When Jake thought of his old man, he remembered his smell: sweat and saw gas. It was the smell of failure, rising like steam.

Jake was wearing a black silk shirt with no tie today, a soft leather jacket and wool slacks. He sat and picked lint off the front of his trousers while Oscar struggled on the couch.

He watched Oscar tip onto his stomach. The old man's cheeks puffed out against the silver tape wrapped around his thinning brown hair. His hands were shaking and turning blue from the tightness of the cords bound around them.

"I'm just in a bad mood," said Jake. He didn't like watching the man on the couch so he spoke up into the air, as if addressing someone in heaven. "I know I shouldn't take it all out on you, but this is business. This is a lot of money we're talking about."

Jake hated this part of his job. He had nothing personal against Oscar, but missing from his storage unit was a large amount of money and, worse, some important business records. Even though he was certain Oscar hadn't taken it, he was almost positive that Oscar knew who had, and, more importantly, knew where that someone was heading. This unpleasantness was just some stupid business foul-up. Jake was a writer, and this was only his day job; like most day jobs, his had its share of irritations.

Jake had been irritated for weeks. Everywhere he went he saw the advertisement for *Stealing Candy*. It seemed like half the buildings in Los Angeles were plastered with billboard ads for the movie. It galled him to no end. Jake could hardly drive anywhere without eventually banging his head against his walnut steering wheel.

Jake had written several films; two of them had been produced so far, erotic films that some people had inaccurately called softcore porn. He had hoped viewers would have been able to see past whatever label brainless money men put on his work. Both of his films had gone directly to video release, a major disappointment. His dream had been to attend a premiere of one of his own films; the limo ride and the flashbulb walk up the roped-off carpet, standing with the stars, waving, laughing, making sly, private jokes with the director. But that was not going to happen any time soon. *Stealing Candy* was scheduled for its premiere, and he would not be invited. He wouldn't even be comped a ticket to the show. It set his teeth on edge.

Oscar struggled to speak, but the silver tape held fast. Jake stood up and threw a windbreaker over Oscar's head. Oscar rolled onto the floor and started thrashing violently back and forth.

"Gracious!" he said, as if calming a feverish child. "Just settle down. Nothing bad is going to happen." He took a couple of wraps around the man's ankles with a spare electrical cord.

Jake had originally written both the treatment and the first draft for the movie that became *Stealing Candy.* Jake's script, called *Who's Your Daddy Now?*, had been well-received by a producer at Paramount; Jake had even negotiated a six-month option and a development deal with Viacom. He hadn't had a star, of course, and he'd foolishly trusted the earnest young Harvard graduate he'd hired to flesh out the script. Now everywhere he turned, he was seeing seven-story likenesses of a Cameron Diaz clone holding a bloody knife.

Jake loved the movies. He loved the feeling inside a darkened theater: the cool air, the expectant rustle of people settling into their seats, all of them facing the same direction, all of them waiting for a new world about to shine right there in front of them. He hated the moment after the film ended, and the lights came up on the spilled sodas and sticky boxes of candy on the floor. This was too much like real life, like the smell of a dirty hickory shirt or the sound of a nagging cough. This was a life he rejected. He preferred success. He preferred the movies.

Oscar had wet himself, and the urine was running in a slow yellow stream across the floor toward Jake's desk.

"I'm sorry," he said, and looked at his watch. He was supposed to be meeting a friend for lunch in thirty minutes. He picked up the nine millimeter in his desk drawer, racked a round into the chamber, and stepped over the stream to shut the door.

"Don't worry, Oscar," he said, a trace of genuine sympathy in his voice. "When the bullet hits your skull, it won't really hurt. You're going to feel a little bit of pressure and maybe some stinging, but not for long."

Oscar shook off the coat covering his head. He looked up into Jake's eyes and seemed to relax; his hands unclasped, his wrists stopped tugging against the cords cutting into him. He just lay there, waiting for the big wind to blow through his skull.

"Wake up now, Oscar!" Jake said softly, as if he really were waking him up. "If you didn't take the money, all you have to do is tell me who did, and we can work together to find it. You hear what I'm saying?" His voice was urgent.

Oscar shook his head violently, nodded up and down to indicate he understood, and Jake reached down and pinched the edge of the tape.

"This is going to hurt a bit," he warned and jerked the tape away.

"Clive McCahon!" Oscar sputtered. "Clive took the money. Three days ago. He said he was picking up some gear for you. He said I could call you if I wanted to, but you know . . . I thought, shit, it's Clive, you know, he's one of your boys. I mean, I know that. He was one of yours. He went to the

86

joint and never gave anybody up. I thought it was all his stuff in the locker anyway. Shit, Jake! I had no idea he was going to rip you off. I had no fucking idea. You got to believe me. Really . . ." Oscar kept babbling.

Jake reached down and patted him on the cheek. "Clive McCahon? He's in jail." He lifted the gun to Oscar's eyes.

"No, no! He's out," Oscar sputtered. "He just got out. You can check that. Really, check it."

Jake stood up straight. He rubbed his chin with the front sight of the gun. "I believe you. I do, Oscar, but still you owe me. You're going to have to give me something, Oscar. You hear me now?"

"Anything," he puffed, struggling to sit up.

"Do you ride a bicycle?" asked Jake, tapping the pistol against his leg.

"No . . . no, I don't." He looked up with a twitchy kind of panic, a tone that hinted he was willing to start riding a bike right away.

"No bike, huh? Do you play basketball?"

"No . . ." Oscar tried to push his way back up on the couch. Jake lifted his foot and shoved down on his shoulder.

"What do you mean, you don't ride a bike or play basketball? Do you jog or anything like that?"

"No, Jake. I don't jog." His voice shook.

"Then this is a piece of cake, buddy." He lifted his gun slightly and fired one round into Oscar's left knee.

Clive was on his knees in the Seattle airport in front of the oversized baggage desk; he was trying to load Little Brother into an expensive, brand-new kennel. It appeared he might never set foot in it.

Clive had tried crawling into it himself. He thought if he showed the dog how easy it was, he might convince Little Brother to load up. The tactic wasn't successful.

"Won't you even consider getting into the crate?" Clive asked politely. The dog stood, his head bowed toward the slick linoleum floor, and said nothing, which frankly relieved Clive because he was afraid of what would come out if the dog did speak.

"Well, I guess we could travel by ship." Clive backed out of the crate. "But I think they will still make you get in a box."

Behind him, a security man, clearing the area for some VIP passing through, grabbed Little Brother's studded leather collar. The growl grew as loud as gears grinding in a Sherman tank; the hair along the ridge of his back stood on end and every muscle was taut, as clearly defined as on a wet, brown bear charging up a river bank.

Every person waiting in line took a step back. The security guard put his hand on his gun. Clive put his hand on the guard's elbow and spoke to him in a friendly, even tone to show he wasn't kidding around.

"Don't do that."

"Yeah . . . Okay." The guard looked shaken, waved to his partner to route the procession to the other side of the concourse. "But if this dog isn't out of here when I get back in five minutes, we'll have to call in the animal control people."

"I think that would be a good plan," Clive said. "Do they have a fire hose? Maybe we can spray him inside the kennel."

Clive was about to say more when the echoing voice of a disembodied pleasant woman came through the air: "Clive McCahon, Clive McCahon, please meet your party at the Alaska Airlines Board Room." Clive looked around and took out a hundred dollar bill and gave it to a Vietnamese man with whom he had struck up a conversation earlier.

"Make sure no one shoots my dog, okay?"

"No problem. He's good here," the man said with no evident concern, and Clive took off down the pre-security hallways of the Seattle airport. He introduced himself to the polite staff behind the Alaska Airlines desk, who showed him to the small board room where sat Jake Shoemaker and the eminently efficient Miss Peel.

Clive nodded to each of them. "Jake. Miss Peel." Everyone in the room knew Jake had once actually had sex with Miss Peel, a fact that she immediately regretted and which he would never let her forget.

"Clive boy, sit the fuck down. You can't steal money from me. What the hell are you thinking? You, you of anybody, know what I have to do to you." Jake had a briefcase in front of him. He was fingering the latches. Miss Peel had not said a word.

"Miss Peel," Clive said, turning to her, "you are looking well. Have you been swimming in the warm ocean regularly?"

"Clive." She looked at the black expanse of desk between them. "I see jail has agreed with you."

Miss Peel — whose first name was Ann, although he had seldom ever heard it used — was a truly glamorous human being. She looked to be of some indeterminate Hispanic descent. Her lustrous, raven black hair was down to her shoulders and clipped up in the front. Her dark eyes were wet and sparkled like wells. Looking at her made men a little crazy, which was why Jake took her to business meetings. But the fact that he never made advances on her led many men to think he might be gay. Clive thought that he might truly be a gentleman, or he was just frightened by that much beauty.

"Anyway, it's good to see you," Clive told her, then turned to Jake. "And you, you little fuck. A: it's my money, it's my paperwork, not yours. B: you are not going to shoot me in the Alaska Airlines Board Room because I know what kind of frequent flyer miles whore you are. I know. I *know* that you gave them your real ID card checking in here, so you can't blast me and walk out. It's stupid. Besides you know they have a camera that photographs each and every one of us when we walk in here and that means that most likely the Port of Seattle Police have probably started asking for the tapes already after hearing your discreet little page of my fucking name. Jesus. How did you ever get this far in crime anyway?"

Jake sat up straight. "Look, man, we talked before. Crime money is hard money. It's stressful. All the fucking assholes — no offense — all the guns, who needs it? You know what I'm saying? Me, I'm taking crime money and putting it into non-stressful businesses. Everyone else is making money. Computers, what a load of bullshit. Dot-coms. Christ! Companies full of zitty kids who sleep till eleven in the morning and produce nothing you can understand and want a million dollars, and they fucking get it. I don't get it. I'm going back into real estate. You can't go wrong buying buildings, you know what I'm saying? Nothing less stressful than that."

"Your stress level concerns me how?" Clive was still looking at Miss Peel, who would not look up at him.

Jake kept fidgeting with the latches on the case. Clive could see Jake's stress now, and it concerned him. "There is this pain-in-the-ass DA. Federal guy. They can make your life miserable, you know what I'm saying? What you have — my money, how you got it . . . The gun stuff, the drugs . . . That could do me in. Twenty years, they are saying."

Clive leaned toward him. "You got no gun stuff. You were strict about that. You never killed anyone. That one thing a couple of years ago, with the Filipino salesman in Yelm, that was a total accident and everybody knows it."

"I know. I never sold to gangs, I never supplied gangs. I only ever sold to these rich dot-com yuppies. But these feds say they can track gangbanger guns to me."

"That's crap. That was your father's bird hunting gun that was stolen out of the milk truck. I told them that, and it's on one of the tapes. They can't use that."

"But if you go backward on me they can put me away."

"Jesus, Jake."

"Listen, kid, keep the money."

"Shut the fuck up, Jake. Don't you hear how you sound? It sounds like you are bribing me to lie. I'm keeping the money and the documents because they are mine. I'm keeping the documents and the money because I'm getting out of the business. I'm retiring. I'm going back to Alaska to get away from you and the life. I'm *not* taking the money to lie for you. If asked, I'll tell the truth that you were not into drugs and guns. You were only into drugs. The Feds love drugs and guns. Well, you were only into drugs. That's it. Sure, you had a gun, but that's, you know, Second Amendment shit." Clive stood up and looked down at Miss Peel. "That's a – m – e – n – d – m —"

"Oh my Lord." She finally looked up at him. "Were you the spelling bee champion of McNeil Island I read so much about?"

"Ann, if you were to marry me, we would have enough leverage with the Feds to get a free home in American Samoa. What do you say?"

"Mmmm, tempting. Unrelenting heat, dysentery, and you. Let me think about it."

"Do that," Clive said. Jake, staring forlornly at his briefcase, didn't say anything. Clive gave Miss Peel a little bow.

"See ya, kids. Got a plane to catch."

As he walked out of the Board Room, Miss Peel put a tidy "X" at the end of the last line she had written. She shut her pad, straightened her skirt, and stood up without looking once at Jake.

When Clive returned to check in and pick up his dog, Little Brother was waiting inside the kennel, apparently having decided it was time to lie down with his new sock toys.

At Clive's seat in first class, the flight attendant wanted to take his heavy parka, but Clive kept it on his lap. She brought him a gin and tonic in a heavy imitation crystal glass.

Clive looked out the window. Outside the plane, the city of Seattle was a tangle of wires and flat concrete. There were homes and sheds and stores and shopping malls all connected by an interlacing web of crushed rock and paving tar. It reminded him of a tangled blackberry patch full of blackbirds hunting through the vines for food.

There was minor damage on one of the cargo hatches, and they were going to have to wait a couple more minutes while it was repaired. Clive heard the captain chuckle; a mouse had somehow crawled up and chewed a tiny part of the rubber seal around a hatch. It would just take a second to get that fixed, and they would be on their way.

For a moment, Clive believed he could hear the merry laughter of mice and raised his glass in a solitary toast.

Soon the plane accelerated down the runway, pushed into the exhaust-scented air, and banked over the bay while the sun set in a red gaseous plume. On the purple sea, an oil tanker ploughed north. Far below him was a cardboard box with his name and his prisoner number written on one end; he was leaving his old clothes and his time in jail all behind.

The captain's voice interrupted his thoughts. The plane was going to have to turn back to Seattle. It appeared there was a caution light indicating a problem with one of the cargo doors. There was no need to worry; he would have them back on the ground in Seattle in just a short while, and after a minor repair they would be up in the air in an hour or two.

Clive took another long drink of his gin and tonic. He pulled his bulky new parka tightly around his knees to warm his legs and lap.

Miles walked back down the boardwalk toward the clinic. Every time he passed Ellie's Bar, he wondered about Mouse Miller. He had seen for himself that Mouse's boat was in the harbor. He had even asked the harbormaster and a couple of other fishermen who lived on the boats whether anyone had seen him.

In the morning Ellie's Bar seemed haunted, but now in the afternoon the old building was unrelievedly lifeless, a corpse with broken-toothed windows that didn't sparkle. A light rain was falling but not enough for water to drip off the eaves; no boards pushed up with the wind, no rusty nails shrieked, no cats hissed. But to Miles, this was when the old bar was at its most frightening.

He hurried along the boardwalk, lifting his collar against the chill. There was no point getting bogged down in useless worry. He had things to do, and he wouldn't be slowed down by ill-considered options.

The rain had stopped; the sun was cutting down through the clouds, and the woods to his left lit up as the clouds moved in the sky. Berry bushes held tiny pearls of rainwater that sparkled like diamonds. The alder trees were starting to show tiny green buds, and the salmonberry brambles had tight fists of well-spaced green leaves at their tips. A varied thrush whirred and chirred up under the dark canopy of the old spruce. A river otter scuttled under the boardwalk and set loose a small cascade of stones back down to the beach. Miles took it all in and was happy to be just where he was.

He got back to the clinic, wrote his notes, went upstairs to the apartment. He put on his sweatpants and flip-flops, gathered up clean work clothes and some shampoo, and headed for the bathhouse.

Like most of the structures in Cold Storage, it was an old plank building sagging on its timber frames. There was a small entryway and a second door leading to a dressing room where painted wooden walls were ringed with benches and hooks.

A set of clothes was scattered on the bench, and a pair of red rubber boots sat underneath. The smell of marijuana smoke overwhelmed the egginess of the bathhouse, and Miles knew exactly who was inside.

Mouse Miller's one deckhand was Weasel, who had taken the name after signing on

with Mouse and kept it long after he quit
fishing on the tiny trolling boat. He liked
being called Weasel much better than he
liked being called Julius, which was his birth
name. Weasel lived ashore now. He spent
most of his time smoking marijuana and
watching movies he had flown in from
Juneau on scheduled food flights. He grew
his pot hydroponically on his float house
and always seemed to have a good crop.

His electrical power came from an old
hydroelectric complex that the cold storage
plant had put in years ago. As long as the
rain kept falling, there was power. And as
long as there was power, Weasel could keep
running the massive lights hanging above
the flat tubs of his growing operation. When
they started putting a drain on the town
power supply, he was told his rates would
quadruple in keeping with a new "prorated"
energy policy. He cut back on the lights.

Some people in town considered Weasel a
genuine gangster. A logger named Tiger
Johnson was convinced Weasel was one of
the major dope operators on the entire West
Coast. He had a theory about him that
included black boats, helicopters, and
midnight runs to private submarines off the
coast. All of that sounded too rigorous for
Weasel.

Besides, it had been made clear to him quite forcibly by Miles that if any of his pot showed up in the possession of any of the school kids, his float house would suffer from an accident involving either fire or flooding. Weasel took the message to heart.

Miles had poked around. It was pretty clear that Weasel sold his crop to a select clientele: familiar adults without kids and visiting fishermen coming in to sell their catch or ride out the bad weather on the coast. The rest of the marijuana Weasel saved for himself.

So while some people had tried to run him out of town and some had tried to turn him in to the drug authorities, Weasel didn't scare off. The drug cops were not interested in coming all the way out to Cold Storage merely for a marijuana bust — or at least they hadn't been before Trooper Brown and his hunt for Satanists. Miles wondered if Weasel's lifestyle would be affected by the trooper's new interest in Cold Storage.

In the bathhouse, Miles crossed the grey-green concrete floor of the main room, passed the old-fashioned claw-footed cast iron tubs against the wall, and headed toward the main pool. A solitary bare electric bulb twenty feet above him shone like a midwinter sun lost in fog.

"Hey, what's going on?" Weasel, a skinny man with hair tied back in rubber bands, sat on the edge of the pool, feet dangling in the water. He smiled up through the steam. "You want some?" He held out a fat, soggy-looking joint to Miles. A sense of propriety made him offer even though he knew Miles didn't smoke or drink.

"Naw, thanks, Weaz." Miles thought about how Weasel could have written a Miss Manners, handbook for stoners. "Hey, Weaz," he asked, "do you know where Mouse is? I haven't seen him around."

"I don't know." Weasel let out a long plume of smoke. "I wouldn't worry or anything, Doc. He's been getting stuff out of his boat. I've been checking, and it looks like he's been going in and out. I bet he's shacked up down at the bar, you know?"

"I was just thinking that I hadn't seen him around." Miles studied the green and white lines left on the wall by the condensed steam sliding down.

"Well," Weasel said, "if I see him I'll tell him to come by and see you."

"That would be great." Miles draped his towel over the stair rail and eased into the hot water. He leaned his head against the concrete step, closed his eyes, and let the heat begin soaking into his bones.

"Missed you at the movies last night," said Weasel on an exhalation of breath.

"I've seen *The Bad Lieutenant,* Weaz." Miles kept his eyes closed. "I wasn't in the mood for it again."

"Naw, we watched *Get Carter* with Stallone. I don't know. No one else was into watching *Lieutenant.* I had just gotten the Stallone tape and I figured, you know, what the hell?" Weasel took a long thoughtful drag on his joint, squinting and cocking his face away from the fire. He washed his armpits with a soapy rag.

"How was it?" Miles asked. "*Get Carter,* I mean. Any good?"

Weasel stepped back from the tub and dipped his head in a plastic bucket of fresh water. He threw his head back in one long wet rope of blond hair. "I liked the original better," Weasel opined. "I mean, this was a fashion show. The guy never mussed his hair."

Miles shook his head. He trusted Weasel's appraisal on this. He might have an unhealthy interest in Harvey Keitel, but Weasel knew how to judge an action film.

"Hey," Weasel changed the topic. "Did you meet Officer Friendly when he was in town?"

"Oh yeah."

"I never even knew you had a brother, man. That's cool."

Miles stepped out of the tub, soaped and rinsed himself with fresh water. "Yeah, it is," he asserted. "It's pretty cool."

Weasel had a limited number of subjects he liked to discuss in the bathhouse: movies, the history of the Industrial Workers of the World, the solo music of Robbie Robertson (after he left The Band), the industrial uses of hemp, and — most recently — the novels of Haruki Murakami. He discussed those stories as if they were holy texts.

Miles didn't think any of these topics would be of particular help with his family problems, so he got back in the tub, submerged his head in the hot water, and stayed there as long as he could.

When he came up, Weasel was speaking as if he'd never stopped. "Hey, you wanna hear something really wild? You know your mom? She came by the boat today and asked me if she could have some pot."

"You're kidding," Miles floated away from the edge of the tub. "No way."

Weasel went on. "She said she had cancer, and she wanted some pot. I didn't know she had cancer, man. That sucks."

"I don't think she knows for sure." Miles tried to be professional, to keep what he felt

102

was confidential information to himself. "Did you give her any?" he asked.

"I kind of felt bad but you know, I thought she might be setting me up or something. I told her I didn't know what she was talking about. She looked sad." Weasel's hands were white and wrinkled from the water now, and he inspected them as he kept talking about Miles's mother. "I almost gave her some after that; she looked so bummed, you know? That sucks big time. Cancer . . . shit!"

"Yeah." Miles looked up into the gloomy steam rising up the concrete walls. "Yeah, it sucks all right."

Weasel dunked his head in the hot water and came sputtering out. "Hey, Miles, have you asked Mouse's ex-wife about him? I bet she might know something."

"Who's his ex-wife?"

"Come on, man," Weasel said. "Mrs. Cera down at the fish plant. She was married to Mouse for years. You know, she dumped him because of his drinking, but she always kind of looked out for him."

"Thanks, Weaz."

The only light came from the cracked skylight above the tub. They both sat silently for a few moments. Fat drops from around the edge of the skylight plopped noisily in the pool.

"Hey, Miles?" he asked.

"Yeah?" Miles reached for his towel.

"Let me know when your brother shows up, man. I'd like to meet him."

"I'll do that, Weaz," he said, toweled off his hair and stretched.

At the northern end of the boardwalk sat the old plant, a collection of buildings covered with green and white wooden siding that looked like they'd grown up out of the ground. The old people in town always referred to the color as "oil company green." The main building was built like a barn with large sliding doors on the ocean side where fishing boats tied up to unload their catch.

In 1952, Old Country Seafoods had built a cannery on the site of what had been the fishermen's bathhouse and recreational camp. The old detective was hired as the manager, and the battered-up logger ran a fishing boat. Over the years, the founders' children stayed on, tinkered with their lives on the inlet. The cannery was changed over to a cold storage when the market for fresh and frozen fish overpowered the canned market. When the fresh fish market became the most lucrative, fishermen started keeping fish on their boats, selling directly to towns like Sitka and Juneau that had airports and jet service. The result was that Cold Storage had been born, thrived and started to wither, almost all within the lifetime of her oldest citizens. That their children lived to see the decline in their parents' paradise gave the town a melancholy atmosphere.

In front of the main building was a small store where you could buy bait and milk and canned stew along with a few belts for your diesel engine. There were a couple of bins of apples and a stack of newspapers by the door. In the main part of the plant, bright lights lit up the stainless steel slides, bins, and work tables; the air held the wet smell of disinfectant and cold fish; generators and compressors hummed, but all Miles heard as he walked in was the guttural throbbing of a boom box.

The cold storage had a skeleton crew of workers who bought fish from a few boats. Recently there'd been some black cod. The crew cleaned and headed the fish, and then sent the commercial meat on a packer down to Sitka.

The matriarch of the large Filipino family was Mrs. Cera. She ran this branch of her family like a crew boss, although that title was technically her nephew's. Her current husband worked for the State Department of Corrections in Juneau as a cook at the Lemon Creek prison; he got good pay and benefits. Her son had been living with his dad and going to high school in Juneau, but three weeks ago he'd got into trouble and Mrs. Cera had made him come out to Cold Storage to go to school even though he was a football player and a wrestler with a statewide ranking. If Anthony worked hard and stayed out of trouble for the spring and summer, she'd let him go back to Juneau in the fall in time to tryout for the team. He'd tried to argue with his dad before being flown out, but he did not bother to try that with his mom.

Mrs. Cera was having a work party. The black cod collars, thin lines of dense meat between the most forward fins and the gills, had to be cut off the heads. The meat was rich with oil, and even though the strips of meat were too small for the commercial plants, they made a good meal if you had enough fish heads and enough time to cut the collars out.

A couple of teachers, Ed and Tina, who were married to each other, stood around a high white table carving up the reptilian-looking heads. Miles's neighbor Lester, the silver carver, was cleaning some of the fish collars while Anthony sulked and smoked a cigarette by an open window in the back of the plant. He considered himself an urban boy now, which made his internment here painful. Mrs. Cera filled out paper work in the office. Three others were stripping out of their work clothes to go rest and eat some dinner; maybe they'd cut cod collars later again, after their Auntie's guests were done.

Tina and Ed had been in Cold Storage for three years, the first teachers to last so long and the first husband-and-wife team at the school. They split all the teaching for the thirty students, dividing kids into classes not so much by age but by temperament. Tina was good with mathematics at any grade level, kindergarten to grade twelve, but lost her patience with the sloppiness of little kids and their endless art projects. She wasn't a finger paint kind of teacher. Ed was. He'd take classes out to trap bugs and make clay models; he'd get them on fishing boats to study the environment; he loved traipsing through the tide pools and didn't mind getting water in his boots to give a third grader a chance to hold a crab or watch the blowing scarves of sea anemones. Tina stayed dry and took field notes. She loved watching her husband, though, loved seeing him in this wild and incalculable classroom. She loved his ability to rekindle wonder in these drowsy kids.

They had been cutting up black cod heads for half an hour when Ed reached into the box beside the table and held up a red fish with a massive round belly. The head alone was almost the size of a football helmet; it had a scary looking snout.

"Isn't this a beautiful thing?" Ed's voice held wonder. "It's a short raker rockfish, a red snapper. This very animal was swimming around before airplanes crossed the oceans. He was alive when Amelia Earhart disappeared in the South Pacific and when the Japanese bombed Pearl Harbor. He might even be older than that. Some people think they could get to be two hundred years old."

Miles and Lester looked at the strange fish Ed was holding up close to his face. Miles thought of Annabelle. He thought of Ellie Hobbes, who had raised Annabelle. Ellie had loved Amelia Earhart.

"Did they ever find Amelia's plane? I thought I saw something on cable TV about that."

"I don't know." Lester shrugged. "I don't have a TV."

Mrs. Cera walked out of the office. A tiny woman, still in her apron and work clothes and her short hair in a net, she smiled broadly at her friends working at the table. She scowled, though, at Anthony in the corner and the music stopped, as if by magic.

"You go on." She gestured to her son. "Go get clean and have dinner. Yes?" Her voice was soft but direct.

Anthony picked up the folder of CDs and walked up the stairs to the workers' cottages on the edge of the woods. Mrs. Cera walked over to Miles and pulled him toward the door of her office.

"Miles," she said quietly, "people been saying that policeman is giving you trouble. I'm so sorry."

"It's not a problem."

"I'm sorry I called him, but I'm worried about Mouse. I really think his drinking might have killed him. I was hoping that policeman could find out where Mouse is." She finished in almost a whisper. "But I didn't want him to make trouble for you or your mother."

"Forget about it," he said. "When was the last time you saw him?"

"Ten days ago. He looked bad, you know. He looked skinny, and his face was white."

"Did Mouse say anything to give you any idea where he might go? Did he mention any friends or anything?"

"Miles, Mouse has got no friends on this side of the grave. You know? Mouse doesn't have anymore real friends. Will you keep an eye out for him, Miles?"

"We'll find him." Miles stood up straight. "Don't worry about it."

He glanced toward the door, but she said, "No. You stay. Get some collars. Get some collars." She gestured toward the cutting tables and raised her voice so everyone could hear her. "Take what you want," she called and pointed to the fish tote of black cod heads next to the table. "We've got some already. Just come up to the house when you're done so somebody can come back over to lock up, okay?" She closed the door.

Miles put on an apron and grabbed a knife.

It was quiet in the old plant. The compressors had cycled off, and all Miles could hear was the hum of the lamps above the table and the rain hitting the tin roof. They worked in silence for several minutes, cutting into the fish heads for the oily strips of meat, each lost in their own thoughts.

Ed's knife slipped off a tough piece of cartilage, and the blade slid down through his rubber gloves. He jerked his hand back and held on to his thumb, afraid to look.

110

Gently, Tina took his hand, opened it and smiled. The blade had only scraped the skin, not even drawing blood.

It was a little miracle, Miles thought. Evidence of the surfeit of good fortune here in Cold Storage. If he had been in Oakland, Ed would have sawn his thumb off, and Miles would be packing the severed digit into an ice bag right now.

He started working on another fish head, smiling to himself.

After a while, Ed spoke. "Holy cow, Miles, that policeman doesn't like your brother."

"I heard."

"Is he really going to come here?" Trepidation hovered in Tina's voice.

"I don't know," Miles said, "but it's not like he's rabid or anything."

"Oh, I didn't mean it like that, Miles. I think it's wonderful that you have a brother." She flipped a chunk of flesh into her plastic bag. "I don't know; that policeman made him sound kind of scary is all."

"Clive's not scary," Miles said. "He's . . . intense and maybe kind of odd, that's all."

"Nobody like that around here." Lester wiped a bit of gill material off his knife.

"Not to change the subject, but," Ed's tone of voice sounded like he wanted to change the subject, "I heard Clint Eastwood was going to come here on his yacht."

"No way," said Tina.

This new kind of gossip had almost become the default setting for conversation around town. The international yachting set had discovered the outside coast, and every summer there were more and more reports of movie stars being seen in unlikely places: Russell Crowe in a fly-fishing shop in Sitka, Minnie Driver at the health club in Juneau. There had been a persistent rumor that Clint Eastwood was scouting locations for some future project from the decks of a yacht; someone mentioned that he'd bought a fishing lodge in south Chatham Strait.

"Well, the truth is my brother is coming to town." Miles hadn't left the first conversation. "He's coming to town and I'll be responsible for him, so you don't have to worry. It will be all right." His voice was more stern than he wanted it to be.

Tina scowled and brushed a strand of hair from her eyes; she looked for a moment at Miles. Ed stopped his work, took his gloves off, and tucked his wife's hair back into her beret.

"It's all going to be fine," Tina finally said by way of not saying much of anything at all.

Miles tried to think of something to say,

112

but Lester beat him.

"I hear Annabelle has cancer."

"She's got a lot of things," Miles replied.

"Weasel is telling everybody in town about it." Lester kept working on his fish.

"Is it true she bought some pot from him?" whispered Ed.

"Well, if she has cancer it makes sense," Tina broke in. "I say good for her."

Miles didn't say anything. He didn't feel like gossiping about cancer, and he didn't know if his mother had cancer. But he knew better than to try to fight the tide of gossip, particularly considering his own ignorance. In Cold Storage, gossip was a semi-official medium of exchange; residents looked to gossip for social context, if not necessarily literal truth. Weasel had become the expert on his own mother's sickness, and Miles had nothing to offer, no expertise, no direct experience to counter Weasel's claim.

"To hell with it," Lester said, and he put down his knife. "I'm going home for dinner. I'll feed any three white people who want to come, but that's it. I'm cooking up a few of these collars — just a few, you understand. It's not the first Thanksgiving or anything." And with that he picked up his bucket of collars and left. The rest of them nodded and kept cutting.

113

"Thank you for the invitation, Lester, but we've got rice on already," Tina called after him.

"I'll be by later with some shiny trade objects," Miles said, and Lester grunted as he shut the door.

The rain was falling again, but not hard. The inlet was dark, and Miles could hear a stream rattling down a rocky chute on the black hillside; he heard the wind pushing the trees around and the faint threads of someone's FM radio leaking through a cracked window.

He turned from the boardwalk and started up the steps. How had Annabelle made her way up and down these last few weeks? He had seen her almost pulling herself up the rail, but the one time he offered to help, she brushed him away as if he were trying to snatch her purse. Miles was going to talk to her one more time about going into Sitka, but if she had enough vitality to climb these stairs, if she had enough vitality to go down to Weasel's float house to buy some pot, maybe she wasn't that sick after all.

Miles had been considering leaving Cold Storage in the last few months. The lack of age-appropriate single women, his bad luck at catching fish, and increasingly, this sense of responsibility for the health of a town that gloried in their bad habits, all of these things made him watch the big blue ferry boat coming in and leaving each month. But each month came and went, and he was never ready to buy a ticket. He was from here. His people were from here and truth be told he didn't feel as good anywhere else in the world. There was no sense in ever loving or hating the place. It was who he was, and that would change only in its own good time.

He walked and thought. Maybe all she needed was an adjustment in her medications and a change of diet. Maybe she was simply out of compliance with her heart medicine and felt depressed. Maybe a lot of things.

But one thing was certain: going to Weasel for drugs was not going to lengthen her life span or even help her with her symptoms if she really had cancer. Miles was going to be firm with her. He went over all the things he wanted to say. He wasn't going to leave with some vague promise from her to "give it some thought." He was going to get her in for some tests.

He rapped on her door, let himself in, and rounded the corner of the kitchen. The tea kettle was sitting on a lit burner, all the water boiled out and the bottom burning black. He turned the burner off. The room was hot, and there was no steam on the windows. He could just see his mother's mouse slippers propped up on the end of the recliner.

"Ma?" he whispered, worried about waking her.

He put the black cod collars in the refrigerator and walked into the front room. His mother sat in her recliner, the remote control for the television resting in her right hand. Her eyes were open, and her mouth gaped wide as if gasping for breath. She was dead.

Miles felt for a pulse, but her flesh had already cooled to a stiff clay. So he sat for several minutes, trying to decide what to do.

He turned on the VCR. There was James Stewart running through the snowy streets of Bedford Falls; there was the front door of his drafty old house, already filling with friends.

The phone rang on the counter in Annabelle's kitchen, but Miles did not move to pick it up. It rang eleven times, but still he did not answer.

CHAPTER FIVE

The plane dipped into the clouds, rocking from side to side so hard that the seats in the first-class cabin creaked in their moorings. Clive looked out the window and saw a grey world of stone and water below. The waves foamed white on the rocks. Small boats tugged on their anchor lines. The plane buffeted through the wind shear, curling up from the peaks. It shook, banked several times, and landed with a gentle thump. Clive opened his eyes, grateful but regretting that he now had to transfer to a smaller plane.

In the Juneau airport, Clive sat, drank espresso, pushed some muffins through the bars of the kennel. Little Brother's lurid, pink tongue licked up the crumbs, swept across his fingers. All the while, Clive talked to him in a calm, almost confessional tone:

"You are going to like Alaska. The climate is a bit standoffish at first, but you are going to like it."

The ugly earless dog lifted his head and stared at him. Clive leaned in close, listening, but all he heard was his snuffling breath. The dog's silence was irritating to Clive, like a manhole in the dark with the cover taken off by vandals.

"And I expect you to be wildly popular," he finally said.

Clive hadn't been able to reach his mother out at Cold Storage, though. He'd called her number several times, but there had been no answer. It had been at least ten years since he had been home. He didn't know anyone in Juneau anymore, and frankly he had only assumed that his mom and his brother were still out on the inlet.

Clive and Miles had grown up around planes and bad weather. Their grandmother had been a fine pilot; she had run a small flight service. It irritated him that there was no one he recognized at the airport. But it didn't surprise him. He had always hated flying. He had never exchanged stories with the ramp rats who loaded gear into bush planes. He never bragged about his grandma's exploits. He had never cultivated his faith in the physics and mechanics of flight. He wasn't a puker; he just didn't believe it was possible, no matter what the available evidence told him.

He had just decided to call a cab, stay in a hotel for the night, and try to fly out again the next day, when a woman came around the corner and told him that they were "going to give it a try." Clive didn't particularly like the idea of a small plane "trying to fly," but he raised his hands, palms up and shrugged. "Let's go!" he said.

The pilot, a Howdy Doody in a plaid shirt and dungarees, smiled sweetly. "I don't think the kennel is going to fit in the Beaver like that, but the dog can be in the seat with you," he said. Even though he didn't like the sound of it, Clive had long ago given up on confrontation.

The de Havilland Beaver was a single engine prop plane with landing wheels tucked under the aluminum floats on the undercarriage. It could land on the runway in Juneau and then land on the inlet at Cold Storage. To Clive, this particular floatplane looked like a piece of farm equipment.

He walked around the tail of the airplane and saw two men loading what looked like his dog kennel, except the kennel was in two pieces; the men had made a nest from the two halves and set Clive's suitcase inside. They were stuffing the whole thing into the cargo compartment behind the passenger seats.

Little Brother stood by himself on the tarmac, his choke chain glittering in the milky sunlight that filtered through the clouds.

"I don't know . . ." The pilot's head poked out from the doorway of the plane. "I guess your dog wants to wait for you . . ." His voice sounded wary. "He seems kind of touchy."

"I think he's just sensitive."

"Well, he's going to love the trip. I bet he sleeps right through until we land; they usually do." He paused and looked at the dog. "You can handle him, right?" he asked.

"Oh, yeah, no problem. Don't worry about a thing."

"He's kind of . . ." The pilot hesitated. ". . . impressive."

"Impressive is a good word," Clive said, starting to climb into the plane without his dog. "Vicious might be another."

A kid loading baggage walked toward Little Brother and stopped about ten feet from the working end of his anatomy. The kid turned his head toward Clive and yelled, "You going to load him on up there with you?"

"I don't think so." Clive kept climbing.

"What do you want me to do?" His voice

quavered.

"Well, if he's still there after we take off, you can keep him." On the tarmac, Little Brother looked sleepy. He turned his head one way and then the other. Then he lowered his head and took a small step toward the plane. The luggage kid turned away, and the pilot started to crank the engine and close the side door.

Little Brother came bounding up the stairs, clambering up the ladder, jumping into the seat next to him. Clive carefully patted the muscled hump between his dog's shoulder blades, and the thin creature settled into the seat, his head on Clive's lap, his breath filling the cabin with the smell of raw hamburger.

The trip west was noisy and bumpy. The plane bucked, the single-radial engine blared, and Clive put his fingers in his ears. Things didn't smooth out as they entered Icy Strait and headed toward the ocean; the plane dipped and rolled against the strong southwesterly wind. Clive watched the pilot scan the water and the clouds and try to adjust his altitude to find smoother air. It was going to be rough.

According to the pilot, everything would be fine as long as the visibility stayed good. Clive quietly gripped Little Brother's collar

121

and stroked his ears. His head — big as a fishbowl — settled down to rest on Clive's new parka. The plane jolted up and down, and the two of them closed their eyes. They might be rattled apart before they got to Cold Storage.

The plane bounced over the mountains of Chichagof Island. The world below them looked like a cauldron of rock, water, and wind. Waves rolled and battered the outer islands, and sweeping spumes of water broke off the tops of the waves.

Clive was about to suggest that someone should either lend him a parachute, or they should all turn around and fly back to Juneau. He opened his eyes, but before he could open his mouth to say anything, the pilot pointed to the water, gave Clive a thumbs up, and put the plane into a dive.

Clive gripped his knees and kept his eyes open. Waves bombarded the aluminum floats, the plane bounced, and they came to rest on the surface. They were in Pelican.

Clive and Little Brother watched silently as the pilot threw a line out to a bald-headed man in a red raincoat. Slowly they were pulled up to the dock, and the pilot handed the man a padded mailing envelope.

"Great, Tommy!" he said. "Thanks for dropping it off. You headed over to Cold

Storage?"

"Yeah, Harry, I am, as long as the ceiling holds. You got something?"

The man reached down and lifted a garbage bag off the dock. "You got room to take this salmon over to Miles? I told him I'd give him one this spring. Poor bastard can't seem to catch one."

"Yeah, I've got room. But if we don't get in," he added, "I'm keeping it. That okay with you?"

"Fair enough."

The man held out a black bag, and the pilot shoved it in under his seat. Tommy would take off again and make the short hop to Cold Storage and then back to Juneau and his home. Clive looked out. He remembered Pelican. Everything in Pelican was pushed together along one boardwalk, like some kind of Russian fishing village. Cold Storage wasn't anything like Pelican. Pelican had smart children and beautiful girls. At least that's what Clive had always felt. Pelican felt like the Paris of southeastern Alaska to a kid scraping along the boardwalk of Cold Storage.

Little brother could smell the fish. His nose came up off Clive's lap. His eyes narrowed, started to look almost primeval, and his muscles tightened. He hadn't eaten well in either of the airports. He tried to get down onto the floor; he rooted and pushed against the seats and against Clive.

"Is there a problem?" Tommy yelled over his shoulder.

A rocky ridgeline lay a few hundred feet below them.

"Just a few more minutes, and we'll be down," Tommy said. "Can you keep control of that dog?"

"We're doing fine," Clive called. "We're having the time of our lives!"

He tried to wrap his new coat up around Little Brother's shoulders, but the dog seemed to be growing. He would soon be the size of a buffalo, Clive thought.

Looking over his shoulder, all Tommy could see was a massive rump of brindled dog pushing against the seat. Above the roar of the engine, he could hear deep growling.

"Just a few more minutes," he said in a weak voice.

Clive pulled against Little Brother's collar, but the dog wasn't interested in calming down. He reached back, and with his teeth he grabbed the coat from around his shoulders. He began to furiously tear at the parka; feathers and dog slobber flecked against the windscreen.

Tommy started pumping the flaps and leveling off for a landing, but hundred dollar bills were floating up over his shoulder and landing in his lap. He pushed the plane down on the water. Feathers and paper money fluttered through the cabin. The dog snarled, Tommy shrieked, and Clive closed his eyes.

When they got to the float, no one was there to meet them. Tommy jumped down; he tied the plane off to a cleat and sat down on the dock with his head in his hands. One thousand dollars in assorted bills were plastered to his hair, and his neck was covered with feathers and dog slobber.

Coming down the boardwalk to meet them ran a flock of children, squeaking with short joyful cries like small seabirds. Miles was walking soberly in their wake.

Inside the plane, Little Brother had finished tearing up Tommy's seat and was busy ripping into the salmon. Blood, scales, and red bits of fish spattered the windows. Bills that had been sewn into the coat's lining fluttered like leaves.

Tommy picked himself up, turned back, and opened the passenger door. Little Brother, the king salmon firmly in his mouth, bounded up the ramp, crossed the boardwalk in two strides, and ran up into the woods. Everyone could hear him breaking through the brush, turning over the stones. No one offered to go after him. No one called or whistled for the dog to come back. They acted as if he were just another spell of bad luck that had happily just passed them by.

Clive clutched the ripped bundle of his coat and jumped down onto the floats. He'd cut his hand on one of Little Brother's teeth and was slathered with drool, feathers, large denomination bills, and his own blood.

Miles pointed to the water beside the dock. A slobbery clump of one hundred dollar bills floated toward the Aleutian Islands and Japan. "That would be your money, I take it?" he said without irony.

"Miles," Clive said softly and opened his arms wide. "Come here and hug me, you lug!"

Miles shook his head slowly from side to side. Behind him over his shoulders trees trembled on the hillside where the big brindled dog was charging up the mountain with the dead fish.

CHAPTER SIX

Jake set down his menu and waited for the waiter to come. It was a fine spring evening in Seattle with the smell of rain on dry pavement drifting in from the parking lot. Jake looked around the restaurant at the young millionaires in T-shirts and jeans. All of them drinking coffee with their meal. All of them giving the impression that they had another eight hours of work to do back in some loft on the waterfront where they were planning the initial public offering of some bullshit idea that would make them dozens of millions of dollars.

Jake was eager to get out of the drug business, and more and more he was eager to get out of computers. It was beginning to have the same kind of tension of the high stakes big deal where you didn't really know what was in the other guy's briefcase until you handed your case over to them. There was too much trust based on bullshit reputations, and the reputations were built by liars or, worse, young cokeheads.

He had understood the drug business. It was substantial and easy. There was a seemingly inexhaustible need for people to get high. There was a substance they wanted, and he provided it by the pound. Classic entrepreneurial supply and demand. But all this computer stuff . . . People were investing in things that had not made — would not make — money. People were sinking money into imaginary products that no one really understood, for Christ's sake. There was a company who hooked up people on the Internet to give and receive free things. Free: as in no money exchanged hands. This was a bad business for a drug dealer.

Jake's first love had been in films. But so far making films had been a money hole. Worse than owning a dozen boats. Films, like computers, had been bad business for a drug dealer.

The waiter brought the calamari and a bottle of Washington Zinfandel. Jake spread his linen napkin evenly on his lap. He slowly expelled his breath and took a sip of wine. Miss Peel had given him a list of subpoenas a private detective had managed to get from the grand jury who had convened on a number of criminal enterprises in the south end of Seattle in which he was included. It was a federal grand jury and a CCE — Continuing Criminal Enterprise — investigation, in which he understood that he was not the main target but was presented as one of the "Capos."

Jesus, he thought, *these fucking guys. How they love Francis Coppola. That guy changed the world. Not one of these Northwest guys is even Italian.*

Jake was anxious to get started on a new script. He had six strong ideas. All he needed to do was flesh them out, send out a few feelers, then take the strongest idea on through to a final script. One was a comedy about a single dad adopting a kid who was psychic. Jake was most hopeful, though, about his story of a husband-and-wife hit team going for marriage counseling; everybody would want this. In fact, he was thinking of shit-canning all the other story ideas and just moving on the hit team story. He'd already titled it *Till Death Do Us Part.*

"Tarantino is a pussy," he said, and took a long drink of wine. It was a tart white, with just a hint of lavender. "I can write violence," he said to himself. *But first I'd better kill Clive,* he thought as he swallowed some more.

He needed to get back on solid ground. He needed money for this enterprise. Clive had taken money from him . . . but even Jake had to admit that Clive had earned at least part of it. The money had come from Clive's milk truck profits. The whole milk truck thing had been his idea and a damn good one. Looking nice, presentable, you could wander around those neighborhoods in the early morning hours and no one gave a fucking thought. But Jake needed the money, and he couldn't risk the liability. Jake exhaled, shook his shoulders loose, and realized that he was nevertheless going to have to kill Clive, even if Clive had kept his mouth shut after getting busted. Crime is almost as dangerous as high tech. That's just the thing you have to accept about being a criminal.

Jake bit into his calamari and calmly scanned the room, as if he had just heard the voice of a good friend over in a corner. He didn't want to look like a gawker, but he had heard that Bill Allen liked to come to this restaurant.

One of the reasons Clive had been such an excellent business partner was that he didn't snort coke. He was also smart and careful, which was unusual for a criminal. Clive wouldn't blow the money; he'd squirrel it away someplace clean and retrievable, so Jake didn't have to worry about that. What he had to worry about was the cops putting pressure on him. Clive was not a natural snitch, but he was not really in love with the life. Jake knew that. Clive was a wild man but not naturally dishonest. He was Alaskan, and once he was home, he wouldn't want to go back to jail. Once he was home the threat of getting sent back inside could make him say anything. It was one of those things that was going to make Jake worry no matter how much comfortable soothing money he had. No matter if he put all his money out of high tech and into real estate and gold bars. Clive McCahon, whose name just happened to show up on this list of subpoenas to be issued, was just going to have to go.

The waiter set a dish of swordfish with mango chutney in front of him. Jake looked down at it. An abstract painting.

"What is it with this town?" he complained to himself. "The portions have gotten so goddamn small." He forked a bite into his mouth, closed his eyes, and imagined buying acres and acres of land inside the lines of America's most prosperous cities. Nothing was more secure than real estate. Real estate never went down. It was as restful as the afternoon nap he was going to take every day when he could finally work on his script full time.

First, though, he had to find Clive, get the drug money, and kill that motherfucker.

The senior center in Cold Storage was still draped in pink and white crepe paper from the last birthday party. Eloise had torn down half of the decorations before Gary decided they should leave them up; since there was no middle ground, they argued until it was time for Annabelle's memorial service to start. The hall stayed half-decorated.

Clive wore a Hawaiian shirt under a blue sweater he'd bought in Seattle and stood in a corner drinking punch from a paper cup. A heater kicked in, and dust swirled through the room, rustling the remaining strands of crepe paper hanging from the ceiling. Miles had hardly spoken to his brother. He hadn't asked about the dog, or the money, or what Clive planned to do in Cold Storage. He had walked Clive up to their mother's house, showed him how to work the oil stove, brought down some old photo albums, and piled them on the kitchen table.

"You might like to look at these," he said, and headed toward the door. His hand was on the knob before he turned around. "If you want to see her . . . her body . . . you can come down to the clinic. She has to be flown out to Juneau and then Anchorage tomorrow. She'll have an autopsy and will be cremated up there." He stopped and stared at the floor. "So," he finished, "I'll see ya."

Clive watched the door close. He stood there looking at it while familiar gulls called out over the inlet. "Hey . . . Hey . . . Hey . . ." they said.

"Good talking to you," Clive said to Miles through the closed door.

By midmorning the next day, the hall was beginning to fill. Men and women carried plates of food, laughed and nodded to neighbors still arriving. Alice brought a baked salmon, and Terry arrived with a pan of halibut enchiladas; there were scalloped potatoes, strips of smoked salmon, a smoked ham, and blueberry pies. The buffet table began to sag in the middle. Ellen came walking in the door with a bag of chips and headed straight for the beer.

Annabelle had been there at the very founding of the town. She had actually witnessed the changes others only remembered through stories. Annabelle's mother had built Ellie's Bar, which had brought

Cold Storage its modicum of regional fame. Ellie's was a destination drinking establishment. Alaska had had only seven governors since statehood, and all of them had had a drink at Ellie's. Anarchists and libertarians drank there. Democrats had their pictures taken sitting at the bar, and Republican legislators wore Ellie's silk bar jackets in the capital offices. This rightly should have been a watershed event in Cold Storage, but Miles was worried it would devolve into another boozy afternoon of overblown memories and bickering.

Chairs had been set up in the center of the room. Miles had wanted the local minister to say a few words about Annabelle, but he was on vacation down at Six Flags in Los Angeles with his niece. Miles had thought of opening the floor to remembrances from people instead but had thought better of it. For one thing, Weasel would be there, and he'd probably bring up the movie club's problems and ask people to pay him the money he was owed. Miles remembered when people were asked to speak at Bob William's memorial. Two had spoken lovingly about their memories of Bob, but then someone mentioned that he had sometimes let his dog run loose on the boardwalk, and the memorial broke down into a melee of charges and countercharges until a fight broke out in the receiving line, which caused the widow to leave early with a sprained elbow.

A Cold Storage crowd needed more structure, but Miles didn't have enough energy to design much of a service. He thought of a few words to say and resigned himself to letting everyone drink as much beer as they brought in for themselves.

Now he looked around the hall. People were already starting to drink. Clive was standing in a back corner talking to Tina; she stared up into his eyes, absently reached behind her head, and pulled a strand of hair away from her neck. Clive looked up to see Miles on the other side of the room; he smiled and then went back to talking to Tina.

Ed sat over by himself on one of the chairs set up for the service. His elbows rested on his knees, and he stared down at his shoes. A little kid ran by and clipped his knee, and he stumbled out of his reverie.

Weasel sauntered into the cold storage wearing a light tan sports coat, and Billy Cox almost spit up his beer. Weasel shrugged and lifted the lapels with the tips of his fingers.

"Yo, check it," he preened. "White Elephant shop. Sitka. Last halibut trip."

Mrs. Cera came in carrying a large tray of smoked black cod collars with Anthony slumping in behind her. Before she had even set it on the buffet table, Weasel had a black cod collar in one hand and a sweaty bottle of beer in the other.

Miles decided he'd better start before people got going on their second beer. He was walking up to the front of the room when he saw Lester come in. He was wearing clean work clothes, pressed and neat; his hair was tied back with a silver clip, and he wore a black silk tie and one of his own silver bracelets. He looked like a delegate from another, more dignified country.

He nodded to Miles. "I meant to give this to her." He took the bracelet off his own wrist and handed it to Miles. It was a thick piece of silver with a traditional salmon design carved into the surface. Before Miles could say anything, Lester softly spoke again. "I can't stay." He gestured around the room as if it were evident. "But come by later if you've got time."

Miles put the bracelet in his coat pocket and continued toward the front of the room. On the table by the flowers someone had put a picture in a frame, a photo of Annabelle as a girl standing at Ellie and Slip's cabin site. She was squinting through the thick lenses of her glasses. Her pigtails were tightly braided, and behind her Ellie and Slippery Wilson sat on the second level of logs laid down and notched into their home.

Miles had scribbled some notes about his mom's life. But these people knew all the details. He could have said how he had enjoyed having a mom who could catch a fish in any season. Or how she could laugh at a dirty joke, eat her own cooking, and burp loudly after drinking a soda, or how she knew more facts about animals than any person he had ever known. Or how she loved his father even after death and the wild north Pacific separated them.

But of course he said none of these things. He stood and muttered his "thanks-for-comings" and looked at his notes. He finally wiped his eyes and turned away. He wanted to be somewhere else.

Then he felt an arm on his shoulder and heard Clive's voice.

"What my brother wants to say is that Annabelle was a good person. She loved her friends. She loved this place. She had two sons, one who is a good guy and likes to take care of people . . ." Clive gripped Miles's shoulder and continued talking. ". . . and another who usually makes a mess

137

of things. But even so, she was proud of her family. And she liked a good party; she liked to eat and drink, and she would hate for us to let this food go to waste. So, let's get started!"

With that, a third of the people in the room lifted their bottles into the air and said, "Annabelle," in loud voices, unashamed and unafraid of the distance that separated them from her. Others called out, "Hear, hear."

Bob Gleason, using his walker, pushed his way up to Miles and jutted out a wobbly hand.

"Best memorial I've been to in a good long while," he said. He turned away, but before he got more than two steps away he doubled back. "Did you hear the story about her beautiful yellow bird?"

"Of course, Bob. That was a famous story. Grandma Ellie told it all the time, about how Mom brought her cockatiel up the inside passage in the dory —"

"And about how it flew away somewhere down south of Dixon Entrance?" Bob Gleason interrupted. "You know I think she half expected that bird to come and find her. Nearly all her life. I really think she did."

"Maybe so, Bob," was all Miles could offer.

"She was a fine gal. I always liked her. I always wanted to kind of steal her away from your father for a little while."

Miles grimaced, even though this was well-known information to him now. He tried to walk away, but Bob's skinny claw of a hand clamped down on him.

"And after your dad's boat went down and she was . . . you know . . . available, well, it just never seemed right after that."

"Yes. I suppose that's true, Bob." Miles took a step away, and the old man turned again.

"But she was a hell of a fine gal," he said, and toddled off toward the food.

Tina came, put her arms around Miles, and kissed him on the cheek. "She did a good job with you, Miles," she said.

"Thanks." He tried to stuff his notes into his pocket, but Tina kissed him again, and he felt the strong muscles between her shoulders holding onto him and he felt the air slowly slide out of him as if he wanted to stay right there in her arms.

But a line of people were waiting for him. Some, it was true, were simply grateful that they didn't have to sit through a bunch of speeches, but all of them knew what Miles was feeling because speechlessness was something they recognized in themselves and each other.

So Miles stood there, hugging people one by one. Friends and people he barely knew: drunks he'd sewn together after countless falls off the boardwalk, angry women who didn't like the tone of his voice or the selection of magazines in the clinic, fishermen who thought he was soft and inept. All of them came with their hugs, their beery breath, sour perfume, cigarettes, and fish slime. They were hugging him because he was burying someone he loved, someone he felt responsible for, and this, too, was something they understood.

Old Walter Williams came up and shook Clive's hand.

"You just got out of jail, huh?" He fixed a stern but wobbly eye on him.

Clive stood flat-footed and stared him right back in the eye. "That's true, Walter, and I've never been happier."

"Well, welcome home, buddy boy." His palsied hand gestured weakly around the hall. "Hell, you know, half of us have done a jag or two, and the rest of them just never got caught. Now get me a beer, would you?" He sat down, and a young girl handed him a plate of food and kissed him on his cheek.

Someone gave Miles a beer, and Tina brought him a plate of food. He sat down in an empty chair and let his eyes roam through the crowd, hoping Mouse Miller might wander in for some free food and beer. Other freeloaders smiled weakly and shouldered their way into the food line, but Mouse wasn't among them.

Clive hadn't eaten yet. People kept shaking his hand and talking to him. The idea of shaking the hand of a man you knew as a kid and was now an ex-con apparently was just too interesting to let go of easily. Kids and old men crowded around him, and some of the younger women stood watching from a distance.

For twenty minutes, Weasel backed Clive into a corner and tried to engage him in a discussion about the films of Harvey Keitel. The problem with Weasel's conversational strategy was that he never paused or asked questions. He lectured. And now he lectured Clive on the subject of Harvey Keitel and America's dark underbelly, which left little for Clive to add.

Mrs. Cera came over to Miles and gave him a special plate of black cod collars. She said some of them "came out of the smoke-house just perfect," and she wanted him to have them. He thanked her, and she held his face in her hands and disappeared back into the crowd.

People who had already had enough to eat were starting to leave. But someone came in with more beer and someone else plugged in a tape player and suddenly the room was full of Glenn Miller. Weasel took his sports coat off and started swing dancing with Tina. Ed undid his tie and began talking to Mrs. Cera about the subtleties of smoking black cod. Miles drank some more beer, even though he hadn't drunk much beer since he got out of the Army.

Now the old people were telling stories. Many were about Annabelle. Miles and Clive walked around the room, sitting on the edge of a group of two or three. They sat and listened. Old women would place their old hands over the boys and leave them there. There were stories of picnics and big salmon. There were stories of bears and long snowy winters. There were stories of unexplainable kindnesses and debts that would never be repaid. Clive and Miles went from group to group, and each group folded them into their own loving company. Glasses clinked. Laughter burbled up, and old friends and people said the names of those who had long left this stormy coast.

The room was quieting down, and most

of the older folks had headed home. Clive was talking to a young woman working in the cold storage for the summer; he was eating huckleberry pie and drinking black coffee and watching her sway in her chair and hold onto her beer with both hands. Tina was sitting with Miles and listening to Weasel tell her about the John Sayles movie *Matewan;* she was laughing at what he said but her arm was draped over the back of Miles's chair, and he could feel her forearm against his back.

Billy flopped down with a cup of coffee, a bottle of brandy, and a plate of sugar doughnuts. He poured brandy into his coffee and ate one of the doughnuts; powdered sugar dusted his chin as he chewed and drank and looked at Miles but didn't say a word.

Tina got Miles up to dance to "Pennsylvania Six Five Thousand," and they spun around the room, bumping into the folding chairs only once. It was dark outside when the song was over.

The people left in the hall sat at a long table where Billy was still eating doughnuts. Miles sat down between Tina and Clive. The cold storage girl was sleeping against Clive's shoulder.

"Forty-nine days," Billy blurted.

"What?" Tina asked.

"Forty-nine days," Billy repeated. "She's got forty-nine days to get a new body."

"Ah!" said Miles.

Tina leaned over to explain this to Clive. "Billy's a Tibetan Buddhist."

"Ah!" said Clive.

"And he's going to paddle his kayak to Seattle so he can meet the Dalai Lama," Miles added.

"I'm going to raise money to free Tibet," Billy said with a mouthful of doughnut.

Clive looked at him and smiled broadly. "Christ, something should be free in this life." He reached into his pocket. "Give this to him for me," he said, and handed Billy ten hundred dollar bills.

"Excellent! Lemme get a picture . . ." Weasel stood up and wove over to the counter for the Polaroid camera kept in the supply drawer. They bunched around the table with Clive and Billy in the center of the group, and Clive handing the money to Billy as if he were a lucky sweepstakes winner. Weasel snapped the picture and waved the exposed print in the air as if he were fanning himself.

"Billy," he said, "you take this with you so the Dalai Lama can see who we are." He lay the print out on the table, and they

144

watched the images ease into being, watched the white sheen of light spread over the slightly overexposed photograph.

Billy took it and held it gingerly in his sugared hands. "I will give this to him myself," he said with purpose.

Billy kept staring at the picture and at the hundred dollar bills. He grinned and put the money and the photo in his front pants pocket, finished his coffee nudge, brushed the powdered sugar off his hands. He licked one fingertip and smiled again. "Sweet," he said.

Out on the boardwalk, rain had started to fall through the dark. Clive had helped the young girl find her feet and handed her off to Tina, who promised to get her back to the bunkhouse. Everyone said goodnight and started to go, but Tina doubled back to give Miles one last kiss, holding up the drunken fish slimer with one arm.

"Have a good sleep, bud," she said.

"Thanks."

"I love you so much!" blurted the drunken girl.

"Thanks," Miles said, and patted her on the back.

The brothers turned to walk to their mother's house.

"You shouldn't have dismissed her like that," Clive said, and turned up the collar of his Hawaiian shirt, shrugging.

"Like what?"

"Like that!" Clive's voice was affronted. "Hell, she spent the entire evening telling me about her deep longing for you."

Miles spun around and watched her staggering home to the bunkhouse. "I don't know that girl," he said. "She was probably in grade school when I went in the army."

"You need to pay a little better attention, brother." He stepped around a spilled can of paint lying on the boardwalk, red drops falling through the cracks. Delicate paw prints ran through the scarlet puddle and along the boardwalk, fading into the darkness.

"You've been here, what . . . a couple of days and already you're critical?" Miles couldn't keep his voice friendly anymore.

"What do you want, Miles?" Clive asked. "You want me to leave right away?"

Miles didn't say anything, and they walked along the slick planks.

"Screwy things happened after you went away." Miles was quiet for a bit. "Pop died . . . and then you just left . . . and then it seemed like all she ever talked about was you."

Wind shushed through the trees, and a raven stood on a rail beside the boardwalk, scratching its beak.

"And I was right here." Miles's voice was tired. "I'm tired of all the attention you got around here," he said.

"I haven't even been here," Clive said.

"I know." Miles turned away from his brother.

Clive wanted to walk away. He wanted to walk back into the silence that had enfolded him in the protective segregation cell. There was no use in explaining anything to a brother who was angry with him. Who had good reason to be angry with him.

"Jesus! You were a dope dealer," Miles said. "While I was in Somalia!"

"I know, Miles," Clive said. "It's not right. I wasn't right. I'm going to try to be better, a better brother."

The raven jerked its head back and forth between the two brothers as if deciding whose side he was on. Clive watched him for a moment. He turned and walked over to the black bird. The bird looked up at Clive and said very succinctly, "Just tell him the truth."

"Cocaine," Clive said finally. "I sold flake cocaine. When I was doing it, I told myself that it wasn't crack. Pure rationalization, it's

147

true. I sold to a select group of rich clients. I delivered early in the morning and they left me cash, and I told myself that at least I didn't sell to kids or people who were reckless around their kids."

"Do you know how you sound?"

"I do," Clive said. "Listen, I'm sorry for leaving you. I really am. I thought about you all the time. But . . . you know those people who talked about me all the time? They didn't know who they were talking about."

"Just as you didn't know the little brother you say you were thinking about."

"What's it like being a hero?" Clive asked.

"Shit," Miles said, looking up and down the inlet. For a moment he thought of brushing his brother off with a canned answer he usually gave about training and instant response, but instead he said, "When it's happening to you, it's kind of a dumb surprise. You just wonder, 'Is this it? Is this what I've been worried about?' And then you see people dying and you kind of figure . . . yeah, this must be it. But there is no music like in the movies, and there is no time to take it all in, you just keep moving and reacting . . . You just go, go, go, and when you make it — if you make it — that's when you get scared. It's weird. You never feel like a hero, you really don't, you just feel bad that you made it and the other guys who must have done that one thing more, that one brave thing, or mistaken thing, that you didn't. I don't know."

They walked on in silence. In the distance, the wind scoured over the trees and out into the darkness. A street lamp cast a shaky pool of light onto the boardwalk.

Miles thought of his mother's empty house. He thought of her being forever gone, and he hunched up his shoulders to the wind.

"I realize that there is so much I don't know about you," Clive said finally, "and that can be added on to the list of things that are my fault." Then he held out his hand to Miles. "I was a criminal, but now I'm not and I'd like to get to know you."

"What are you now?" Miles asked, still a little shaky on his feet.

"I'm not sure, brother."

"Is that money from your coat going to get us in trouble?"

"Us?"

"Well, you."

"No. I don't think so. It's my money. Even the guy I stole it from knows that."

Miles looked up at his brother. "Somehow I don't find that very comforting."

"Money doesn't really belong to any one person. That's why they call it money. But we're splitting hairs. Tell me the truth: have you seen my dog?" Clive smiled at his brother.

"That is an ugly dog, Clive."

"I didn't ask for your opinion of his looks," Clive said. "Have you seen him?"

"No." Miles said. "No, I haven't seen your dog."

They looked at each other. The wind washed up the hillside in a wave, and the trees flung their arms in the dark. Fat raindrops started falling, sounding like a gamelan hitting the tin roofs and the buckets all around town. "We can look for him tomorrow." He stepped forward to put his hand on his brother's shoulder. "Thanks for helping me out back there at the memorial," he said, "when I froze up."

Clive returned the gesture so they were arm in arm as they had once been walking down the boardwalk. "Don't worry about it."

They started up the stairs to Annabelle's house. The wind was shrieking now, and a branch of a tree scraped against a metal roof. They stopped in the dark and looked up toward the noise. There, at the peak of the roof, sat a strange yellow bird with orange dots on its cheeks. Clive saw it clearly as a fever dream. He pointed without saying a thing, and the bird flew away.

"Look," Clive whispered even though the bird had flown.

"What?" Miles said, following his brother's gesture but seeing nothing.

"I must be imagining things."

Just as they reached the dark porch they heard a deep-throated growl. Miles pushed past Clive, picked up the flashlight stored on a shelf, and pressed the switch. He swept the beam of light into the darkness.

Twenty feet away was Clive's brindled dog. Black tree limbs swirled above him. He sat, the stubs of what were once ears erect, taking short puffs of breath and holding a dead cat in his jaws; red paint daubed the pads of the cat's feet.

"I would like to take this opportunity to apologize for my dog," began Clive.

"Whoever owns that cat is not going to be happy," Miles said, as if to himself.

"Well, they can take that up with the dog." Clive turned to go into the house.

"What's his name?"

"Little Brother!" Clive called through the closed door.

"Perfect," said Miles. The sigh of the wind

in the trees blended with the growl of the ugly dog with a dead cat in its mouth.

CHAPTER SEVEN

It was a clear morning; the sun hadn't risen yet above the ridgeline, and the sky flared blue and silver above the inlet. Out to the west, a layer of fog rolled in from the coast. It should burn off by the time Billy reached it, but if it didn't, he could hug the shoreline of the outer coast.

His kayak, loaded and heavy with gear, was tied up at the floatplane dock. She sat low in the water, but every inch of her looked buoyant, long and narrow like a eucalyptus leaf caught in a back eddy. Billy had built her from strips of Sitka spruce and canvas following a modified plan of an Aleut design, and the bow swept up to a large, flat holding point shaped like a dragon's head. Billy had painted a pair of eyes up there to watch over his progress.

He had packed a few clothes, a small tent, a sleeping bag, and some charts. He planned to build fires most of the time but had a small gas stove along, just in case. He had dehydrated pinto bean flakes, rice, cheese, vitamins, and chocolate bars. He had a small fishing rod and a spinning reel with a box of lures, since he was almost certain he could jig up rockfish just about anywhere he put in. On top of the boat, he'd lashed two extra paddles.

Tina had given Billy a gift for this trip. She had wrapped it in a waxed canvas bag and tied it up with a length of tarred twine. *The Tibetan Book of the Dead.* It was an old library book by Dr. W.Y. Evans-Wentz. Billy flipped through the pages, scanning each page as if he were reading a map.

"I thought you might need it."

"Cool!" He hugged her and closed his eyes as if he were committing the moment to memory. "I knew you believed in me."

"I never said that." She whispered into his ear, "I just want you to come back, one way or another, and this might help." She held him a little longer than usual.

Billy had ordered a brand-new dry bag from Seattle. It was bright yellow and carried all of his most important papers: his passport, his money for the trip, Clive's money for the Dalai Lama, and some flyers he'd made that described his trip and requested donations. Inside all of these

154

papers, he had placed the photograph taken at Annabelle's wake. He added Tina's new book to the bag.

Billy took off his boots, rolled them up, tucked them behind his seat. He put on his warm slippers, eased into the kayak, and wriggled around in the tight cockpit as if he were putting on a new pair of blue jeans. He put a bottle of water on his lap and slid his rolled up slicker under his thighs. He pulled his spray skirt over his head, stretched it tight over the hole in the cockpit; he slipped wrist gaiters over his long-sleeved shirt and looked around.

A few gulls were floating like chips of ice on the surface of the inlet. Tina had disappeared. A couple of kids were running up the boardwalk pulling a red wagon, clattering like a bucket rolling on its side. Smoke was sliding out of the chimney of Lester's house and rising up, ghostly white, against the sides of the mountain. Billy undid the painter line from the dock and pushed away.

He had hoped a few more people might have come down to say goodbye, even though he knew that his sentimentality about the place was an illusion. He had Clive's money and two thousand dollars in pledges if he made it all the way to Seattle, but he knew that was an illusion of sorts, too. The substance of this trip was compassion. And even though compassion was supposed to flow from him and not toward him, he was still a little ticked off that no one had noticed his leaving.

He pulled his paddle through the water. "I take refuge in the Dharma," he murmured sadly, thinking that he must still be a pretty crappy Buddhist.

He pulled his way through the water and past the pilings of the cold storage. Fat drops of water plunked into the water from a broken pipe. With each new stroke, his boat felt sleeker and stronger as if she, too, were looking forward and pushing ahead. A fat raven flew down from the roof of the cold storage and landed on the bow of his kayak, and he stopped paddling, sat still. The bird cocked its head from side to side and looked at him expectantly. Billy had a peanut butter sandwich in his coat pocket; he fished it out, broke off a corner, and tossed it toward the raven. It made a loud cry, jumped, caught the bit of bread in midair, and flew low over the water back to the shadows under the wharf. Billy watched it weaving between the pilings. He could hear the air pushing past its wings as he started paddling toward Seattle.

He made it around the first point out of

town in a few minutes. A squall from the west was blowing through, and fog lay ahead. Should he cross the inlet? He looked to his right and saw the sign.

They had hung the sheet about twenty feet up in the trees at the end of the boardwalk. A white sheet with some kind of red design that was hard to decipher because the wind pushed the tree limbs around and pulled the sheet in all directions. He tried to identify the pattern but couldn't, so he turned to face the sheet head on and stopped paddling.

The squall passed. The branches hung motionless. A group of people stood beneath the sign, and Billy saw Tina reach up and pull on a rope tied to one corner of the sheet. The red lettering on the sign snapped into focus; it read: "We love you, Billy. Whatever is here, that is there."

The kids who had been running along the boardwalk were now standing on their wagon and waving, as if he were floating away in a hot air balloon. Clive was standing beside his brother, and Billy heard Miles call out over the water, "I put some extra medication in your boat. Some ointment and antibiotics. I thought you should have some just in case."

Billy raised his hand and shook it in a

short embarrassed wave.

Weasel pulled his pants down and mooned him.

"Meeeee, tooooo!" he screamed. And the children started swaying with laughter, almost falling out of their wagon.

Clive was waving as if he were the Prince of Wales.

Someone shouted, "Give our best to His Holiness!"

And the girl from the cold storage yelled, "You go, boy!"

Billy waved again and started paddling toward the head of the inlet where fog was easing in from the coast.

Clive drank a cup of coffee, walked along the boardwalk, and tried to decide what to do. Radio reports had tracked a storm off the coast, but for the time being the air was clear. A light breeze drifted across the inlet, teasing the steam rising from his mug.

Clive had spent a week going through his mother's house. Some evenings Miles would come over, and the two of them would start packing boxes and end up cross-legged on the floor or parked at a table, flipping through piles of loose photographs. They would talk, try to help each other remember names or places, and drift back into their separate reveries.

Only a few boxes were filled. Annabelle's clothes still hung in the bedroom closet, and her sheets lay untouched in the linen closet. Clive slept in her bed but borrowed bedding from Miles because he didn't want to use hers. There had been no more discussions about Clive's past or about the money sewn into the down parka.

Little Brother ranged on the hillside and over in the far river valley; Clive left food in a bowl and found it empty in the mornings. No cats were reported missing, not even the white cat that had been killed the night of the wake. Clive had been prepared to make a substantial payment to the aggrieved cat owner, but none appeared and Miles wasn't surprised. Most of the cats in Cold Storage belonged only to themselves; they had to survive on scraps from the fish plant and from the garbage cans along the boardwalk.

Miles was at the clinic tending to Teddy, whose knees and elbows were full of splinters from a particularly spectacular bicycle wreck.

Clive was restless. He didn't want to look at pictures and the inside of Annabelle's house was beginning to feel close. A storm was expected to blow through soon, and

Clive felt a headache coming on.

He eased around the southern border of the boardwalk and walked into Lester, who'd clamped a music stand onto the top rail of the walkway to make himself an easel. He had a piece of fiberboard set up and was scratching at it with a tiny putty knife.

"Hey, Clive," Lester murmured.

"Lester," Clive nodded.

He squinted at the drawing on the board. It was a traditional Tlingit design of a raven; thick black lines surrounded the stylized ovoids, the eyes and the beak reflecting the same circular forms.

A raven flew across the tide flat, back around the point and out of sight. Lester wiped the palette knife on a rag, then daubed at the canvas, watching the bird. Clive looked at the stylized drawing, then to the bird, then back at the canvas. He started to ask why he was watching a raven when Lester obviously wasn't drawing from life. But he held his tongue, remembering enough of the manners he learned from before he left Alaska the last time.

"Can I ask you a question, Lester?" he finally said.

"I don't suppose it would hurt," the artist replied without taking his eyes off of his work.

"Do you think animals can talk to people?"

Lester put aside his palette knife on the top of his supply box. "Before I get into that let me ask you something."

"Okay."

"Were they giving you some medication in jail that you stopped taking? You know what I'm asking? The pills that made the voices stop?"

"I don't need medication, Lester."

"At the risk of employing a cliché, Clive — that's what they all say."

"Come on, Lester. What about all the old stories? Animals used to talk to people, didn't they?"

Lester wiped his hand on an oiled cloth. "You are serious about this, aren't you?"

"Yeah, I guess I am."

"And you're not talking about parrots and mynah birds, are you?"

"No. I'm not."

"Because there is a girl up at the cold storage who has lost her parrot, and she's going crazy looking for it."

"Somebody really lost a parrot?" Clive thought back to the vision on top of his mother's house.

"Okay . . ." Lester bullied his way through the silence. "It's not like the animals talked

161

to people. It's more like people used to be animals. It wasn't such a big deal. Like you talk to your dog, you don't really expect the dog understands everything you say, but you talk and the dog gets your meaning because . . . I don't know. Because you have a relationship. It used to be that way with animals and human beings. They all were related somehow. They talked to one another, and even if they knew all the meaning wasn't getting through, they could still understand each other."

"Could it happen now? Could someone start understanding the animals now?" Clive asked in a low voice, obviously embarrassed now.

"Are we back talking about the pills thing? Maybe you should talk to someone about that."

"No. I want to know. Could it happen to someone now?"

"Why the heck are you asking me?" Lester snorted. "You're not some new age nut job who is going to ask me to lead them on some frigging dream quest, are you?"

"No. I just remember the old people talking about it when I was a kid. Even some of the old Norwegian fishermen, they'd tell stories about hearing seals talk and the birds. I remember the Indians talking about how to act around bears and what to say and stuff. I'm . . . I'm just . . ." And he stopped speaking and turned to walk away.

"Hold up," Lester called to him, and Clive turned. "Yes. Yes, it can happen now."

"What would cause it?"

"All it takes is getting over yourself as a human being. Living with animals for a long period could do it."

"Is it a bad thing?" Clive asked.

"Are any animals telling you to start killing Indians?"

"No."

"Then it sounds fine." Lester snapped shut his supply box. "But again, I'm not sure why you are asking me."

"All the square-headed Norsky fishermen are dead." Clive smiled.

"You'll be fine," Lester said as he unscrewed his makeshift easel. "Just don't try and go Native. That's just so eighties. Schizophrenia is what's happening now. Go with that."

"Thanks for the tip," Clive said, then waved and walked down the boardwalk.

Up to his left, he could hear a large animal walking along the rocks of a steep-sided stream bed; he had heard that there had been a bear in the garbage cans out in front of the restaurant, and in fact had heard dogs

163

barking in alarm early in the morning when he was cooking his breakfast. The trees rustled fifty feet away, and Clive started whistling the tune to "Don't Fence Me In," hoping that the bear would recognize him as a kindred spirit and give him a wide berth.

So he was whistling when he turned the corner and saw the fallen-down bar. Actually, he saw Little Brother sitting on a loose piece of roofing lying out in front of a salmonberry thicket some ten feet from the boardwalk. The big dog was lying in the sun with his head on his front paws; his eyes were barely open, and he seemed to be content.

"It's good to see you," said Clive as if greeting an old friend at the post office.

The brindled dog lifted his head just slightly, turned, and said nothing.

Clive headed toward the dilapidated structure. The sun was breaking over the ridgeline, and the building started to glitter; steam began to rise from the roof. Clive stopped and watched for a moment. The thicket came up and around the back of the roof; just up the hillside, two gnarled hemlock trees leaned out from the forest with their trunks almost shading the bar. This was a magician's hiding place, Clive

164

thought, and something he later recognized as optimism rose in his chest.

This was Ellie's Bar. The wildest and most storied drinking spot along this stretch of coast. From World War II and onward, fishermen had yearned to make port here. Now its spongy boards were melting into the moss. All he had to do was push the wooden door aside, and it came off of its hinges. He ripped some of the plastic off the windows to let the light in, and when he had, he knew he had taken the right path. Chairs were stacked on tables in the center of the room and old high-backed booths lined the walls; dusty bottles stood at the back of the ebony bar; the ceiling was water-stained plaster. Wet dollar bills hung over the room like wilted leaves from tacks that had been pinned there years before. All around the bar and on the edges of every booth, people had carved the names of their boats: *The Defiant, The Lisa M, The Samuel R Wiks, The Point Hope, Willie's Raider.* There were hundreds of names of fishing boats carved around the room. There were tin beer signs, and an old horsehair dart-board, green with mildew. At the back was a slate pool table with leather pockets; one of the legs had broken through the flooring and the whole table listed forward like a ship gone aground; colored balls rested in the leather pockets, mossy with neglect.

Clive pulled a chair off the top of one of the tables and sat staring. He could smell something underneath the mildew and spilt heating oil. He could smell burgers cooking, and perfume; he smelled beer foaming over thick glass mugs. He could hear the gurgling of the coffee maker as morning regulars came in to chat; he heard music and women laughing at badly told jokes. Something about the bar's decrepitude attracted him. This was the opposite of his old concrete bunker in protective seg. This was some place the forest was going to eventually get back; this was only a temporary shelter from the storm. Unlike prison, this place was designed for impermanence and escape. Clive sat with his eyes closed and imagined such a thing.

Little Brother walked in and lay down on a mat at the end of the bar.

"You want to be a bouncer?" Clive asked the big dog. "You are family now. I could probably put you on."

Little Brother raised his head and looked down behind the bar, whimpered softly, and put his head back down on his front paws.

Clive went over to where the dog lay. A pad and a ring of candles in shot glasses

166

rested on the floor; a fairly new sleeping bag was spread out, and a backpack stuck out from under the bar where the garbage cans had been. A sour smell of rotten meat reached out and enveloped them both.

There was a foot in a rubber boot, attached to a leg.

Clive walked past the dog and over to the body. Half of the sleeping bag was resting over the shoulders of the short, bearded man. Clive rolled him over. The body was stiff, hard as wet clay under the damp wool jacket; small animals had already started in on the exposed flesh of the face, but Clive could still make out the features.

"You must be the famous Mouse Miller everyone's been talking about," said Clive. He patted the old fisherman's shoulder and eased him back down.

A gust of wind rattled through the bar and sent a flurry of dry alder leaves swirling behind the bar. One landed on Mouse Miller's dead open eye just as the storm from the outer coast announced its arrival.

CHAPTER EIGHT

Bonnie had booked an Alaskan cruise on board the *SS Universe* as a last attempt to bring order to her life. It was beating down on her, like a hard rain, just how mistaken she had been.

She was standing on the port side of the lower stern deck dressed as Little Bo Peep and carrying the empty swimming pool's lifesaving hook as her shepherdess crook. The ship was on the first sailing of the season, southbound from Valdez. By nine o'clock, the seas were darkening to a bruised color, but the steep slopes of the Fairweather Range still shone with a brilliant, rose-colored light. On the deck above, the band from Oberlin College was playing "You've Got to Ring Them Bells," and a tiny boy from Belgium, dressed as some kind of fuzzy space monster, was boxing with two Japanese girls dressed like lambs.

Bonnie had seen whales spouting near the

ship that afternoon, rubbery grey forms with slick backs slowly lifting their tails up in the wake of the ship, then disappearing into the whitewashed foam. She thought she could hear one of them make a long groaning sigh, almost impossibly low and mournful.

She looked down at herself, at the blue Bo Peep dress billowing out away from the rail in the brisk wind. "How stupid is *this*?" she asked the sea, hissing below her.

Bonnie's mother had insisted that she take the Alaskan cruise, had sent the ticket for her twenty-seventh birthday. It wasn't lost on her that her mother hoped she'd meet a man, and she had met men, almost all of them over fifty and traveling with their second or third wife. All the forced gaiety of the cruise made her feel sad: the dances where retired people swayed to big band tunes, the lectures where retired professors and engineers dominated the question-and-answer sessions, trying, Bonnie supposed, to regain some of the authority they'd left behind in their old jobs.

But why was she sad at this particular moment? She didn't know. She'd just started to cry while sitting on the bench before the costume parade, sitting by herself, waiting alongside three people in black garbage bags who were planning to dance to Marvin Gaye's "Heard It Through the Grapevine" like the California Raisins. She hated herself for being sad and judgmental. After all, she was dressed as Little Bo Peep, and no one had made her wear a costume. But still, she hated herself and these people she didn't know.

She took a bottle of vodka out of the front pocket of her pinafore, took a long drink. She looked down into the grey water curling around the stern of the ship; no fish cut the surface, no life rose up from the darkness. She felt something lift inside her chest. Her right foot began to rise up to the lateral rail support, but as she felt her weight come down on the raised foot, she knew she wasn't going to climb over the rail. She couldn't kill herself because she knew her problems didn't have the gravity of a suicide. Her vague sadness now wouldn't compare to her mother's grief later when she heard from the Coast Guard that the search for her daughter's body had been suspended. Even though there wasn't a clear reason to go on living, there wasn't a clear enough reason to take her own life.

The sun sank over the starboard side; the Fairweathers darkened and stepped back into the grey-greenness of southeastern

Alaska. Bonnie looked out to sea. The band barreled into a medley of songs from *Cabaret;* a balding man with a cardboard shark fin taped onto his head peered over the railing above her, scanned the horizon, took a sip from his glass, and stepped back inside the deck lounge; and Bonnie imagined her life proceeding at its own implacable pace throughout the rest of the evening, the rest of the voyage, on and on through a long cycle of years. She'd live her life, learn to pull up her socks, accept whatever fate brought her.

She started to turn toward the stairway but something caught her eye; about fifty yards from the ship, a long ridge cut the water from beneath the surface. Another whale, she thought, but no blow appeared, and the ridge was straight, not nearly as pliable as the backs of whales. She looked again and made out the straight line of a piece of wood, a drift log perhaps. But then a pale arm reached up out of the water.

Bonnie screamed. She threw the useless shepherdess crook overboard toward the figure fading behind the ship; she threw an emergency life ring hanging from a nearby wall. And as two of the California Raisins came out on the upper stern deck, she jumped from one foot to another and screamed, "Man overboard!" and various unintelligible syllables in a high-pitched voice.

The emergency beacon lit up as soon as the life ring hit the water. The Raisins saw the small blinking light lost in the darkening Gulf of Alaska and heard the loud blast of the ship's whistle. They cupped their gloved hands over their ears and looked at each other in dull surprise as the engines of the *Universe* started to slow.

Billy was not making great progress down the coast. The prevailing winds had been against him the entire week.

"I take refuge in the Buddha, I take refuge in the Dalai Lama, I take refuge in the Dharma, I take refuge in the Sangha," he repeated to himself as he paddled.

His boat rode low in the sea. Billy was not a big man so his torso above the spray skirt didn't make up a lot of sail area. Even so, the weight of the wind pushing against his chest felt like a hand holding him back.

The clouds were spun from iron filings, silver to grey to black. They smeared across the pale grey, sunless sky. The wind shrieked across the top of the waves, drew claw marks across the water.

Billy rode up the waves, topped the broken

whitecaps as if sledding down a fast river. His spray skirt filled with water at his lap, but no water came into his boat.

"I take refuge in the Buddha, I take refuge in the Dalai Lama, I take refuge in the Dharma, I take refuge in the Sangha."

Billy had to make a decision. He could try to find a safe place to land, but then he risked getting caught in the big surf the storm was throwing up against the rocky bluffs to the west; a ten-fathom shelf caused ocean swells to steepen dramatically on this part of the coastline. He could try to paddle out past the shelf where the swells would flatten out, but then he'd have to battle the wind to stay upright until he could find a headland to hide behind or a broad passage he could take back to inside waters.

He stopped paddling. He rode the waves up and down; steadied himself with his paddle and kept his bow pointed into the wind. If the wind built much more, the waves would start cresting hard enough to roll him down the face of the swells. He'd rolled his boat before, first in a swimming pool in Sitka and then a couple of times in a lake for practice, but he didn't know how long he could maintain his strength in cold water. He didn't think he could fight the storm all night long.

173

He thought he was going to die. He thought about his parents back in California, about the early mornings when he was a baby and his baby feet left faint impressions on the lawn and how his footprints were never there just a few moments after. He pushed his paddle into the waves and felt himself growing weaker, felt himself fading away just like those footprints. He felt sad. Then angry. Then he heard easy laughter, the low rumble of the storm, and . . . "No fighting," he said to himself. He turned his boat with the wind and spread his shoulders to catch the storm.

The wind blew straight onto the steep coastline; the sea pounded against slick rocks, sending the broken teeth of the waves thirty feet into the air; white foam churned up, and Billy tasted saltwater in his mouth as his slender kayak plunged through the tumult.

He floated giddily above his fear. He shifted his weight almost imperceptibly; the boat cut into a wave and sledded down the slope.

He pulled the boat toward a narrow channel of green foam-mottled water and felt the sudden boost of a shore wave building beneath him; he cut back. He slid down a broken wave, and just before the white water tumbled over his shoulders, he and his boat were tossed out into an eddy of water behind a bluff.

It was like walking into a quiet room off a busy street — suddenly calm. The green sea rose and fell with the swells, but no water broke through the mouth of the small bight. Billy's hand shook; he reached under the spray skirt for a bandanna to wipe the seawater from his eyes. High above him in a cranny in the bluff, a peregrine falcon split the wind with its call. Three hundred feet up the rock wall, Billy saw trees surging back and forth in the wind.

There was no flat beach from which he could crawl out of his boat, and so he floated on water relentlessly rising and falling against the steep walls of the island. He ate flakes of fish that he'd caught and cooked the previous night; he lay them out on top of his spray skirt and ate them with two pieces of soggy pilot bread and half a piece of chocolate. He washed it all down with the last of his fresh water. And his boat dipped into the trough of a wave.

The wave didn't break, but the force of it slid up the side of the bluff, rebounded; rocks appeared and water eddied in circles. The tide was rising. The small ledge protecting the tiny bight was about to become awash and time was running out for Billy. In a few minutes, the waves would break through and his little seedpod of a boat would be ripped wide open. If he had to ride out a night at sea, he'd have to stay well clear of the rocks.

Billy hadn't thought of trying to get on the *Universe,* although he'd seen it moving down from the north; its lights had served as a frame of reference in the descending darkness. But it was lit up like a birthday cake in the tenebrous night, and its resplendence seemed remarkably close, and so Billy paddled. He pulled his boat up over the swells until the booming and sucking shoreline was behind him, and the wind died.

The lights came nearer. Billy saw the railings, the lights from the portholes, the lone figure of a woman in a long dress standing on the back deck of the ship and holding some strange kind of fishing pole. He felt like he was on a collision course with the *Universe.*

He didn't want to be caught in the wake, in churned waters that would snarl the already confused sea. But his hands shook and his spray skirt was undone; his legs were wet and he shivered. The adrenaline that had rushed through his body and carried him through the surf was leaving, and he felt light-headed, weak, and cold. The flakes of fish, the bread, the chocolate had been burned up half an hour ago, and now his teeth chattered.

"No fighting," he said out loud and reached for another chocolate bar. His paddle dropped. He reached for it reflexively, and a wave crested. He felt his boat give way and he tried to recover, but another wave slapped him in the face, then pulled him into the sea.

His gear drifted out of the boat. Sealed food bags, half-filled with air, floated like jellyfish; his yellow bag of documents drifted downwind, and he tried to swim after them but the water was too frigid, his strength was too feeble, and he felt the weight of his body pull him beneath the surface. He turned, raised his arm high into the air, and brought it down on the overturned hull of his floundering boat.

The lights of the ship spilled out over the water. Billy heard the engines churn, felt the wake of the bow wash over him, and threw out his arms to grip onto something in a world turning black.

The *Universe* had come to a stop, and Bonnie stood on the deck pointing and shouting. A boat crew began lowering a lifeboat from station number eight, and before they could stop her, she jumped down into it. The crew wanted to lift the boat back up, but the sailor in charge motioned to lower away and another crewman put a life jacket on Bonnie. She allowed him to attach the straps but continued to point out into the darkness where just moments before she had seen the human arm rise up out of the water.

The lifeboat floundered in the water until they were able to start the motor and pull away from the ship. The waves rocked the little boat from side to side, but even so Bonnie stood on top of the middle seat pointing. Three crewmen held onto her legs, asking her politely to step down and be careful.

The lifeboat motored out into the darkness and as soon as it did, a spotlight on the deck of the *Universe* flashed a burning hole into the night. Bonnie could see a kayak overturned in the water, and the boatman steered toward it. But a half-dozen yards upwind, Bonnie could see someone floating just under the surface of the water. As soon as she saw it, she dove into the water and swam.

The water was so cold she felt as if she would pass out. The cold coursed through her body almost immediately, as if it were a drug being pumped into her veins. She flailed her arms, trying to swim, but the bulky life jacket kept her from moving well, so she unhooked the jacket and swam free. The sounds of the men on the boat were a slurry of voices. She found herself fighting back against a kind of sleepiness that was overtaking her. She started slapping the water with her arms, aware of breathing each new breath and pulling herself toward the man sinking in the water.

The spotlight followed her progress through the waves. The shaft of light turned the black water green and when she stopped swimming, she opened her eyes and saw a man with pale white skin suspended just underwater. With his arms out at his sides, he drifted there as if the light were holding him up. A few bubbles came from his mouth, and he looked up at her as if he had been waiting for her. What she remembered most clearly before she dove down to grab hold of his jacket was that he was smiling like a saint.

They both woke up in the infirmary on the boat. They were covered in warm blankets that felt as if they had just come from the dryer. Hot pads sat on their chests and bellies, the extension cords running out from under the blankets.

The ship's doctor leaned over Billy and asked him if he knew where he was.

"I'm in the *Universe,*" Billy said with a smile on his face.

"Exactly," the doctor said, and patted the shivering man's shoulder.

All of Billy's gear scattered in the darkness that had closed in around the wake of the ship. Once the lifeboat crew had gotten both of the people out of the water, their only thought had been to get them back on board the *SS Universe.* Billy's tent, sleeping bag, the paddle, and the boat itself lay to the stern on top of the water. The bags of food had been wrapped too tightly to maintain buoyancy and drifted down and settled some six hundred feet below the surface where only the long-lived short raker rockfish swam among the bare stones.

But the yellow package with the money for the Dalai Lama, Billy's passport, the photograph of his friends, and his unread copy of *The Tibetan Book of the Dead* floated on the surface of the great black sea, mindless and undisturbed.

CHAPTER NINE

There was barely a memorial service for Mouse Miller. Some of his friends brought the leftovers from Annabelle's service down to the deserted bar. Mrs. Cera brought some fresh black cod and some potato salad, but she did not stay. She hugged Miles and Clive, thanked Clive for finding Mouse, and left. Her eyes were rimmed red, and Miles thought that he had never seen the strong woman look so sad. He walked her to the boardwalk and touched her on the elbow as she turned silently toward home.

Weasel had a forty-five pound white king salmon that he brought straight up from the docks and laid on the bar with the shaved ice still stuffed into its belly. Within an hour, someone had set up the half-barrel grills in the yard, and the coals were almost ready for cooking. Someone had put a photograph of Mouse over the bar.

Fishermen balanced themselves on the uneven floor and passed around a bottle of schnapps. In a corner, a deckhand from Juneau played cribbage with Jerry Hughes. Miles and Clive walked in, and since it was only ten in the morning, both of them asked for a cup of coffee. Weasel poured some from his insulated jug, and the three of them toasted the portrait above the bar.

"Here's to strong hearts," Miles said, and drank his coffee.

"Was that it?" asked Weasel. "His heart gave out?"

Miles nodded. Mouse's body had been shipped to Anchorage the same morning Clive had found him, and they had gotten the report two days later. Mouse had died of a heart attack. "He ate badly, drank two fifths of whisky a day, and had a history of heart disease in his family. He was what they call in the trade 'at risk.' "

"Aw," said Weasel. "That's not it." He took a long pull on a bottle of beer. "He loved Ellie's barmaid, Kelly. She had black hair and a huge" — he held his hand out in front of his chest — "vocabulary, she really did. She was a master of the crosswords," and he laughed. "It near killed him when she died. You know how he liked the cross-words." He belched and wiped his mouth with his forearm.

"Did this Kelly with the huge vocabulary ever love Mouse in return?" Clive asked over the lip of his coffee mug.

"Not really. I mean she liked him and all. But you know, she basically ran the bar and Mouse liked to drink. It was more or less a professional relationship."

"To unrequited love," said Clive. He raised his cup, and the three of them drank. "The glue that holds us all together." They banged their drinks on the bar.

"What's up with this place?" Clive asked Miles. "Who owns it now?"

"Aw, it's a mess, like most every piece of property in this town. Mom didn't want it so she sold it to a guy who got divorced and his ex-wife's daughter sold it on a contract to some guy from Juneau who said he was going to open up a hotel, but of course he quit making his payments after the bank disapproved his loan for the hotel, and she's never gone through the process to call in the note."

"You think I can find the guy's name in the city office?"

"I suppose so." Miles stood up from the bar. He intended to go back to work. "Why do you want it?"

"I'm going to buy this place," said Clive,

"and I'm going to open up my own bar slash church."

"A *what*?"

Clive explained. He had looked into getting a liquor license when he first came to town, but the town council, which met on a semi-regular basis, had discovered an old ordinance that allowed only as many liquor licenses as there were churches. The hardware store had a liquor license and sold beer and hard liquor, mostly by the case, to people in town and on the fishing boats; there was one church that allowed the town Catholics, Lutherans, and Unitarians to hold Sunday services, in that order. When Ellie's bar had closed down last time, so many people had moved out of town that the second church had closed. In order for Clive's new bar to receive a liquor license, there needed to be another church in town.

Of course Clive could have asked the town council to change the ordinance, but since there hadn't been a quorum at any of the last two dozen council meetings, this seemed a poor option. But the idea of closing down for drinking on Sunday and opening up for worship instead didn't seem like a bad one to him.

"I've seen you studying the Bible," Miles said. "Do you mind if I ask you, are you a

Christian now that you got out of jail?"

Everyone at the fallen down old bar leaned in. Most of them had expectant smiles on their faces.

"Brother. I'll tell you," Clive said. "I love Jesus the way Mouse loved Kelly. Unabashedly. I love Jesus like I love Duke Ellington and the great Satchmo, like I love the music of Bonnie Raitt and Joni Mitchell. I love Jesus like I love the opening paragraph of *One Hundred Years of Solitude* and all the books of P.G. Wodehouse. I love Jesus like Elvis loved his momma. For in Jesus is forgiveness, love, joy, and happiness." Clive lifted his beer as if to toast them all. "That love will always be unrequited for the gift has already been given, and we just have to get used to it. So one more time to the great Mouse Miller, to his love, the beautiful and unattainable Kelly, and to Ellie Hobbes, the anarchist mother of us all!"

The beers went up and a loud cheer could be heard far back up the hill into the forest.

Miles was of two minds about his brother's attempt to buy Ellie's bar. It was a good idea, and he knew that Clive would do a fine job of running a bar. But the money still bothered him. Miles knew that somehow or another the cash sewn into the jacket

185

would eventually bring a storm of bad luck down on all their heads.

But Clive had no such concern. For some reason the conversation with Lester and the finding of Mouse Miller had put Clive's life in a new perspective. He was either suffering from some new psychosis or he had developed a superpower, one that allowed him to hear animals speak. And neither possibility frightened him, as long as the animals didn't start telling him to kill people or to start picking random numbers for a distant lotto. So three days after Mouse Miller's wake he flew to Juneau and found the current owner of Ellie's bar sitting in the Triangle Club downtown. He spoke to him about a price, and when the owner said he was asking four hundred thousand dollars, Clive held up an envelope with twenty-five thousand dollars in cash and a contract to take over all payments and liabilities (which included several tax liens and a potential disastrous environmental clean-up necessitated by the fuel oil spill under the building). The owner took the cash, signed the contract, and ordered a round for the house.

Clive had already contacted Ellie's former legal representative. She was living down in Lewiston, Oregon. He proposed that he begin making payments on the property where the former buyer had left off, and she agreed, figuring some money coming in was better than no money, lawyer fees, and a rotting bar a thousand miles away.

Miles took the news of this new venture with a mixture of strong emotions. The thought of his ex-con brother in a legitimate business, most likely a very lucrative business, created in him a kind of giddiness that only other worried siblings may know. But on the other side of the emotional color wheel there was the rising of a kind of sharply focused dread. Clive was spreading the money around the region with equanimity, which was sure to attract attention: the attention of the police and eventually the attention of the original owner of all the parka money.

Clive continued with his project, showing little concern for his brother's fears. He began work down at the site in early June. He had rough-cut yellow cedar brought in by a young boat builder down the inlet, and he bought new pilings to shore up the foundation. He had an engineer come and give an estimate for cleaning up the spilled oil, and he paid a couple of local kids to dig out the contaminated soil with shovels for less than half the estimated cost.

Clive patched the roof, and any afternoon that had more than an hour of sunshine, he scraped and painted the outside of the building. He painted it white, added red trim, and hung a new sign over the door. The sign was much larger than the old one, and it hung prominently over the boardwalk. Clive called the new bar Mouse Miller's Love Nest.

Billy ended up enjoying life on the *Universe*. He was given a room in the crew quarters right next to where the members of the orchestra bunked, and he was allowed to eat in the dining hall with the passengers. After being fished out of the north Pacific, Billy seemed to have developed a large appetite. He ate as if he could end all suffering at the three offered meals and lined up for every midnight buffet and sundae bar.

Bonnie had never saved anyone's life before, and she wasn't quite sure of the protocol. The captain was horrified that she had gone into the water and threatened to fire every member of the lifeboat crew. But the cruise director eventually convinced him of the public relations value of declaring them all "heroes" and even agreed to have Bonnie and Billy sit at his table two evenings in a row, nodding and making a show to each of the passengers who passed and stared, some of them being bold enough to come and shake Bonnie's hand and marvel at her courage.

Both Bonnie and Billy were dumbfounded. Billy was mostly overwhelmed by rich food and sat at the captain's table in a caloric haze. Bonnie meanwhile was on new emotional ground, having saved someone's life. After coming out of the ocean, her old life, her old melancholy, seemed to have been left behind somewhere in the wake of the lumbering ship.

She liked this new feeling, but she couldn't quite give words to it. She couldn't describe it to her mother when she talked to her on the ship's satellite phone. She could not describe the feeling to herself.

And so, she fell in love with Billy, thinking that since he was the most tangible evidence of her adventure, she had to keep hold of him if she were going to preserve this new life in its current form.

She moved out of her room for the rest of the cruise and bunked down in the crew quarters with Billy.

"It's not like love," she said to him as she squeezed into the narrow metal bunk bolted to the bulkhead, "it's more like waking up from a dream."

She kissed him, and they took each other's warm breath into their own lungs, and their hands felt the warmth of skin created by their bodies' burning calories. They were alive again, together, and this was something Billy enjoyed. Looking back on it, he saw that he enjoyed eating crab cakes and fresh asparagus. He enjoyed making love to a beautiful woman who had saved his life.

The four noble truths taught that life was suffering, and suffering could be overcome by overcoming desire. But he had to admit to himself that he didn't simply enjoy this new life, he craved it now, all the more so because he had spent his entire life not knowing that there was such pleasure possible on this earth. He craved the feeling of his own warm body after he had been taken out of the Pacific. He suspected all the more now that he was a crappy Buddhist. He still wanted to meet the Dalai Lama, but there was no getting off the *Universe* until it came into port. So he kissed Bonnie and lay in that narrow bed beside her as if he had fallen out of the sky from a jet airplane and had landed safely beside her. So they drank and ate and slathered their skins against each other's in the narrow bunk. At night they clattered up the metal stairs in borrowed formal clothes and danced to the ship's little orchestra.

The kids in the band were all music students from Oberlin. There were only seven of them, but the ship insisted on referring to them as "the orchestra" even though they were clearly a band. Rick was the tenor sax player and had put the band together after the Christmas break the year before. He had cajoled, and sometimes bullied, his friends into joining him on this northern gig. Rick looked a bit like Bono, and he knew how to work any room made up of any age group. Earl was the drummer. He was black and had a wispy goatee and horn-rimmed glasses. Nix was a young white girl who played the bass as if she were dancing with it. She had short brown hair and multiple piercings, all of which she had to either hide or allow to heal up while she worked on the ship. Rick had explained that you simply couldn't play Cole Porter while wearing a goat head stud through your tongue. Nix had rolled her eyes but took the stud out. The rest of the band reminded Billy of children attending a wedding, faces flushed from their ill-fitted formal shirts.

But they loved to play. They performed three sets a night and then backed up various solo performers. They played '40s music at seven, '50s music at nine, and something called "contemporary" music at eleven. Every other night they played for the cabaret singer or did the Broadway medleys for the operatic duo from San Francisco.

The band was intensely interested in Billy. The idea of him paddling through the dark of the north Pacific struck them as something almost mythic. Late at night, they would pile into the tiny room and hunch onto the floor to eat junk food (which the band seemed to prefer over the ship's cuisine), smoke pot, and talk about Alaska. Billy held court during these sessions, and he relished the role of the storyteller pulled from the sea.

Nix, particularly, was interested in the stories about Cold Storage. She liked hearing about Lester and Clive. She tried to imagine a community clinging to the side of the mountains with no roads, no cars, and virtually no sense of the outer world. She ate handfuls of greasy cocktail peanuts and leaned her head against the hard bulkhead and tried to imagine such a place.

Nix had a boyfriend in Portland. He was a fiddle player, and sometimes he would fill in on guitar. He would play anywhere but preferred traditional Irish music. There was a big Irish scene in Portland, and Nix had sat in on many of the all-night sessions in one of the three pubs that hosted them. She liked the sessions but was getting tired of her boyfriend, who was in danger of becoming an IRA-style Catholic. Nix had taken the Alaskan gig with her old schoolmates as an easy out from the situation. She had moved all of her things out of their apartment and into storage before her boyfriend had noticed anything was wrong. She had said goodbye over the phone from a booth in Vancouver.

Billy would sometimes tell stories well into the early morning. He'd talk about whales rubbing their backs on the bottom of his fishing boat, and about the fights in the movie club, and the time a brown bear got into the café and had actually crawled into the chest freezer. He told about Mouse Miller being in love with the barmaid and disappearing from sight, and he told about the time a fisherman was beaten to death by a giant halibut that had landed in his boat, and how they had served the same halibut at his wake.

The band from Oberlin listened and snacked and dreamed their own Disneyfied version of Billy's adventures. Earl beat his sticks against his thighs. Nix practiced her finger exercises. Bonnie sat up on one elbow with a blanket covering her bare body and played with the ends of Billy's hair as Billy told story after story about the world he had left behind.

The boat put into Vancouver on the last day of the cruise. Billy found out that afternoon that the Dalai Lama had canceled his appearance in Seattle after some security issues were discovered, and Billy breathed a sigh of relief. He knew he wasn't worthy. He hadn't been meditating, he hadn't finished his journey, and he had lost all the money, anyway. He felt a certain sense of peace when he learned the Dalai Lama's plans had also changed.

So Billy decided to stay on the *Universe*. The band hired him on as a percussionist and backup vocalist. There was not much of a problem getting on the band's roster, because they had sailed with one musician short when the original trombone player broke his leg skateboarding the week before the first sailing. Billy just had to fill out a few pieces of paperwork, and he was on.

Bonnie got a job in the ship's library. This job was a little harder to get, but Bonnie had dropped a couple of hints that she might have suffered a back injury as a result of her rescue from the water. The ship's lawyers claimed not to be concerned about any liability, but when an assistant librarian quit because of seasickness, Bonnie was offered the job.

On that afternoon the *Universe* sailed from the dock at Vancouver with Bonnie and Billy as staff members, the sun was glittering off the water, and a few people waved from the dock. Bonnie stood out on the deck and waved to her mother, who had flown to Vancouver to try and take her daughter home. Bonnie waved and blew kisses while her mother wept. Billy was looking resplendent in his new black pants, white shirt and formal red bow tie. He was knocking on a wood block as the quartet played a samba on the back deck. And so the *Universe* moved slowly away from the dock for its trip back toward Alaska.

CHAPTER TEN

It was the second week of June, and Jake Shoemaker was sitting at his breakfast table in Seattle harassing Miss Peel over the telephone. Miss Peel was upset; Jake was trying to calm her down. The police had been around again. They'd raided the warehouse and hadn't found anything incriminating, but they kept coming around trying to bully everyone into snitching off their boss, and Jake was having to do a lot of hand-holding.

Clive had been right about one thing: Miss Peel needed to be kept happy. She knew so much that she could put Jake away for a very long time. He also knew that she was smart enough to have hidden copies of everything in some safety deposit box somewhere. Miss Peel had many admirers — sports stars, several of them, famous men who were in the papers nearly every week. One of them clearly loved her and sent her flowers as often as he was in the paper. If anything bad were to happen to Miss Peel, it would be noticed. It would be investigated vigorously. Also, Jake was sure there were portions in her will and testament that read, "If anything of a suspicious nature should happen upon my death . . ." At least she could be trusted. The ballplayers were insurance both ways; she wouldn't want her gangster connections coming out while she was still in play.

Jake had been riding a seesaw with his fortunes. On one hand, it turned out to be a good thing that Clive had cleared the money out of the unit; if he hadn't, it would be sitting in some evidence room right now and Jake would have no hope of ever seeing it again. On the other hand, it was a bit of bad luck that he had shot Oscar in the knee because it had pissed the man off and sent him running. He suspected Oscar had snitched him off; the cops kept asking about a gun and about Oscar's whereabouts.

Jake said that he'd be happy to talk with the police and get all of this mess cleared up; they just needed to set up an appointment with his lawyer; and the cops took that and walked away, lumbered down the steps leaving Jake smiling at their back. They'd soon discover that his lawyer would no more set up an interview to talk with the police than waive his fee.

Life in Seattle was heating up. Real estate was looking good. Banks for some reason were loving to lend him money. But the computer kids were total pains in the asses. When they weren't sulky about not having a basketball court in their office suites, they would complain about the coffee, for Christ's sake. Jake was ready to drown the whole lot of them like kittens.

Adding to his peevishness was the fact that Jake's lawyer had started hinting around that he should be putting together cash for bail money, and had flat-out advised that it might be a good time to go on a long fishing trip in Mexico. But Jake didn't want to leg it; start running and you have to be ready to keep running, and he wasn't ready. He had to be somewhere his agent could find him; he had to be somewhere where he could entertain producers and money men if they ever became interested in one of his scripts. So he smoothed Miss Peel's feathers and helped her get the bail money together from his various interests.

He was focusing most of his creative energy into *Till Death Do Us Part*. He'd decided to make it a bit more topical by making the lead roles — a couple who worked together as covert CIA operatives — Jewish, while their therapist would be Arab-American. He'd already drafted the early scenes where the husband and wife go to the marriage counselor for the first time, and it was funny — or it would be as soon as he smoothed it out. He could see any number of stars fighting over it. He just had to get away from the cops, lawyers, and the cokeheads for a few months. And if he could just get that money back from Clive he could solve all his problems in one fell swoop. But no one knew where Clive was.

Jake put out feelers. His lawyer's investigator had contacts at McNeil, where Clive had been inside. No one had a line on him. The investigator had run records and talked to the usual jailhouse snitches but had come up dry. Jake had received a report from the investigator, along with his last outrageously inflated bill. The only information in the report was from a cabdriver who had given someone who matched Clive's description a place to stay for the night, someone who called himself Stilton Cheesewright, which was no doubt Clive. The cabbie mentioned something about this Cheesewright going to pick up his dog. Jake snorted and tried to rub the sleep from his eyes. He knew for a fact that Clive's fleabag of a dog was dead, and the ugly new guard dog was missing.

Jake was angry. It wasn't easy to find someone who had no home, no car, and no mailbox or email address; it was even harder to find someone who was traveling on cash. The investigator had worked a source in the probation department but had come to a dead end. They wouldn't give up any addresses, just told the investigator that Clive had family in Alaska. But unfortunately Alaska covered a lot of fucking real estate.

He was in a situation where he was spending money to recover money. This was not something he enjoyed. He considered making another call to this shit heel of an investigator and telling him to get back on it, get him a name of a relative or something. Jesus! How hard could it be?

But he didn't want to bring on any more unnecessary stress. So he took some deep breaths and a sip of fresh orange juice and opened the paper. It was there on the third page of the second section in a two-column AP story that Jake found the answer to what he was looking for. His eyes widened, and he started smiling in a grateful kind of disbelief.

"I'll be a son of a bitch!" he said, reached for his orange juice and knocked it over in his excitement.

■ ■ ■ ■

It was the first week of June, Billy was in the middle of his third cruise of the season. He was standing on the bandstand up in front of the band, singing, "Do Nothing Until You Hear From Me." He was singing more and more solos on each trip, and he loved it. He loved standing in front of the band with his eyes closed and his hands gripped around the mic stand. Billy sang, and he felt the ship sway under his feet. As he sang, he imagined the *Universe* flying through the green water of Dixon Entrance north of Vancouver Island; he imagined the flat, sandy bottom of the ocean three hundred fathoms below his feet. He felt his mind unspooling as he sang. He glimpsed the dancers, felt the sway of the ocean in his legs. He imagined the waves, and the whales swimming through the gloom beneath the ship. He imagined his lost gear — the kayak, the packet of money for the Dalai Lama — floating over the north Pacific, and he felt no yearning, no loss, only a sense of lightness as if the top of his head had been removed and his mind were able to rise up out of his body.

So it was more than a surprise — it was

almost a collapse of his imaginative world — when he went to the Vancouver Post Office three days later and opened an envelope that contained his battered passport, *The Tibetan Book of the Dead* and a letter.

There on page three of Jake's copy of the *Seattle Times* was a somewhat overexposed picture of some people jammed together around a table. In the center of the group was a goofy long-haired man being given some money. Two things struck Jake immediately: the first was that the man handing the money over was Clive McCahon, and the other was that it was *his* fucking money Clive was giving away.

The headline above the article read: "Lost Donation Finds Its Way to the Dalai Lama." Above the first photo was a larger one of a smiling Tibetan described as "a secretary to his Holiness the fourteenth Dalai Lama happily displaying the watertight package found in the Pacific and forwarded to Dharamsala, India."

A quote in a box next to the article said, "Good fortune has allowed this small package to survive a dangerous and uncertain journey. His Holiness is grateful to Mr. William Cox of Cold Storage, Alaska, and to the person who sent his generous donation on to India."

The article described how the package appeared in Dharamsala with a postmark in Kodiak. Some anonymous fisherman had apparently found the waterproof pack and sent it on to the Dalai Lama. The reporter noted that William Cox had been located and was working as a shipboard musician on an Alaskan cruise ship. He had not been contacted for comment. The photograph represented friends and well-wishers from the small fishing village, and one resident, the local health care provider, Miles McCahon, was quoted as saying, "We're happy that Billy is all right and glad that the money found its way to His Holiness."

"Son of a bitch!" Jake said once again and reached for his telephone.

In Cold Storage, it was a beautiful summer day. Clive was finishing up the painting on the outside trim and playing an old vinyl record of Spike Jones. He smiled, bounced on his feet in time to the bicycle horns and slide whistles squealing out from the rattling big band panic. Little Brother lay on a piece of tin roofing, soaking up the heat of the day, slowly raising his head as a raven hopped along the railing of the boardwalk with a brown strip of a potato peel drooping out of the side of its beak. The raven strutted along the rail and teased the big earless dog.

"Ugly. Ugly. Ugly," was all the bird said.

Clive waved his paintbrush at his dog. "You're scaring the customers, you know." Little Brother glanced over at Clive, saying nothing, then went back to languidly watching the big black bird.

"Your job is to throw them out when they get rowdy, not keep them from coming in."

He put his brush into the paint can and walked over to Little Brother, came to within three feet and started to put his hand out. But the brindled dog stood up. He backed away, the heavy roofing underneath him buckling. He didn't growl or show his teeth, but he stared at Clive with eyes that burned like cigarettes.

"All right, all right. I was just asking you to consider the options." Clive turned to go inside.

At the bar, unofficially open now, five men sat and talked about Billy's amazing rescue; dance music loped in and out of the open windows. It was a fine sunny day in rain country.

"The lucky bastard was flopping around out there in the dark, and he gets scooped up by a cruise ship."

"How'd you hear that?" asked Clive.

"Are you kidding? Reporters have been calling all over town. They're loving this story. Haven't you talked to any of them? They'll talk to anybody who will pick up the receiver."

"Reporters?" Clive watched the raven outside; it stood barking at the big dog, taunting him with his prize potato skin.

"Yeah, reporters. They're loving this story about how the money you gave to Billy found its way all the way to India."

"They asking about me?" Clive asked tentatively.

"They don't know your name, but they want to know who was in that picture. But you know, we don't say anything about you or nothing. We just say the money was raised by the community. That's okay, don't you think, Clive?"

"Yeah . . . yeah . . . sure, it's okay." Clive watched the raven drop the potato peel, bark twice at the woofing dog, and fly up into the blue summer sky, saying, "Bye. Bye. Bye."

"Yeah, that's fine," he repeated.

"Good, now can we try some of that new tap beer? You know, for quality control purposes."

"Absolutely." Clive reached down for the

hose attached to the rusty keg beneath the bar. Little Brother came back inside and sat on the sleeping bag laid out in the spot where Mouse Miller had died.

Billy read the letter from the Dalai Lama's secretary with a mixture of panic and amazement. Billy had been living on the ship for the last forty-nine days like a man who had been born again into a life of satiated desire. He had been pulled from the sea by a woman who wanted to love him; he had been eating his fill of rich food and telling stories of his old home, embellished stories to feed his ego, and they had started to become almost like fables in his mind.

But now here was his old passport — his old identity — and it smelled like home. He held the passport up to his nose, picked up a whiff of sulfur water and fuel oil. He flipped through the pages and inexplicably felt as if he had been taken prisoner by that village. The stories in his mind sank away into his chest, where the reality of that place — the rain, the bickering, and the depression — seemed to have always resided. Unlike a cruise ship, Cold Storage was well-suited for the life of denial.

In the letter, the secretary explained that he'd gotten Billy's new address in Vancouver from a member of the press; he'd assumed that "Mr. Cox" would want his official papers and reading material back. The secretary thanked him for his kind donation and wished him health and good fortune on his journey.

Inside the book, the secretary had placed a small photograph of His Holiness. It was a postcard-size official portrait of the Buddhist monk in his robe sitting and staring at the camera with an expression of dignity and intelligence. But staring at the photo, Billy knew the Dalai Lama had been suppressing a laugh, as if he knew exactly how silly Billy looked in his tuxedo. He slid the picture back into his book and, with a heavy heart, took the longest possible route back to the ship.

On the night after Billy had recovered his passport, the fabric of his new life began to come unraveled.

There had been dissension in the band before this. The cruise director, a perky Australian who had been a singer in a dinner theater company in Key West before signing on the *Universe*, felt directly responsible for the enjoyment of every single passenger who came up the gangplank. She took her job very seriously. For the last two trips, she had been forwarding complaints about the band to Rick and saying that the "contemporary" music was getting "a bit wild." There had been reports that they'd done a version of "Roadrunner" by Jonathan Richman.

"Do you really think that was appropriate?" she'd asked the band leader.

"Roadrunner" had been Nix's idea. She was going stir crazy. On each cruise, she made friends with the two or three younger passengers and encouraged their requests for newer music. She'd tried everything, even ska versions of rhythm and blues tunes and playing Richard Thompson's waltz time numbers with horn accompaniment. She watched couples in knitted Irish sweaters and deck shoes happily dancing, not paying the least attention to the twisted lyrics about red hair and black leather. But the cruise director heard.

Billy and Bonnie's cabin had become the unofficial club room of the band, and it seemed the best place to clear the air, even though Bonnie was in bed trying to recover from a cold.

"Listen, Rick, I never signed up for this kind of gig." Earl threw a stick onto the dresser. "You told us there would be a variety of material. You told us it wouldn't be a painful boom-chuck–Imperial Room–cocktail lounge-off-the-interstate kind of scene. Christ! It's way worse. You said we would have one set a night where we could choose the material. If that's not the case anymore, I want to know right now."

"We signed a contract," Rick sighed. "We work for the cruise director, and she told me we would have one set, but she also told me the music had to suit the audience, that we couldn't play free jazz or experimental music."

"This is hardly Sun Ra," Nix said. "We're just talking about something with a few different rhythms. They could have gotten a polka band if that's really what they wanted. Besides, there are plenty of people who like Richard Thompson." She sat beside Bonnie, who rolled over and put a pillow over her head.

The argument sprayed out. They discussed the subtleties of the tunes in their repertoire; charges and countercharges were laid, the trumpet player threw some cheese curls at Rick, and Rick's face darkened in anger.

Outside, Dall's porpoises played in the wake of the ship. They pushed through the water like torpedoes and burst onto the surface, their black and white bodies shooting into the sunlight. Passengers on deck cheered while the musicians argued about the changes in their arrangement of "Stardust."

"Listen, Rick!" Nix said. "I'm not saying Hogie Carmichael isn't a fucking genius. I just want to play some different tunes." She bounced up and down on the bed, her arms held tightly to her sides, like a child about to break into tears.

"Wait," Billy said from the upper bunk. He had not said one word so far throughout the entire argument. All the players stopped, stared up at him. "I know exactly what we can do."

CHAPTER ELEVEN

By late July, the salmon were starting up into the rivers to spawn and die. Once in fresh water, they became humped and hook-nosed, their bodies already beginning to rot. But out in saltwater, these late season fish were bright and quick. These were the fish Miles was determined to catch.

Miles had heard nothing from Trooper Brown, but he knew that there was a visit coming. Clive had been making too many things happen not to be noticed. There was the liquor license, and the business license, and money changing hands. And Weasel seemed busier than usual: talking on the public phones at the head of the dock, using the one computer at the library, even taking his old wooden boat out past the inlet. Each day that he didn't see Trooper Brown walk into his clinic, Miles felt lucky; each moment that he didn't need to be in the clinic, he wanted to be out in his skiff, if

211

for nothing else than to be somewhere else when Brown did blast through his door.

Besides the occasional prayer made to Japanese outboard engines, Miles was extremely practical when it came to fishing. He was good with all manner of salmon but king salmon, and this flaw was irritating him. Lester had told him that Tlingit elders believed that the fish only came to those who were worthy of catching them. This, Miles believed, was a faith promulgated by a core group of successful fishermen. He was beginning to wonder if there was a religion for the consistently unlucky.

He rounded the point and ducked into the lee of two small islands out near the northern opening of the inlet. He could feel what was left of the swells moving from the outside; these little swells were lifting his boat up and down, but there was hardly a breath of wind on the water. Miles went about rigging his gear and lowering it into the water; he set the engine on the lowest possible idle and started pushing along at a moderate trolling speed.

It was then, with the motor geared down and his line taut against the pull of the flasher, only then that he forgot about his brother's criminal enterprise. He forgot about his mother's sudden absence from this world, and he had finally forgotten his bad luck as a fisherman. He was just sitting in the sunlight, empty headed, and here, as if empty headedness was the one element that was necessary for his good luck to come, was the exact moment when it did.

The line pulled tight as hard and fast as if the whole world were on the other end. He jerked back on the pole. He cranked on the reel, and the pole bowed. He reeled, and the drag spun, letting the fish run; he tightened down the drag and pulled harder. Thirty yards off, the salmon broke the surface of the water and flashed in the sunlight. Miles breathed hard, his knuckles white from the pressure he was putting on the pole.

The line twitchcd and jerked, and Miles leaned back. The salmon dove under the skiff and for a moment Miles thought it was off, but he kept reeling, putting more and more strength into his grip until he saw a flash of silver close to the rail. He reached over carefully with one hand for his net. He held his pole up high and gently pulled his net toward the head of the tired fish from behind.

There was a flash, and a tug, and all of the shaking, silver energy of the ocean teetered on the lip of the net. With one arm, he tried lifting the big fish. He struggled. He lifted again, but his line went slack and the hook flipped out of the lower jaw; Miles dropped his pole and lunged with the net.

But the fish was gone, the pole was in the water, and all of the earth's slippery energy dissipated into the dark.

"Fuck it!" Miles said, and threw the pole out of the boat. "Goddamn son of a bitching motherfucker," he swore. He slapped his hands against his thighs. He looked at the engine and slapped the housing. "And you shut up!" he threatened.

But then, of course, when he pulled on the starter cord hoping to recover the pole floating thirty feet from the boat, the engine would not start.

"I'm sorry," Miles said. His voice had the faint quaver of a man who was either going to find religion or give up fishing.

"I'm sorry," he repeated and sat there waiting for forgiveness.

The opening day of Mouse Miller's Love Nest took on the atmosphere of a solstice festival in Cold Storage. Flags flew from porches all around town, and from the flagpole in front of the bar flew both an American and an Alaskan flag. Clive had given six tours to groups of citizens, including one group of kids from the school.

Into this atmosphere, Trooper Brown arrived for a second visit. The plane landed just after nine in the morning, and Miles had come down to pick up some clinic supplies arriving from Juneau. The pilot was handing Clive his three boxes from the cargo hold when Ray Brown stormed down the ramp in his blue uniform.

Clive looked up, smiled and put his hand out. "I'm Clive McCahon. I bet you want to talk with me."

Trooper Brown skidded to a stop, and all the creaking leather on his utility belt became silent.

"Yeah, well, I have a federal subpoena for you to appear and produce records for the US attorney in Tacoma, Washington."

Clive looked at the papers. He looked down at the ground around him. "What do you think, Trooper? Are we above mean high tide?"

"What do I care?"

"Just wondering," Clive said as he fished into his own jacket pocket. He pulled out some old paperwork sealed in the kind of plastic bag that one might freeze salmon in. "It just means that as long as we are above mean high tide we are on Township land, which is good for you on one hand but bad for you on another."

"Cut the crap, McCahon. The US attorney in Tacoma wants you down there pronto, and I don't have to waste any more time with you."

"Now that's true, Trooper. But have you ever met Willa Perlmutter in Anchorage, Alaska? She's a lovely woman. Are you single, Trooper? Willa Perlmutter is single, I believe. At least she was when I went into the joint. Lovely woman, the mind of Voltaire and the body of a Brazilian swimsuit model."

"I'm married, wise guy."

"Too bad. A runner. Very spirited. Hardly rests in the pursuit of the interests of her clients. Willa Perlmutter of Anchorage, Alaska, is my attorney."

"Listen, I don't really care."

"I realize this. But for one thing, you have no fucking authority to be serving a federal subpoena on township land, flat foot. And for another, if you can read, which I doubt, the US attorney has been notified by the lovely Willa Perlmutter, as noted and acknowledged by the US attorney himself, that she herself — the lovely W. Perlmutter — would be the point of service for all legal notices and subpoenas for said Clive McCahon in perpetuity or, as far as your fat ass is concerned, until hell freezes over."

"Bullshit, McCahon, this is a Washington case." Trooper Brown started frowning now so that great deep furrows of fat curled above his nose.

"Not that this matters in the least in this instance, fat boy, this being a federal case, but did I tell you, Trooper, that among all of Willa Perlmutter's lovely features, the loveliest is the fact that she is a member of the bar of both Alaska and Washington? So, you can take this subpoena and hip hop on up to Anchorage, and/or Bremerton, where the LWP has one of her fine-ass offices, and serve her there. And when you do, she and I will begin the months-long process of asserting my Fifth Amendment right against self-incrimination by whittling away what questions I can and cannot answer and, when it comes down to it, I will answer the big payoff question that everyone wants to ask and the answer to that is this: Jake Shoemaker is a doof who wants to make easy money and watches too many movies. He is not a federal grunt or a gangbanger. He loves his Second Amendment, but he is no gangster."

"So you must of shot the warehouseman?"

"What the fuck?"

"Oscar Laurentis, if Jake is such a Gandhi.

You must have blown Oscar Laurentis's knee off."

Clive wasn't feeling so smart now. "I don't know anything about that. Talk with my attorney, talk to Willa. This conversation is over."

Brown grunted, turned toward the waiting airplane and slammed the door shut. Clive watched the thin door bow out as Brown fumbled for the seat belt and got the ends connected. The trooper slapped the pilot on the shoulder, and the engine sputtered to life.

At twelve noon, when Mouse Miller's Love Nest's doors officially opened to the public, a crowd of people poured into the bar. The turntable was spinning an LP of the Turtles singing "Happy Together," and Weasel was sitting there at the corner of the bar wearing aviator sunglasses and his best Hawaiian shirt, looking for all the world like a Jimmy Buffett-style drug runner. By twelve thirty, people were dancing to Kitty Wells. By two, they were listening to The Doors, The Kinks, and Marvin Gaye. People brought food, the barbeque was once again set up in the front yard, and Tina and Miles helped tend bar. Ed was learning his way around the tough lies on the pool table, and Clive was behind the bar thumbing through the Bible, brushing up for his first service.

He had considered showing a church service from a television broadcast since he could hook up on satellite, but he decided he was going to refuse to allow a television or any high-tech entertainment in the Love Nest. The Love Nest was to be a haven away from American pop culture. If someone wanted to listen to a sporting event, Clive would try to find it on the radio, but people were going to have to look at each other while they listened. He had an expensive stereo system with a shortwave and FM receiver, as well as a new turntable. Carl Erickson, who had been a logger until he was laid off three years ago, had volunteered to climb the spruce tree behind the Love Nest and place an antenna at the very top. This dramatically improved the radio reception. The first night Clive had tried the shortwave, he listened to dance music from Cuba while finishing the plumbing repairs under the bar.

Since televangelism was out of the question for this church service, he flipped through Luke and John, cruising through the New Testament hoping to find a long passage about the power of love without referring to the need for obedience. He didn't want to scare off potential customers with his first sermon.

But the music kept distracting him. His head bobbing along with Marvin Gaye, he considered playing "What's Going On" at the service and throwing the floor open to discussion. He slammed the Bible shut and started thumbing through the LPs.

In his mother's house, he had found a large collection of vinyl, including his old records from childhood. He envisioned keeping these in a cabinet next to the bar; if customers wanted to hear a particular record, they could ask whoever was working to put it on for them. There would be no video games to ruin the solemnity of the atmosphere.

Clive had done his best to recondition the ancient pool table. The floor had been shored up and the table itself was level, but the felt and the slate top had somehow warped slightly and developed some interesting characteristics that greatly improved the playing advantage for players with local knowledge. One had likened it more to putting on an undulating green than playing pool.

Clive had reattached the money that had once hung from the ceiling, and people were encouraged to stand on the bar and pin up more. The beautiful barmaid loved by Mouse Miller had died of breast cancer, so Clive pledged every dollar on the ceiling and some percentage of the opening day's receipts to a women's health center in Sitka, and he had hung a picture of Kelly at one end of the bar with the only known portrait of Mouse beside it. The photographer had caught Kelly standing behind the bar, gently scolding him, trying to avoid having her picture taken. Her awkward pose and laughing face told Clive that she was a woman almost certainly worthy of Mouse's unrequited love. She looked both intelligent and modest, a woman with whom it would have been a pleasure to spend a couple of hours on a stormy afternoon. There was also a photograph of Ellie Hobbes and Slippery Wilson, the original founders, at the crest of the roof beams.

The portrait of Mouse was some twenty years old and showed a healthy young man wearing a dirty white cap and grey halibut coat; he was standing in the trolling pit of his little wooden boat and working the gear. He looked strong and capable: one of the last hunter-gatherers. In the photograph, the sun was painting strips of light up the side of the boat and onto the fisherman at work.

The night before the bar was to open, Clive had mounted the two portraits with heavy screws that showed through the frames; he intended them to be a permanent fixture in the bar. He drove the last screw and put the driver into his back pocket, looked at the interior of his new life's adventure, wiped his hands on a bar rag he had stuck in the front of his belt, and gave a satisfying sigh. The Love Nest would be a dignified shelter for both drinking and prayer.

After dinner, the bar thinned out, and kids ran back and forth with plates of food. Clive changed records, and Weasel kept asking for Frank Sinatra doing "Fly Me to the Moon"; Clive played it twice but when Weasel asked for it a third time, he exercised his imperial discretion.

"No," he declared. He played one entire side of The Band's *Music from Big Pink* while Weasel sat quietly on his stool.

Little Brother didn't seem to notice all the people. He stayed close to his pad near the corner of the bar, slept sometimes but raised his head whenever he sensed a cross tone of voice or heard the sharp thump of a chair.

"That dog's going to eat somebody," observed Lester.

"I just hope it isn't somebody I like." Clive set a glass of iced tea in front of him and waved off Lester's gesture to pay.

"Don't take this the wrong way . . ." Lester paused a moment. "But I've been thinking about what you asked me about a while back."

"About the animals . . . umm . . . talking?"

Lester nodded and looked around the bar to see the happy faces of the patrons. "You talk to anybody else about that?" He steadied his eyes on Clive.

"Just a couple of mice in my room." Clive smiled.

"You ever get anything out of the ugly mutt?" and he nodded toward Little Brother. Neither Lester nor the dog were smiling, and both of them were staring at Clive.

"It's a funny thing . . ." Clive leaned in and spoke softly. "The big dumbbell never says a thing. Silent like a tomb."

"Dumb . . ." Lester said, almost as if to himself. "It's just this . . . If he does ever say anything, will you let me know?"

"Sure, Lester, but . . ."

"To the owner of the Love Nest!" Lester lifted his glass of iced tea, raised his voice. Everyone looked toward him as he said,

"And to the best bouncer on the coast."

"To the Love Nest!" Voices roamed around the room, fell silent. Everyone swallowed and slammed their glasses down.

The evening wore on peacefully enough. The opening day crowd gradually wandered out, and a core group of drinkers and pool players were left listening to Dolly Parton on the record player. Robbie Robertson and Pearl Jam were replaced by *West Side Story.* Clive cut some drinkers off before they were ready, but no insolence lasted long in the festive atmosphere.

By closing time, Clive was serving more free coffee and soda pop than mixed drinks. Tina and Miles had gone home. Weasel and Ed had left to watch some movies that had come in on a plane that afternoon; they'd invited Clive over to watch *The Piano* after he got off work, but he'd told them not to wait up.

Finally the place was quiet, and Clive turned off the stereo to listen to the wind washing through the tree limbs above the bar. The place smelled fine, more like coffee than cigarettes, and the furniture didn't seem tired yet after this first night.

"Good night," he said aloud to the room and turned to the dog. "What are you going to do? You can come up to the house if you want. Or you can stay here. What will it be?"

Little Brother stood up, stretched. He too cast a glance around the room, although more suspiciously, and walked to the front door and stood there, staring straight ahead.

"Home it is, then." Clive grabbed his cash bag full of the night's receipts, and they walked out into the night.

The late summer sky was dark. There was a hint of silver on the western edges of the horizon, and Clive stood for a moment looking at the dark outlines of the islands humped up to the west. The wind continued sighing, and he thought for a moment about going to watch the movie with Ed and Weasel; then he thought of hunting up the girl who worked at the cold storage but he had heard that she had found her parrot and had gone fishing with a guy from the longline fleet and wouldn't be back until the fall, if she came back to Cold Storage at all.

So he turned and walked south toward his mother's house. The alder trees and the thick bramble of salmonberry vines darkened the way, and the great ugly dog stopped at the steps to Annabelle's house to wait for Clive.

Except for when they'd flown into town six months ago, Clive had not touched Little

Brother, nor had anyone else in Cold Storage as far as Clive knew. Little Brother was clearly a fixture at the bar and it could not be said he was a feral dog, but neither could it be said that he actually "belonged" to Clive.

Now he saw the dog watching something hidden ahead of them. A deep growl, like grinding rocks, came from his chest. His eyes were fixed on some phantom in the brush. Clive moved to walk around him, but the dog took two steps ahead and blocked his way.

"I'm going to go to bed. You can take care of whatever's out there." He stepped around the bristling dog. "But if you kill another cat, it's coming out of your wages." He tried once more to walk around him, but the dog would not let him pass. Clive reached out and nudged him three times with the toe of his right shoe, but the dog would not move.

Clive took a step back and raised his leg as if to actually kick at him. That's when Little Brother turned and looked straight at him and said, "What have I done to you that you have struck me these three times?"

Clive froze. Along the boardwalk, footsteps padded toward them.

"What did you say?" Clive asked, surprised mostly by the dog's strange diction.

Then Little Brother said, "Look up."

And he did, straight into the high-caliber revolver at the end of Jake Shoemaker's outstretched arm.

"Hey, Clive," said Jake, businesslike. "I really need to talk to you about something."

Little Brother showed an alligator smile of teeth.

"You should have stolen a better dog." Jake pulled back the hammer on the big six-shooter. "He's sure enough ugly, but he isn't worth a damn for protection."

"What did you say?" Clive asked again.

CHAPTER TWELVE

Little Brother leapt for the arm holding the gun. Clive ducked and rolled off the stairway into a tangle of salmonberry bushes, rolled until he came up hard against a thorny stalk, and looked back to where the big dog was standing over the fallen Jake, shaking the man's arm back and forth as if it had come unhinged at all of its joints. Jake was crying out in a wordless howl, his head thumping on the decking, while the dog worked almost silently, breath heaving out of nose and jowls as he tore at the limp man's arm.

Clive circled back down under the boardwalk near the water, taking his time, listening to the animal grunting into his work. Jake's voice became more and more faint.

For a moment, Clive considered walking down the beach to Miles's house, letting the dog finish what he had started. He even considered going back to the bar and listening to records for a while.

But then he heard Jake's voice floating out over the tide flat, calling for help in the same kind of faltering voice Clive used to hear from under the door in his old cell block. It was the last bleating of a dying animal. Clive didn't want to have to explain to anyone how his former partner in the drug trade had had his throat torn out on the steps of Clive's new home, so he walked back toward the boardwalk, found a cross brace to climb, and lifted himself back onto the decking.

The gun lay just under the stairs of the house; Clive stepped over Jake and picked it up. The dog had stopped trying to tear Jake's arm away, but he still clenched what was left of the arm between his teeth. In the thin light from the porch, Clive could see that the forearm was broken, the wrist and hand flopped at an unsettling angle, and the shoulder was dislocated. Little Brother blew air from his massive lungs like a racehorse at full sprint.

"Get . . . him . . . off," Jake managed.

"Jeepers, Jake!" Clive knelt down beside his head. "I'm sure he'll let go when he's ready. There's not that much I can do."

"Shoot . . . it," Jake wheezed.

"Aw, cripes! I can't do that, Jake. I mean, you were going to shoot me through the head. Probably would have, too, if my dog

229

hadn't helped me out. I can't just shoot him now that he saved me. That just doesn't seem fair."

"Do something . . ." Jake's voice grew fainter.

"I tell you what." Clive sat cross-legged on the decking with the pistol resting in his lap. "This dog likes to hear good news. You can't boss him, but you can use a nice tone of voice on him and tell him that all the money in that storage container was rightfully mine."

"Fuuuugghhhyewwww," Jake sighed.

"And tell him that I will be keeping all that money to help run our new enterprise here in Cold Storage."

"Fine," he said weakly.

"And that you will never ever try to hurt me again for the rest of your life."

"Yes . . . I will never try and hurt . . ."

Little Brother still held on.

"Then I don't know." Clive shrugged. "You could tell him he's a good dog."

"Good dog." Jake's eyes closed. His head rolled to the side, his cheek nearly flat against the planking. Little Brother's breathing eased, and the boardwalk grew silent; Clive could hear the wind in the trees up the hill but nothing from his former employer.

Clive looked over at the dog. "I think you killed him." His voice was somber.

Little Brother stared up with sad brown eyes, looked almost sheepish. "No," was all the dog said.

Once Jake's body had gone limp and the tension of the fight was over, his floppy arm had dropped from the dog's jaws and fallen to the deck with a slap like a dead fish.

Little Brother studied Jake, contemplated Clive. He looked tired of the conversation. Without saying another word, the ugly dog shouldered past Clive, padded up the steps, scratched the outer door open and went inside.

"I'm surprised he didn't kill him!"

Clive stood under the clinic's unduly bright lights and watched Miles wipe away the blood on his former partner's arm.

"This is an amazingly clean break," Miles was saying. "I mean considering that the dog snapped his arm, then pulled his shoulder out of the socket."

Jake was hooked up to an IV and a blood pressure monitor. His eyes weren't focusing; they were open but rolled around as if he were lying back in a convertible, driving through a tunnel of trees in autumn.

"I've got him on so much Demerol that

he shouldn't be feeling much of anything," continued Miles, "which is a good thing because he's got a little bit more to go through before we get that shoulder back in place."

"Well, I'm just going to leave him here," said Clive. "I need some sleep before I have to open up in the morning."

"I need you here." Miles's voice was calm but firm. "First to stitch him up and watch his BP, but then to pull this shoulder back so we can pop it in. It's going to take at least two of us." Miles looked around. "Unless you can get your dog to do it."

"Come on, I can't get that dog to do anything." Clive took his jacket off. "Except eat and pass gas."

"That," Miles added, "and chew up men who want to kill you."

"Hey! I had nothing to do with that. Whatever happened was between Jake and the dog. They had some old business."

"All right," said Miles. "Just stick around to pop his shoulder back in."

"Sure. I'll help. Just lose the tone with me, okay? I didn't do anything criminal."

"I'm sorry, brother. I know. Let's just get this back in, then do the stitching, all right?" Miles stood up on a chair, grabbed the injured arm below the break and wedged his knee behind Jake's shoulder. "You better hold him," he said gently to his brother. "He's apt to flop around some."

By the next afternoon, Jake's eyes were beginning to focus. He writhed, tried to get away from where his splinted arm was suspended, and saw Clive and Miles standing at the foot of the bed; they were smiling. Jake closed his eyes and reopened them; felt as if half his body had been stung by bees; closed his eyes again. The room spun, and a vague electric current pulsed up and down his arm.

"I'm going to have to get you to a hospital so they can take a look at my handiwork," Miles was saying. "Get you a bed where you can heal up for a bit before you travel."

"No," breathed Jake. "No police."

Miles turned to his brother. "I take it this is the owner of the money?"

"Former owner, Miles." Clive looked over at the bed. "We've worked all that out, haven't we, Jake?" He leaned across the broken arm while Jake recoiled, tried to move to the other side of the bed. He was pulled up short by the tension on his elbow and winced, rolled back in agony.

"More drugs," he pleaded.

"Soon," said Miles.

"I am the sole proprietor of the money, and all she has purchased. Well, me and the dog. I think I'm going to have to cut him in for a full share after what he did for me."

"This guy could turn you in to the cops, Clive. I mean, your dog did mess him up pretty bad." Miles directed a sympathetic glance toward Jake, huddled at the far end of the bed.

"First off, somebody is going to have to prove I'm responsible for that dog. I mean, he lives on his own. But more importantly, if Jake goes to a hospital and says one word about that ugly meat-eater being my dog, I'm going to have to give federal law enforcement the whole poop on Jake. I don't have anything to lose. I've got old business records that can account for all that money. My records might not stand up for long, but they will stand up long enough for the cops to get a load of Jake's interest in me. I've done my time. I haven't violated parole . . . at least, the spirit of my parole. I've got a new life going, and then this drug dealer came and attacked me. So my dog ate him." Clive tapped Jake's splinted arm. "Well, ate half of him anyway."

Jake sucked air through his nose, tried again to escape to the far side of the bed.

"No," Clive went on, "if federal law

enforcement puts his name into their computer, the thing will light up like a pinball machine. Jake's not going to a hospital if he can help it."

"We've got to put him someplace." Miles was running out of patience.

"Can I say something?" Jake whispered.

"He could stay with me." Clive turned to face Miles. "But I don't think the dog would care for it. I don't know, that ugly bugger might wake up feeling peckish in the middle of the night." Clive smiled at the thought.

"Excuse me," Jake's voice quavered.

"He can't stay with me. I do not take patients home. Christ, if I did that I'd have half the town wanting to bunk with me. I'm not doing it, Clive." Miles was turning away from the bed as if he were going to walk out on the conversation.

"The more I think about it, I'm certain he can't stay with me," said Clive. "What would our buddy the trooper think of me living with this chewed-up old crook? I've got my new, clean reputation to think of. No way, he's not moving in with me."

"You. Doctor. Listen to me!" Jake yelled, hauling his head up from the pillow. "If you don't scurry around and get me some more pain killers, I swear to God when I get up out of this bed I'm going to shoot your nuts off."

Miles glanced at his wristwatch. "I suppose I can give you some more Demerol. But listen, you are not staying with me. I don't care which body part you threaten to shoot off."

Jake lay his head back down and let out an exhausted moan.

A few hours later, Jake sat in a sturdy camp chair in front of Lester's wood stove.

"This is one chewed-up-looking white man," observed Lester. "Did your dog eat him, then spit him back out?"

"I tell you, Lester, he's not really my dog." Clive carried in a bag of groceries, set them on the counter. "I got some hamburger and some canned stuff. There's milk and cereal and some bread here. I think there's a jar of peanut butter. Hell, Jake's not a picky eater." Clive smiled over at the men sitting in the sunken area around the stove. "But I have to tell you, Lester. Little Brother. He speaks."

"What he say?" The Indian man leaned forward.

"The first thing he said was, he complained about me tapping him with my foot."

"You kicked him?" Lester said with alarm.

"No. Cripes. It was just a tap."

"He say anything else?"

"No. He just warned me about Jake."

"Is he an angel or something?"

"Who, the dog? Hell, Lester, he's just a mutt."

The carver sat quietly for a moment, staring at his wood stove. Finally he turned to the injured man and asked, "What brought you to Cold Storage, Jake?"

"I wanted to kill him and get my money back." Jake pointed with his chin toward Clive.

"Oh . . . okay." Lester put some more wood into the firebox. "So you got some assassination travel package: airfare, hotel, ammunition? That sort of thing?"

"Is everyone in this town a goddamn comedian?"

Lester continued feeding sticks into the stove, the flames lighting his face. "No, actually most of the people in this town are drunks or depressives, but we have our funny moments."

No one spoke for a few seconds; the fire popped; Clive folded the grocery bag.

"Like when a hit man gets eaten by a dog," Lester said flatly. "You've got to admit, that's funny."

"I'm out of here," said Clive, but then remembered. "Hey, thanks, Lester." He looked over at Jake. "If you feel up to it, come on down to the bar. I'll buy you a cup of coffee." He started to leave but doubled back again. "You don't keep any guns here, do you, Lester?"

"I've got a deer rifle and a bear gun. But I keep 'em locked up."

"Good." Clive's hand was on the doorknob. "Just keep them out of reach of old Jake here. We're getting along so well now, but if he gets a little more bounce in his step, he might try to blow my brains out. Okay. See you later." He was gone.

Lester slapped his hands together; he stood up and held them toward the stove for warmth and asked, "What other kind of work you do, Jake, besides killing people?"

"I'm in the movie business." He didn't look at his Tlingit host.

"Get out of here," said Lester. "What were you in?"

"I wrote the script for a film called *Stealing Candy,* but they made a fucking mess out of it." Jake leaned back, but there was no way to sit comfortably in a camp chair, especially with his arm in a fiberglass cast. He grimaced.

"No kidding. I read about that movie.

Hell, Jake, you must be a player. Why you need to keep your day job of killing people?"

"It's a long story," he lamented.

"Yeah, everybody's got a story." Lester went over to his workbench, put on his jeweler's glasses. "I got a story. In fact, I've got a book I've been working on, and it would make a hell of a movie."

"Oh, Christ." Jake groaned.

"That's okay, I trust you. It's called *Circling the Wagons*. It's a crime story, but it's really about white people in North America. There's this Indian undercover cop, see . . ."

Lester started talking; the wind rattled under the eaves; if he'd been listening, Jake could have heard the yawp of a heron fishing on the tide flat underneath the house. The fire in the wood stove popped; the tea kettle rumbled on top of the iron; Jake closed his eyes and tried to shut out every sound in the universe.

In other parts of America, August was the height of summer, but in Cold Storage, it was the beginning of fall. The first two weeks of steady rain had already fallen. Those who were not used to this were emotionally pulled up short. Miles was cleaning up the clinic; he wanted to go home early and get a nap. He was tying the top of a garbage bag when the bell above the clinic door clanged. He put the sack in a box for burning and walked out to the waiting room.

There was Tina, her hands up to her cheeks, crying.

"Are you hurt, Tina?" asked Miles. "Has something happened?"

Miles had been in battlefields, scoured ground and dusty expanses littered with burned trucks and strewn bandages, smelling of diesel and desperate women under the hot sun. His job at home had different kinds of battlefields. People often came to his office to cry. Some came because of some recent pain, a pain that had taken them by surprise. Others came on a kind of schedule; it could be the moon, the weather, or some personal orbit that brought them back to an old injury that continued to overwhelm. There was plenty of old pain in Cold Storage.

In any northern village there is a darkness lurking: the differing terrors of childhood; the men who have victimized children and inoculated them with dread that will last for the rest of their lives; the refugees from family wars who are as shell-shocked as any soldier on the front. Some grow up swearing they'll never again end up in that situation, but most do. Some, from sexually battered families, know no other emotional territory and can't leave. In happy circumstances, they feel like foreigners whose papers have been revoked; they're always waiting for the knock from the secret police to take them back to their real lives. There are more than 700 villages in Alaska. No matter how much oil lay in the ground on the north slope and no matter how wisely it was allocated, it was at times hard for Miles to imagine how a twentieth century mind could navigate a Paleolithic world without a lot of chemical coaxing. Most of the people in Cold Storage drank, some of them lived alone and avoided human contact, but all of them periodically became unhinged and ended up in Miles's clinic.

Miles suspected Tina's pain was recent. "What's happened?"

She lifted her head up out of her hands, looked up at the ceiling, and held her breath.

"What happened?" she repeated. "Oh . . . I'm sorry, Miles, nothing happened . . . It's just . . . It's just . . ." and she started crying into her hands again.

He put his hand on her shoulder, led her gently to the examining room. "Come on in," he said softly. "No sense in you standing out here."

She sat on the edge of the table and talked; her shoulders heaved; her words came out in spasms. Miles sat on a low stool with his elbows on his knees and looked up at her, listened to her voice float around the small room.

"It's just the weather," she explained, blowing her nose. "You know we get more than two hundred inches of rain a year here?"

Miles shook his head.

"People in Seattle think they have a lot of rain, but they only get some thirty-seven inches. I mean, really . . ." Her tears kept flowing. "Thirty-seven. That's nothing . . . but the worst of it is, we only really get some fifteen really sunny days a year. Fifteen!" Again she started sobbing, for the fifteen clear days, Miles supposed.

"What else?" asked Miles.

They stared at each other for a while. Rain ticked down on the tin roof; they could hear kids rumbling by, pulling a wagon down the boardwalk.

"How's Ed?" Miles asked, and Tina's dam broke.

There are so many people with broken hearts: there are parents and their children,

242

husbands and wives, the hard-hearted and the sensitive. They do horrible things to each other with whatever weapons they can muster. These emotional battles in Cold Storage were like drunken broadsword fights: sloppy and inaccurate. But the blows, when struck, were often crippling. It wasn't the rain filling the fishing streams and creating the gamelan of their tin roofs that made people sad. It was the wrong turns their love had made. But the rain didn't help.

As a teenager, Miles had been unsympathetic to these people. People in books and films — people in the real world had survived worse. Whole orders of magnitude worse. And they still did, every day. Not that the teenage Miles knew how they did it.

But when Tina let words push past her tears, a recognizable story began to unfold: Ed did not love Tina, or that was her fear. Ed was pulling away from her. School was starting, and he was sullen and distant. He disappeared out on his own to gather specimens for their classrooms, and when he returned, he would hang up his slicker and say nothing. In bed he rolled away from her, feigning sleep. Tina stared at his back and her mind rewound where they had been and where they were going, and discovered she couldn't imagine a coherent future, or even a story of one.

It hadn't always been that way. Ed and Tina had shared a common story, or so it seemed to her, from the moment they met. This was the story of two young people who went on an adventure to Alaska to touch, walk, and study the wild country other people only imagined — two people who each needed the other to reach their destination: the driver and the navigator. But now it seemed that Ed had always been happy to both drive and navigate and was ready to go on ahead by himself.

Miles was growing impatient. A thought was building up pressure in the depths of his mind: *Why should I care about this woman's sadness?* he thought to himself, while at the exact same moment he knew that he did care. A world away, his friends still walked a battlefield where smoke roiled up from charred holes in the ground, and widows wailed for the missing. Brave men died while rescuing strangers, and here he was listening to this mildest form of suffering. But he listened for there was nothing else to do. Pain, no matter how slight, has a magical way of filling whatever container it finds — much like happiness but apparently more often.

Tina told Miles about the time she and Ed came up on the ferry. They had to back their rented moving van onto the ship in Bellingham. Tina stood in back and waved the directions. She waved and yelled and gestured, and all the while Ed was swerving back and forth in the lane. Finally, when the van pushed up against a parked car and broke off both vehicles' side mirrors, Ed got out yelling.

"I was giving you good directions," she countered.

"But you weren't standing where I could see you," he yelled.

"Now you tell me, Miles, whose fault was that?" Tina tried to pull herself up straight in her chair, but all she could muster was a defiant kind of slump.

Miles's shoulders jerked, and he stirred himself. "He could have adjusted the mirror," Miles said, "or he could have stopped and figured out a better way."

"Or maybe I was standing in the wrong place, at the wrong time, trying to talk to the wrong guy." She blew her nose again, smiled.

Miles smiled, too, and reached out and touched the top of her hand; she took her other hand and covered his; they said nothing. They stared down at their hands on her lap until Miles stood up, but she kept hold of him.

"Thanks, Miles, for letting me talk. It helps. It does. What about you, do you need anybody to talk to?"

"No," he said, "my life's not that interesting."

She squeezed his hand and said, "You look funny."

"I'm all right, I guess."

"What are you thinking?"

"I'm thinking that I'm a crappy salmon fisherman." His voice held more seriousness than he'd expected.

"That's pretty bad, Miles."

She cupped his face in her hands and kissed him on the mouth, hard enough and long enough that he had to put his hands around her waist to hold her there. The rain, which was neither tears nor music, continued to fall on the tin roof, making a fine rhythm in the room, and slowly smeared down the windows.

CHAPTER THIRTEEN

The clinic's door opened, and they heard Ed's voice out in the waiting room. "Miles, you with somebody?"

Miles had his arms around Tina; he brushed her cheek with the back of his hand, and she looked straight up into his eyes. She did not look startled, she did not look worried, and she did not look guilty. Miles felt almost inordinately happy.

"Just one second," he said to her and walked out to the waiting room.

"Tina came in; she's in the examining room; she'll be out in a minute."

"Is she okay? What's the problem, Miles?" Ed stood up on his toes to look over Miles's shoulder, as if Tina were standing there. "She just ran out of school. I had to finish up by myself."

"She was upset."

"Well, I mean, what's the problem? Is she going to be okay?"

"I think she's going to be okay. But she needs to tell you what the problem is."

"Does she need medication? Can you give her something?"

It occurred to Miles that Ed was asking him a lot of questions considering she was his own wife.

"No," he said, "I don't think she's going to need any medication. If this keeps up I think I could get her a telephone appointment with a counselor in Sitka. Maybe she just needs to talk things over with someone else."

"Someone else?" Ed let the words linger in the air.

"A counselor in Sitka," Miles said again to snip off the thread left floating. "I'll see how she's doing."

Miles walked back, and Tina grabbed him — forcefully — kissing him even harder this time.

He ran his hands over her shoulder blades and down the curve of her waist. He pulled her toward him, feeling her legs against his, her breasts against his chest, his hands shaking against her strong back. Then he pulled away.

"I don't know, Tina. You've got to talk to him. Tell him the story about backing the van onto the ferry."

"I want to sleep with you, Miles," she said. "I've just decided."

"Well, that's something to consider." Miles made it sound like they were talking about alternative therapies; quite possibly they were. "But I can't see you here in the clinic, and I really want you to talk to Ed."

"You are a good guy, Miles." She kissed him and pushed past him out of the room.

Miles stayed; he didn't want to be in a room with those two right now. He pulled the paper lining down from the table, checked the connections on all the telemetry machines, even looked down in the trash basket to see if there was anything there that needed his attention, before opening the door to the waiting room.

It was empty, so he went to his office and filled out his log, identified Tina's visit as a "wellness-consult, no treatment schedule."

He had a stomachache. Sleeping with Tina would definitely qualify as a change in his circumstances. It would be a happening in Cold Storage once word got out, as it surely would. Tina probably hadn't considered that yet; perhaps she was new enough to town that she thought that keeping something of a sexual nature secret was a possibility, which it certainly was not.

People would know. There were the obvious tip-offs, of course — being seen walking out of someone's door at an unexplainable time or being seen kissing through a partially closed curtain. These things were common risks in a small town but didn't explain people's near-miraculous ability to divine the sexual quality of any relationship. The people of Cold Storage had an uncanny sensitivity to the body language of lovers and their slight changes in habits.

Edna Whelaby, while sitting on the examining table, had once told Miles that she couldn't keep a boyfriend in town because of "everybody's damn sex radar." Edna was eighty-three years old at the time and between boyfriends. Miles had known her all his life so it was with some trepidation that he asked her to explain "sex radar" and to his discomfort she was happy to oblige:

"Ah, Christ Mary on a crutch, Miles. Everybody in the coffee shop, everybody at the post office or the library can tell if you've been sleeping with somebody. They just know. It's like radar. It's the least little thing. Lipstick on when it usually isn't. Teasing somebody when you usually don't, *not* teasing somebody when you should. These are all the signs, Miles, and the people around here just have a sense for it, I swear. One night in the sack, and there's hell to pay when you go for your next cup of coffee. There's not enough men around who can stand up to that kind of treatment," she complained. "I've been thinking of moving to Juneau."

Miles had been skeptical. He thought the old woman was just elaborating to show off her superior knowledge of life. But after, he had been alarmed when his own sex radar started to kick in. He saw a woman flush at the mention of someone's name. He noticed a fisherman, who had always slapped his money and the check down on the counter, was handing them to the waitress instead. It wasn't just that he handed it to her, either, for that could be just his attempt to flirt. It was the way her fingers curled up quickly around the money in a furtive attempt to touch the tips of his fingers; it was how she leaned forward on the dairy case and smiled as he came in and would sometimes walk around the counter when he left.

These were things that told Miles that the two of them were sleeping together. And he knew this because he hadn't been sleeping with anyone in the years since his return. He had become finely attuned to all aspects of desire, as if the loneliness he hadn't even admitted to himself had honed his senses. Lonely people recognize those in love like a parched tongue senses moisture. It may not be their own love, but it feels like a blessing to them.

Miles opened the door to the empty waiting room and stepped out into silence. Weasel waved from the boardwalk, and Miles had a sick feeling in his stomach. He had become accustomed to thin rations of affection, and these two kisses, as thrilling as they were, had given him a stomachache. It was as if he had eaten a rich meal much too quickly.

Jake was lying on a pad on the floor on the upper tier of Lester's studio/home. He had a phone cradled against his shoulder and was listening to Miss Peel speaking with a kind of urgency that reminded him of a typewriter key striking a roller on the end of the line. She was holding onto a subpoena to appear in front of a grand jury. Jake tried to soothe her, even though the pain in his arm was twisting up his torso and into his brain like an electric drill bit. He was making it clear that he was not advising her to avoid responding to the subpoena, then he paused and read an account number for a bank in Arizona plus two addresses in Tucson. "Yes, yes. Now read those back to me please." He paused. "Good. Thank you,

Miss Peel. You, too, dear. You, too. Good luck and have a good trip. Yes, God bless."

He hung up, gritted his teeth until the pain subsided, stared up at the ceiling as Lester carved on a two-inch strip of silver that would become a bracelet.

The pain passed, and he eased back down onto his sleeping pad. "So, how come you live here then?" he asked. "I mean, why don't you live in one of those, you know, Indian villages?"

"I'm on a scouting mission." Lester peered through his jeweler's glasses down onto his design.

"You said you been here ten years. That's quite a scouting mission. When you going to make your move?"

"We're a patient people."

"That's bullshit." Jake tried to heft himself up onto his good arm so he could look at Lester. "My bet is you got thrown out of whatever life you had before. Just the little I've seen of this place, I can't believe anybody would live here if they weren't hiding out from someone."

"This place grows on you." Lester didn't look up from his work.

"Yeah, like toe fungus," agreed Jake.

"Exactly." Lester looked over at Jake sprawled out on the mat and started to add something. He was almost tempted to justify himself, to launch into an explanation, but he stopped and looked down at the bracelet he was making instead.

It was a bear design. Bear had been the clan crest of his mother's people; he thought of telling Jake about the different clans with their strict rules and the rivalries between them; he thought of telling him about the complex structure of protocol, politics, and ancient grudges that a contemporary Tlingit person needed to understand in order to live peaceably in a village. He thought of telling him about how he had quit drinking only after it was too late, but he stopped himself. Lester was not in the mood to teach Indian 101 to another uninterested white man.

"So," Lester said, "tell me what you think of my story idea."

"It's got no arc."

"What do you mean, no arc?" Lester was a little irritated.

"Christ, man. Arc. You know, what connects the story from beginning to middle to end. Listen." Jake took a deep breath and broke into a professorial tone: "Movies are really about one thing happening to one person. That's it."

"That's not true," Lester threw down his

carving knife. "*Jurassic Park,* what was it about?" Jake stared at the ceiling.

"It's about people's greed and arrogance toward natural systems they don't understand," Lester explained, took another tool and started back to work.

"That's the message, but that's not what it's about. *Jurassic Park* is how a snotty scientist discovers that he really loves kids. That's the one thing that changes during the entire movie. In the opening, he hates kids, and by the end, he's cuddling with them in the friggin' helicopter. That's what's going on."

Lester gestured toward Jake. "The lawyer gets eaten."

"True, and that was a great moment. But it's a perk, an extra bit of action that happens while the snotty scientist is learning to bond with the kids. Your story is all perks. Little bits of action strung together with an implausible mission of this Indian cop, but the main character doesn't really change. He's a sarcastic shit heel in the beginning, and he's a sarcastic shit heel at the end. He's just eaten up a hundred and twenty minutes sleeping with sexy women and killing irritating white men. It's an interesting setup, but it's no story."

"You know, you don't have to sugarcoat

your opinions for me. Just spit them out." Lester picked up a tiny fleck of silver and placed it carefully in a jar of similar flecks. "James Bond doesn't change," he added, almost petulantly.

"Fucking James Bond is a franchise. He's not a character. The problem with your guy is he just keeps killing the bad guys off, but he never rescues anybody. He doesn't learn anything, and nobody is going to give a shit about him by the end of the movie."

"So, you want him to change?" Lester looked up through his jeweler's glasses.

"Hell, man, I spent ten minutes with your snotty fucker, and I was begging for him to change."

"This is a white thing, isn't it? You're saying to make him dance and shuffle, make him some mystical holy man, make him 'sympathetic' to the mass audience, aren't you?" Lester's annoyance was obvious.

Jake continued to stare at the ceiling. He could hear the rain falling on the roof. No rush of freeway, no car horns, no sirens. Just the rain, the fire in the stove, and the wind against the house. He lay there, examining the hand-hewn beams above his head.

"Hey, Lester," he said. "I think you should use your left hand to carve that bracelet. It would give it a rougher, more primitive effect."

Lester stopped carving. "You don't know shit about carving or about me or about anything, as far as I can tell."

Jake didn't look at Lester. He just spoke calmly. "You are two-thirds right. I know dick about silver carving and I know nothing about you, but I know about movies and your idea sucks, at least as it stands now."

Lester was standing now, ready to take a step toward the injured man lying on the floor.

"And don't give me that 'make him dance' crap. I don't care if your guy kills everybody in Washington, DC, and declares himself emperor. I don't care if he is a mystic or a Republican. I'm just here to tell you that if you don't know who he is, and if he doesn't meet some challenge that substantially changes him, if you don't get him to help somebody — even himself — you aren't going to get fucking Sitting Bull to watch your movie."

Lester took a step away from his workbench, a step back, and sat down. "I'll give it some thought," he said.

"You could give him a pet," Jake suggested. "That would make him sympathetic."

"I'll give him an ugly dog who eats white people."

"That could work," Jake agreed. "You could make it a buddy movie."

There were footsteps in the outer porch, a stamping of boots, and Jake leaned up on his good arm to watch Miles walk into the room and hang his coat on a peg by the door. It wasn't wet enough to hang by the stove.

Lester lifted his head slightly. "Hey, Miles." He kept working.

"I've come to announce that Tina Mc-Carty wants to have sex with me. She just told me. I know you guys will hear about this sooner or later so I wanted to tell you right off the bat."

The fire popped and sent a small spark soaring out through the grate down onto the scarred piece of tin beneath the stove.

"Christ, Miles, that's old news. Everybody knows she wants to have sex with you." Lester was nonplussed.

"I've only been here two days, and I knew it," chimed Jake.

Miles, deflated, sat down on the splitting stump. "I know you're lying," he said to Jake, "but Lester, come on, you didn't really know she wanted to have sex with me, did you?"

"Come on, Miles, there's a betting pool." Lester reached into his pocket and pulled out a small scrap of paper. "It was a twenty-dollar buy-in. I bought November sixteenth." He waved the stub at Miles.

"November sixteenth? So the person who buys the closest date to the actual date we . . ."

"Will be two hundred and forty dollars richer." Lester looked up through his jeweler's glasses. His eyeballs looked like wobbly saucers.

Jake reached into his pocket with his good arm. "Let me in on some of this." But Lester waved him off.

Miles lowered his head into his hands. "She's a schoolteacher! She's married to a schoolteacher!"

"Oh yeah," he said, "that's why the pool sold out in two days." He put the slip of paper back into his pocket.

"Well, I'm going to disappoint you, Lester." Miles sat up and straightened his shoulders as if someone had just called his name. "I'm not going to have sex with her. I've just decided that."

"Yeah, we'll see. I still have three months. I'm thinking my November is looking good. It gets mighty cold and lonely around here in November. I say right around the election time. I'm cashing in on your sex life because I put my money on Gore, and I think he's tanking."

"Well, I'm not." Miles sounded shaky but resigned.

"What? You're betting on Bush?" Lester said with disgust in his voice.

"No. I'm not having sex with Tina."

"I'm glad that's cleared up," Lester said without taking his eyes off his work.

"What's the coverage in December?" asked Jake. "The holidays could be tough, you know. A little eggnog, a little mistletoe."

"You might buy in, but it's a waste of money because November is still a lock. I don't care what this mook says. Anytime a man announces that he's not going to have sex, either it means he already has or is just about to. This guy" — here Lester nodded to Miles — "is a little more earnest than most white people, so I'm giving him until November. You might as well give the money to me." Lester stood up and walked over to Miles, gave him a slap on the back, then went over to a desk in the corner and took out a spiral notebook.

"Don't worry about it, Miles. Nothing's really different," he said. "Everybody knew about it before, and everybody knows about it now. Nothing's changed." He took his notebook over to Jake. "Speaking of which . . . Jake here is going to help me out with the 'arc' of my story. You're just in time."

Lester pushed his jeweler's glasses up on his forehead and sat down on the floor beside Jake.

"Let's talk about change," he said to the crippled gangster.

CHAPTER FOURTEEN

In the Madera Canyon Sports Medicine Rehabilitation Center, just southwest of Green Valley, Arizona, the September sun was like a luscious orange in the sky. Oscar Laurentis sat with his leg unwrapped after his sixth surgery, soaking up the sun as he waited to go to rehab. It was the one thing that he had insisted upon when he worked for Jake: Oscar had the best healthcare plan that money could by.

But he had little else and that was why he had milked every ounce of his coverage to get his leg back into shape. He told the surgeons right from the start that he had been a top prospect for professional soccer clubs in Europe, that he had just been out of shape on a new training regimen. He was going to get a leg like Pele's, even though he barely knew who Pele was.

Oscar spent a lot of time reading crime novels in his various hospital beds. He began to seethe with the need for revenge. He also watched Bronson movies and Tarantino films. He loved how sexy damped-down rage could look. He thought that was what women must love: the man who could control his rage and release it in service of justice. This is what all the books and films seemed to teach. Chicks dug it. Oscar had a good cause. He was a victim. He was going to have a new kick-ass leg. All he needed was a big-ass gun. He was going to get an insurance settlement. Ann Peel helped him get policy limits from the insurance company as long as he kept Jake's name out of the police reports. Fine. No big deal. Chicks didn't like the whole courtroom bullshit. They wanted the *mano a mano,* we-take-care-of-our-own approach.

Yes. He would definitely do it. Someday. He would stick here a while. It was nice here. He didn't know where Jake was anyway, and it was probably a long ways off.

It was some big deal visitation day. Some baseball player was supposed to sign shirts and cards for the patients today, to raise their spirits and everything. Oscar looked down the veranda, shading his eyes, and saw a massive Hispanic man.

"Who's the meat?" Oscar asked the patient

next to him, who wore a full lower body cast.

"I dunno. Manny Something. Hit over three hundred last year."

But there, standing next to Manny Something and waving like a little girl on a Ferris wheel, was Miss Peel. In seconds she was clicking down the marble tiles to his raised and sutured leg.

"Oooooscar! Oh my gosh, you look . . . well, you look . . . good. You've gained weight, even! They must be taking care of you! How *are* you?"

She bent over and gave him a makeup-preserving kiss, her right hand spread over her chest to protect her gold jewelry from hitting him or to prevent him from looking down her silk blouse.

"I'm, uh, good, Ann . . . ah, Miss Peel."

"Oh, Ann. Please. So, have you heard from Jake in Alaska?"

As Manny spent the next two hours signing baseballs and having his picture taken, Oscar and Miss Peel caught up on the intricacies of life in the world of Jake Shoemaker and what the world might hold for the financial security for his former employees.

The autumn moved down from the north.

Hunters ranged closer to town, afraid to be caught out in the storms. Kids stayed closer to home because there wasn't enough daylight to wander past the boardwalk and up into the river valleys. The plumage on the diving ducks began to change. The mergansers appeared whiter, and the old squaw ducks showed up in shimmering white rafts near the inner harbor.

The bears stopped coming into town for garbage, and the dead salmon carcasses washed out into the inlet with the heavy October rains. The water of the inlet itself appeared brown as tea for a few weeks during the heaviest of the rains, and sometimes the ghost fish floated near the surface with their hollow eye sockets and rotted flesh staring into the sky.

The bathhouse stayed busy even though people weren't covered in summer's grime. Men came during men's hours and women during women's hours. They came to warm their pale bodies as the chill of the turning year started gaining a foothold in their bones.

Mrs. Cera let Anthony go back to Juneau, and he turned out for the wrestling team. He'd eventually win State at 164 pounds, break a finger in the last match, and come back to Cold Storage.

Little Brother began eating from a bowl in plain view of people. He stopped wandering up the hillside and never ate another cat that anyone missed. Every evening after Clive locked up, the dog walked down the boardwalk and up the stairs to Annabelle's house. He waited for Clive to open the door and walked in ahead of him, settling himself onto a blanket beside the oil stove. He'd lift his jeweler anvil head and stare at Clive's ankles as they passed by his resting place. The two had grown more relaxed in each other's physical presence, but Little Brother had not spoken since he had tried to eat Jake's arm. Clive spoke to the big dog as he lay on the bed. He would make small talk, discuss the weather or his unimportant list of errands for the day. Little Brother would lift his head with effort and simply stare back at Clive as if to say, "Are you talking to me?" and then, "Why?" then plop his head back on his paws. Clive was getting the impression that his dog was not much of a conversationalist and would only speak if, and when, he had something important to say.

Every Sunday, Clive preached a sermon at the Love Nest. He stuck closely to his major theme of love and slowly circled around the whole issue of obedience. He read the story of Jonah, mostly for the character of the worm who God commanded to destroy the shade tree. He stayed away from the crushing tedium of Ecclesiastes.

It snowed on Halloween, but the flakes were fat and soggy so that as soon as they hit, they disappeared into a sloppy film on the boardwalk. But three hundred feet above town, the branches of the spruce and hemlock trees gathered white pillows of snow.

The contested election came, and people were pissed off for a few weeks. But no one in Cold Storage could really muster much enthusiasm for the race. Almost everyone agreed that there was certainly some sort of criminality involved, but no one could decide exactly the nature of the crime or the mastermind behind it, although theories abounded.

The movie clubs continued to meet, and eventually Weasel brought a monitor and VCR into the Love Nest for one evening a week for the men's movie club. Clive made an exception to his no-pop-culture rule and offered the use of the bar to both the men's and women's movie groups, but the women politely declined — not because they didn't approve of the surroundings, but because they had a nice setting of their own along the water side of the back of the library. And because, as one man said, "They don't want to mix their pleasures, lest the whole thing go sour."

Some American sailors were killed in Yemen by a group of people unhappy with the US. Several people in Cold Storage hung yellow ribbons on their fences, but most of the people in town were not sure what the ribbons meant, other than a vague sense of patriotism.

Miles didn't have sex with Tina McCarty in November, for which Lester barely forgave him. Instead, Tina and Ed took a three-day weekend trip to Juneau after the second parent-teacher conferences of the school year and came back with gifts for the schoolchildren. Tina brought Miles a sweater from an Irish woolens shop, and he noticed that Ed had begun to drink beer at the Love Nest late into the evenings, even on school nights.

Jake's shoulder stayed sore for weeks. He scratched under the cast with thin pieces of firewood and complained loud and long whenever he saw either Miles or Clive. Miles pleaded with him to go to Sitka for X-rays, but Jake refused. He tried calling Miss Peel on her cell phone, but there was never an answer; eventually, he was greeted with a recorded message that the phone had been disconnected. This seemed to satisfy him for some strange reason.

Jake spent his days sprawled out on the floor of Lester's shop, working on their story ideas. Jake had convinced Lester to put the novel aside and work out the story as a film script, and he sat on the floor, cast propped up on pillows, with a large board that Lester usually used for cutting up meat on his lap. Twenty large sheets of butcher paper were attached to the top of the board; each sheet was divided into six sections, and each section represented a page or approximately one minute of running time.

Jake and Lester argued over the relative merits of each plot point and every subtle change in the character's growth. Jake wrote in pencil, often rubbed out whole scenes with a fat pink eraser while holding the pencil in his teeth. Sometimes at night he lay on his pad listening to the wind in the trees; somehow they didn't sound as lonely as he'd once imagined they would.

As the days went by, Jake could see that he and Lester were shaping something original and unexpected, something that had the feel of the familiar but was, upon second look, completely new. And Jake forgot about the ranch above Santa Monica; he forgot about dot-com holdings and real estate. All he thought about was Lester's story and the strange transformation of the beautiful land mass now called North America.

Lester sometimes sketched out scenes or props that Jake couldn't visualize, and Jake would tape them onto his flopping butcher papers. The manuscript grew; he'd forgotten about his other script ideas and never even mentioned *Till Death Do Us Part.* Since that ugly dog had nearly torn his arm off, he'd learned something about himself: he was a natural critic. He was such a good critic, in fact, that he couldn't bear to work on his own ideas, and it finally became clear to him that he was the kind of writer who enjoyed talking about his stories but couldn't really bear to be in their company. A husband-and-wife hit team going in for marriage counseling was a good idea as long as it stayed an idea, but just the thought of trying to write it up started to make him sick because his first impulse always had been, and always would be, to rip ideas to shreds.

In Lester, he found the perfect partner. Lester was a fountain of ideas, most of which were terrible, Jake had to admit, but for some reason having a terrible idea didn't seem to bother Lester or impede his progress. He just kept on spinning out new ones.

Lester had a definite point of view. It was hard for Jake to understand this, but Lester *was* somebody, as opposed to most of the people he'd met in the movies who had only wanted to *be* somebody.

Even if Jake had been willing to risk the possibility that the police were still looking for him, he didn't have enough money to travel very far. As it was, Clive footed most of his expenses: food, coffee, and medical treatment. In the end, though, it was neither the lack of money nor the fear of the cops that kept him in town.

There was something amorphous about the place, about the smell of the wood stove and the clattering sound of the carts in which people carried their groceries up and down the boardwalk. As hard as this was for him to admit, Cold Storage was a place his father would have chosen for himself. Jake could imagine his old man sitting at the corner of the bar or wrestling a big fish up the dock to show his cronies, and when he thought of such things Jake's body became somehow more solid, as if there were something in his chest besides his bruises that made him feel like he didn't want to muster the energy to move on.

Jake liked the easy rituals of the days in Cold Storage: coffee, work, visiting with people who seemed to spend their afternoons wandering along the boardwalk. He looked forward to walking down to the Love Nest every evening at nine o'clock. Once in a great while, Lester would come along, too, would drink coffee and listen to old records with him. It was on such a night in the middle of November, that an event happened that would change everything in Cold Storage for years to come.

The first real snow of the year was falling on the boardwalk, and the only footprints to be seen were those of Lester and Jake. Inside the bar, Ed played pool with the young visiting Lutheran minister, and Clive listened to Charlie Parker records. Visibility had been down in all directions, and no planes had landed in the inlet for three days. Weasel had come into the bar earlier to say that a small boat had tied up to the dock. "Who'd be wandering around in weather as crappy as this?" he'd asked.

Lester was lifting his coffee cup to his lips and bouncing his head to the looping sax of *Ornithology* when the door of the Love Nest opened. In a perfect cinematographic moment, the falling snow on the boardwalk made a silhouette of two figures standing there in the doorway.

Little Brother looked up and growled.

Bonnie Sue Mellon and Billy Cox walked in with packs on their backs and pushing padded cases on pieces of plywood in front of them. They'd come in answer to the ad for a new house band.

Clive sounded stunned. "There's never been an ad," he said.

"Then there shouldn't be much competition for the job," said Bonnie and put her amplifier down next to the bar.

CHAPTER FIFTEEN

"You are going to have to play before I sign you on," Clive said to the group. "I'm mighty fond of this record machine."

The band didn't hear much; they were busy searching for electrical outlets and a place to set up. Nix was taking off her coat, looking for a hook on which to hang it. She had a gold stud through her lower lip and a golden rose through one nostril; her short golden brown hair shimmered with blue highlights, and to Clive, she looked like a fairy child sneaking into his bar to warm up before flying out of a window, back into the forest.

"Hey, puppy!" she squealed and leaned down beside the ugly dog.

"I really wouldn't . . ." Clive started, but she was already on the floor, Little Brother's head in her arms. She was hugging him as if he were a childhood toy. ". . . do that . . ." Clive's voice trailed off.

The dog's eyes drooped serenely. He was panting, and his tongue lolled out the side of his face.

"You are just a big lover, aren't you? Just a lover . . ." Nix was cooing and hugging him close.

Little Brother's spotted tongue licked her face, and she rocked back laughing, wiping her cheek on her sleeve.

"Yuck, sloppy kisses on our first date!" She stood up, still laughing, while Clive watched her in amazement. "I'm Nix," she said. "I'm the bass player. You're going to love the band." She held out her hand.

"Do you have this kind of effect on all animals?" Clive motioned to Little Brother, standing next to Nix now, looking up at her with adoration.

"Oh yeah," she said. "I'm an animal person. A big animal person." She took back her hand from Clive, who seemed to have taken temporary possession of it.

"Then you should go over well in this place." Clive kept staring at her.

She looked around the room and smiled winningly at the three patrons. "Oh yeah, I think we're going to be good for business. Definitely." She held out her hand again. "I'm Nix, by the way."

"We've already done this, you know, Nix."

Clive held onto her hand again, though.

"That's right, we have." She held on and smiled. "We have."

Lester called, "Did you say your name was Nix?"

"That's right," she replied.

"That's really funny because I think Clive has your name tattooed on his ass." The Indian carver-turned-screenwriter eyed them over the lip of his coffee cup.

"Really?" Nix turned to Clive with an interested twinkle in her eyes, and for the first time since he could remember, he started to blush.

"No . . . not really . . . he's just fooling around." He picked up a clean glass, started wiping it down with a dirty bar rag. "Don't listen to him."

But she pointed her index finger at him and winked. "More about this later," she said, and picked up her bass, bringing it over to the corner of the room where her bandmates were setting up. Little Brother followed close on her heels.

"You are cut off," Clive hissed at Lester.

"That's fine by me," he said, and rapped his coffee cup down on the bar. "I'll never get to sleep as it is anyway."

The orchestra from the *SS Universe* had

been fired in Vancouver after a spectacular fight with the cruise director. They had been playing livelier and livelier music and been making continuous, subtle modifications to their costumes until Nix was wearing Billy's tuxedo and Billy was wearing a strapless evening gown. The two of them had been racing through a medley of songs by The Talking Heads. This was grounds to terminate their contract, proclaimed the director, but the union got them the rest of their season's salary and part of the next season's as a severance package. They decided to start a new dance band. This had been Billy's idea, and he'd been working out the details even as he'd zipped up the back of his gown.

So now they were a seven-piece band: bass, drums, guitar, saxophone, trombone, trumpet, and vocals. Bonnie, their manager, insisted they find a "wood shedding gig," that is to say, a place where they could work on their sound away from the public eye. This was important. They were looking at forming a band that crystallized the cross-influences of swing, The Squirrel Nut Zippers, and the Canadian folk tradition, with perhaps some spare kind of New York electronica reminiscent of Arthur Russell. Nix had been playing her bass with a bow. Bonnie said that the band was shooting for a kind of hep-cat hallucinatory maritime swing sound, and they already had a name: Blind Donkey.

They'd spent some of their severance money on a portable sound system, and in a matter of minutes they were set up in the corner behind the pool table and launching into their first number. They were a bit ragged at first. Because they wanted to impress the owner, they ripped into a swing version of "Sailor's Hornpipe," but their fingers were cold and the horn section slurred a little, so they bailed out of it after the second set of changes and pushed on into a ska version of "The Wreck of the Edmond Fitzgerald" that came off quite nicely. Billy sang to the enthusiastic applause of the audience and took a deep bow. He was happy to be home. He smiled at everyone; he even smiled at the pool table and the dog in the corner.

They played an original composition to close out the audition, an instrumental ballad that Billy introduced as "Love Is the Answer, But What Was the Question?" The horns started in together in kind of a minor key fanfare until the saxophone picked up the melody and played it through twice before coming back to the turnaround with the rest of the band. There was something lonely and ardent about the tune; it sounded like a foghorn at night or a train running past a slaughterhouse. It made you sad, but there wasn't an ounce of self-pity in it. It said that this life is just too goddamn short, and we're lucky to be here. This was the song Mouse Miller would have wanted to dance to, the melody he would have been humming while he pinned dollar bills on the rotten ceiling of the abandoned bar.

Miles walked in during the middle of the ballad and stopped short. He didn't even close the door. He was surprised to see a live band, surprised to see so many strangers, surprised to see Billy back from the sea. But mostly, he was surprised to hear a strange and affecting melody coming from the saxophone.

"How do you like the new house band?" asked Clive.

"They'll do." Miles didn't want to talk. "They'll do all right."

Bonnie was leaning against the door, watching the band, watching them make all the changes she'd heard them rehearse a hundred times, and she smiled. *Not everything is an accident,* she thought.

The song ended. Bonnie applauded along with everyone else as the band nodded, took their bows. Rick kissed his saxophone and walked to the bar.

Lester, Jake, and the minister stood around Billy; Lester made introductions, and the minister slapped Billy on the back. Ed talked with Nix as she wiped down her bass guitar and unplugged the cord. Clive looked at his ledger and tried to total up some numbers.

And Bonnie turned to Miles, since they were the only two people in the place who weren't engaged in something else. "I'm Bonnie Sue Mellon," she said, and Miles introduced himself.

"You know the guy who runs this place?" she asked.

"He's my brother. But don't take that as it sounds. I'm not really that familiar with him."

Bonnie squinted at Miles, tried to figure out if he was serious or not. "Think he'll give us a job?"

"He'll give you work," he said. Ed was laughing at something with Nix, and Clive appeared to notice.

"Will he be sneaky and try and screw us over?" Bonnie was conscious of how she sounded, but she was taking her managerial position seriously.

"No. If anything, he'll screw you right up

front. Are you their manager?"

"It sounds lame, doesn't it? Manager." She shrugged and wrinkled her nose. "Did you know people in high school who were managers of things? Manager of the fencing team, manager of the chess club." She turned her head away in a sudden spasm of embarrassment.

"You know it's not the same thing, being the manager of a band. These guys are really good. How in the world did you get hooked up with Billy?"

"I pulled him out of the ocean." She didn't look at Miles.

"Now see? That's not lame. Those guys in high school didn't have answers like that."

"It's true, you know. He had fallen out of his kayak. I'm the one who pulled him out," she said. "I'm not kidding."

"I know you're not kidding." They walked over to the bar, and he rapped the bar for service. "And I for one would like to thank you for bringing him home. Now, what would you like?"

"I'd like to meet the owner." She watched Clive walk toward them, and she held out her hand.

Clive was the older brother and as such had always felt superior in the biological sense; that is, he never gave much thought to his younger brother as they were growing up. When Miles was toddling around the living room, Clive was playing in the woods up behind the house. When Miles played T-ball, Clive was in Little League. When Clive was a criminal, Miles was a student. It wasn't until now, as this young woman walked toward him, that Clive realized that he didn't want to be out ahead of Miles.

Bonnie and Clive bantered back and forth about what Clive would be willing to offer Blind Donkey in the way of remuneration. She tried to smile but kept nervously brushing her hair back; a poker player would've called it her "tell." Clive nodded and tried to look serious while tapping on the closed ledger book.

Miles knew that Clive was reaching the end of the money that he'd sewn into the lining of his coat. He knew that there had to be some new source of income soon.

Business in the autumn was lively but hardly profitable, even in a small town of alcoholics. And the truth was that Clive wasn't catering to the alcoholics. There was too much sunlight in the bar during the day and too much laughter at night. The hard drinkers stayed at home drinking in their caves where no one could see them, and they didn't have to deal with the world.

But it was December, and no one could pay for a seven-piece band in a town like this. Then again, it was December, and Miles hoped that they stayed.

He looked at Bonnie dickering with his brother, and he smiled. She had a nice way of being forceful, as if she really were looking out for your best interests even as she tried to put forward her own agenda.

"That's what I can offer. Does this look like the Copacabana?" said Clive.

Bonnie looked around. The band had more than doubled the population in the bar. Now that the music had stopped, Lester and Jake were putting their coats on and were getting ready to leave. Ed was deep in conversation with Nix, and the minister had already gone home. It was Saturday night.

"This bar looks like a place that really needs a band," she said.

"I couldn't agree more," said Clive, "and so here is my offer. You all can live with me up at the house. There's a small cabin out back we can turn into an extra room. I'll provide dinner every night and a five-dollar bar tab per player. You play a minimum of Thursdays through Mondays, and if we start turning a profit on a weekly basis, I'll give you a percentage of the bar. *If* we start

283

turning a profit. Which we might have a shot at between Christmas and New Year's. That's all I can do."

Billy came up, whispered something in Bonnie's ear. She nodded and turned back to Clive. "The band can buy food and supplies in Juneau, and you will pay the shipping. And you'll let me look at the books so I can see for myself when you start turning a profit."

Clive smiled and shook his head. "She's tough, Billy. You're lucky she was there when you dumped your sorry butt into the ocean." He held out his hand but quickly added, "No special flights. I'll pay your freight as long as it's coming out with the supplies for the bar."

Bonnie glanced back; Billy shrugged, nodded. She shook Clive's hand, and it was done: Blind Donkey was the official house band for Mouse Miller's Love Nest.

Clive brought out a bottle of champagne someone had given him when the bar opened. He'd had it buried down in the ice machine, but now he started pouring it into beer glasses while the band members came surging toward the bar.

"And," said Clive as if proposing a toast, "I want you to play that last song, that instrumental, every night at closing."

Blind Donkey raised their beer steins of champagne to their great good fortune.

"Love is the answer," toasted Nix.

"Hear, hear!" came the answer from the bar.

They drank their champagne, and the band started to unplug. Clive chatted with the horn section about creating a small riser on which they could play; they were pacing off distances in the bar and looking for a new place for the pool table. Nix came up to Bonnie and Miles, Little Brother still beside her. The ugly dog was apparently keeping Ed at a respectable distance.

"So we're good to go?" asked Nix.

"Looks like it," Bonnie said.

"Ed — I think he's the biology teacher or something — said he could show me where we're staying. He also said he'd take me out kayaking tomorrow, if that's cool with you." Her voice was tentative, as if she didn't really know if she needed to ask permission but wanted to all the same.

"Sounds good, just be careful, okay? Crazy things happen kayaking around here." Bonnie smiled.

"I'm nothing if not careful." Nix headed for the door, and Ed held it open for her. Just as she got to the threshold, though, she bent down and cupped the ugly dog's massive head in her arms, kissed him on the top of his coffin-shaped snout. "Good night, puppy," she cooed to him. She waved gaily to the room, winked at Little Brother, and walked out the door with Ed. She was gone, but something of her still lingered, like an echoing bell.

Little Brother stood flat-footed, contemplating the door for a full minute, then walked slowly over to his pad, let out a low groan, and flopped down, hitting his lower jaw on the floor. He let out another long breath, a sigh which sounded for all the world like a moan.

"Oh, just great!" groaned Clive.

"What?" Miles asked him.

"Just what I need now. A love-sick bouncer."

The next day Ed met Nix down near the floatplane dock. He'd carried the kayaks there so she would have an easier time getting in. It was still snowing, but there was not a breath of wind. The snowflakes fell silently into the milky green sea.

Nix, already bundled with a hat, a pair of mittens, and a fleece coat, put on the float vest Ed gave her. She listened to a few instructions on paddling and some reassurances: the water was very cold but they weren't going far, and there wouldn't be any need for sudden movements. She sat in the little slipper of a boat awkwardly but when she pushed away from the dock, she felt as if she were suspended in air. She moved as easily as a cloud gliding through the sky while snow gathered on her hat, on her mittens, on her kayak.

Ed got into his boat and paddled toward the wharf of the inner harbor. He loved showing people the world around Cold Storage. He especially wanted to show Nix everything there was to see; he wanted to talk his head off. He wanted to explain about the rain forest and the tidal environments, the rivers that flowed into the inlet. He wanted to tell her everything about the place, and as he dipped his paddle into the green, he started thinking of every story he knew: the stories about deer and bear and salmon, the stories about the black cod and the shorebirds and the diving ducks. He wanted to tell her everything all at once. But he had sense enough not to talk.

The tide was approaching the low water mark, so he was able to paddle under the wharf of the old cannery building into a forest of tarred pilings. Some were cocked at odd angles. Water dripped from a broken water pipe, and everything sounded cavernous. Alongside them, a few gulls paddled about, making a clucking sound as they swam, nodding back and forth, searching for the small fish darting beneath the surface. Further away, some gulls swam on the surface, riding the tide back up the poles to fresh feeding areas. Others stayed by the pilings, picked at encrusted mussels. Red starfish clung to the sides of the pilings and below them drooped flaccid sea anemones. Just under the surface, Nix could see anemones coming to life, billowing like silk flowers in the water.

Ed pointed toward the back of the wharf near the shoreline where the shadows were the darkest. She looked back at him and saw a heron that had been watching them let out a great yawp and lumber into flight. The bird seemed prehistoric as it flew over, its long neck stretching out, its nearly six-foot wingspan beating the air in half-stalled flight. The heron pulled itself awkwardly through the pilings, but once clear of the wharf, it lengthened out into a steady rhythm, flying through the falling snow. Nix laughed and pointed after it with a clumsy mittened hand.

They paddled for another hour, drifting slowly along the shoreline, watching river otters darting up the beach, coming upon a seal that watched them with curious human eyes. Nix loved everything she saw but she started to shiver, and Ed suggested they paddle hard to help warm up on the way back to the dock.

Ed was full of things he wanted to tell Nix. He wanted to tell her about his students and about the projects he'd planned for them; he wanted to tell her about the age of the short raker rockfish and about collecting smolts in the streams in spring. Nix held the aura of the exotic. Ed looked at her and felt a door opening. He didn't know where this door led or who might be on the other side, but it didn't seem like a problem. He just looked at her and felt opportunity, felt that if he passed it up now he might never get another chance. He hadn't expected this fullness in his heart and he knew it was both stupid and dangerous, but he hadn't been in love long enough with Tina to know that he should be taking the small feelings of restraint more seriously.

Nix was awed. She was grateful and flushed and looked for all the world as if she were in love, but she wasn't, not with Ed anyway.

It was this place, this forest in the sea, and it was the experience of paddling through the snow. She'd thought that Ed might have a crush on her, but that wasn't unexpected. Many men fell in love with the bass player; bass was a sexy instrument. And it was easy enough to shake men off in bars. There was always lots of space to fade into, and other people to fade away with. But this morning, as she paddled back to the dock and looked at the tiny village, at how much it looked like a little town inside one of those snow globes, she realized that her tactics had better change.

The bow of her boat bumped the dock, and Ed was already out of his own and ready to help her tie up.

"That was amazing," she said. "Thanks, Ed, I'll never forget it."

"Aw, don't worry about it." He was slapping his gloves together and shifting from foot to foot. "Listen, I have a sauna out in back of my place. I was thinking of getting it warmed up later. You all could come. You could bring the whole band by. We could eat something, take a sauna, you know, get warmed up."

"That might be great. I'll ask the guys. Would we get to meet your wife?" Nix beamed wholesomely. She didn't want her question to sound like a sleazy accusation; she wanted to sound casually friendly, but she saw Ed's expression change.

"Yeah . . . yeah . . . you could meet Tina, and we could take a sauna. That would be great. Maybe in an hour or so the sauna will be hot."

"You know, Ed, I think I'm going to pass this time. We're talking about getting the stage set up and getting our gear and set list together. Why don't you bring Tina to the club tonight? We'll meet her there. I tell you what, the drinks will be on me. We can talk about a sauna then."

"Sure . . . good." For a moment Ed started to despair in the way only desperate lovers do. But then it occurred to him that she was saying she wanted to see him again, and he was buoyed by blissful optimism in the way only desperate lovers can be.

"Yeah, great, I'll see you tonight then," and he waved as she walked up the ramp to the boardwalk.

The great blue heron had flown up to the top of one of the light poles in the harbor, had settled there to survey the vastness of the inlet. It watched Ed stuff the spray skirts into the boats and Nix walk up the ramp and the entire world fill up with snow.

Back at Clive's house, the rest of the band was just waking up. Bonnie was making scrambled eggs, and Rick was cutting up green onions; Clive was standing in front of the window drinking a cup of coffee; Earl the drummer was wrapped in his sleeping bag on the couch watching *It's a Wonderful Life* on television. He'd worked a week in a rhythm and blues band in Victoria and got tired of it; he'd turned down a salsa band in Winnipeg; he'd decided to follow the band to Alaska.

"Man, I *hate* that fucking Mr. Potter," he said. "I mean, the man *has* that fucking eight thousand dollars. It pisses me off every time I see this movie. I tell you he'd be missing something more than his legs if I worked at that bank. You can believe that!"

"They needed you in Bedford Falls, man," Rick called out from the kitchen.

"Damn," said Earl. He got up and ambled to the kitchen in his underwear. "I'd get Uncle Billy his eight grand *long* before they have to have that party and shit." He cocked his thumb and pointed his forefinger at the side of Rick's head. Rick laughed and scraped the green onions into the eggs.

Earl was showing off for Clive, and the other band members knew this. They knew Earl was always a lot more "black" around club owners, a sort of defense mechanism or something. They liked him both ways, but they knew he wasn't really "street." He came from a wealthy family in Toronto with a father who was an orthodontist and a mother who taught piano in their home. Before attending Oberlin, he'd studied at McGill. Before that he'd probably been a hockey player. He was a hell of a good drummer, and Rick wanted to hold onto him.

Billy was down on his boat checking his gear. Weasel had promised to look after things and he'd done the minimum, but the old boat felt cold and dank. Mildew had set in on the pads and the bedding; rainwater had started to leak in from the top of the house next to the radar pulpit. Nothing feels as cold as an old wooden vessel that's been left unattended; it's a bone-cold that goes all the way through you. Billy sat on the edge of his bunk and wondered what he was doing back in Cold Storage. As soon as he'd walked onto the boat, his old life had come up and hit him in the face. His old life felt like this boat. It was cold, cramped, and impractical. It took a force of will to enter the dream world of Cold Storage, and Billy didn't know if he had the strength to reclaim that life. He didn't know if he wanted to.

He rummaged around, trying to get the stove started so he could at least get the stink out of the bedding. He unpacked some of the gear he'd brought along from Vancouver, found *The Tibetan Book of the Dead,* and held it in his hands for a few moments before putting it back in his pack. He turned off the oil stove, plugged in an old heat lamp that worked off of the shore power, grabbed everything that wasn't mildewed, and trudged back to the boardwalk. He would live in the house with Bonnie and the band.

Billy's old life was gone; it had left him when he went into the water off the coast. It was yet to be seen what his new life would be or to whom it belonged, but one thing was certain. It didn't belong on this boat in the winter.

The winter eased along from one dark day to the next. Lester and Jake worked on their script, and Blind Donkey played at the Love Nest. Trooper Brown was apparently off chasing crooks in some other part of the state because no one in town reported any contacts.

For two weeks in January, the snow piled up along the boardwalk until a northern high pressure system stalled over the outside coast. The clear skies brought temperatures in the low teens, and the town was encrusted in a frosting of snow. The school children got out early to go skating up on the little lake behind the main water supply for the fish plant. Ed took the kids up there, but Tina stayed in school, preparing lessons.

A few fishermen came in with winter king salmon, and a local diver hauled king crab up from the inlet. After Christmas, the café started offering a "Feast of Kings" buffet on Sunday mornings. It featured crab, crab omelets, eggs any style, poached salmon, and bagels flown in from Juneau; it cost twenty-five dollars a head but was all you could eat, at least until something ran out.

The Sunday morning buffet became a regular event for the band after their Saturday night gigs. If they could make it to the café before eleven o'clock in the morning, they could count on having a meal that lasted them the rest of the day. They were under contract to play a full sct on Sunday after the church service and usually rehearsed Sunday evenings while the regulars listened, playing records between sets.

Miles finished off his crab omelets and watched kids bundled in hats and gloves run along the boardwalk. Their toboggans slipped along behind them and through the windows — steamed up from the coffee urn, which had overflowed earlier in the morning — they looked like Christmas decorations. Miles was content.

He drank the last of his tea and was about

to get up when Tina came in the door. She smiled at the waitress and waved at the two other people sitting on stools at the counter but walked directly to Miles's back booth and sat down.

"If I get a divorce, will you be my boyfriend?"

Only a few months ago, before Clive had returned to town and reopened the Love Nest, Miles might have answered differently, but now he thought for a moment and asked, "Would you be a Betty or a Veronica kind of girlfriend?"

"Betty or Veronica?"

"You know, like in the Archie comics." He got up, grabbed another pot of tea from the counter.

She opened the menu. "I'm a Betty. Definitely a Betty."

"Jeepers, I don't know. I've always been more of a Veronica kind of guy," said Miles.

"First of all," she said, leaning in with real urgency, "you are not a Veronica kind of guy. Every man thinks he's a Veronica kind of guy, and that's just crap. You want to have sex with Veronica, you might even marry Veronica for her money, but you'll divorce her and end up with Betty. But whatever. I can change. Betty . . . Veronica . . . I can change." She brushed her hair back from under her collar and sat back in the booth. Clearly irritated now, she went on, "What I want to know is will you be there for me if I got a divorce?" She closed the menu, turned her head, looked at him.

Miles stirred some milk and sugar into his tea and looked down into the muddy swirls. The kid washing dishes in the kitchen dropped a salad bowl, and someone was swearing at him.

"I don't think you can change that much," he said. "I think you just have to be either a Betty or a Veronica. It's like saying you could become a Reggie or a Moose if you were really a Jughead . . ."

He stopped mid-sentence, embarrassed now. She stared at him for a long moment. Someone in the kitchen cracked an egg on the hot grill.

"Are you making fun of me?" she said.

"Ah . . . I don't think so," he said through a painful grimace, wishing now he could turn back the conversation like a page of a book.

Clive came in, pulling off his mitts. He looked around, walked over to their booth.

"Which character from the Archie comics do you think I am?" Tina asked, her voice rising.

Clive pulled off his hat, slid in beside Tina,

lifted up the lid on the teapot and peered in. "Oh man . . . Let me think . . ." He snapped down the lid and looked her up and down three times before speaking again. "She is secretly a Veronica, but she wants the world to think she's a Betty." He pulled off the scarf wrapped around his neck, looked at her again for a long moment, then shook his head in confirmation of his own judgment.

Tina was becoming upset. "Fine. I'm a Veronica. Fine. But will you be my boyfriend if I get a divorce?"

Now the cooks were out leaning their elbows on the counter waiting for the answer.

"Wow . . . This is a different conversation than I thought." Clive turned and waved to Meredith in the kitchen, got up and walked over to the buffet.

"And I suppose you guys think you're both Reggies?" Her voice was rising in pitch as if she were about to start screeching for her butler.

"That's a *very* Veronica thing to say," Clive called. He kept loading bagels, cream cheese, and prehistoric-looking crab legs on his plate.

"Yeah," Miles said, as if he were reappraising Tina in a new light.

"But . . ." Clive sat down and cracked one of the fifteen-inch crab legs against the corner of the table. ". . . to answer your question, I only *think* that I'm a Reggie. In fact, I am much more a Jughead but with some of Dilton Doily's intelligence."

"And your brother?" Tina leaned back and crossed her arms.

"My brother wants the world to think he's an Archie, when in *fact* he's really Mr. Weatherbee."

"Mr. Weatherbee?" Miles didn't have much fight in his voice.

"Oh, yeah," Clive insisted. "The B. Ever since he was a kid, he's had that frustrated authority thing going."

The door opened and Nix came in, looking like she'd been skiing or sledding. Her nose was running and her face was flushed and Little Brother was following close behind her. She stopped and said to him, "I'm sorry, sweetie. You wait outside, and I'll try and bring you something later."

He looked at her for a moment as if pretending not to understand. She pointed at the door and scowled at the dog. He slowly backed out, turned to jump onto a snow-covered table by the window. He circled twice and settled down, his head level with the bottom of the glass, his sad eyes scanning the inside of the café.

Nix walked through the steamy clatter, pulling off her stocking cap and unwinding the long scarf around her throat. Clive jumped up and waved Nix over.

"Whew, it smells good in here. I'm hungry." She sat down opposite Tina and slipped the parka off her shoulders but awkwardly kept her arms in the sleeves. Clive smiled, offered to buy her breakfast, and she was about to go over to the buffet when Tina reached over and grabbed her arm.

"Don't you think I'm a Betty?" she pleaded.

"You mean like Betty Rubble in the *Flintstones*?"

"Oh, Christ." Tina put her head in her hands and almost started sobbing. Outside, Little Brother lifted his head and squinted to see what was going on.

"That could be it," Clive exclaimed. "Betty Rubble."

"She's hot." Miles smiled as if remembering an old affair. "I always had a kind of secret thing for Betty Rubble."

"Me, too!" Nix put her hand on Miles's shoulder. "I'm so glad to hear you say that. I thought I was the only one. That nice little shape, the short skin dress. Rowww." Nix got up, ambled lazily over to the buffet table.

"Betty Rubble was married to a dope," Tina moaned.

"But she was sexy as all get out," Nix called over, "and besides, her husband was a lovable dope."

Meredith made Nix some scrambled eggs with crab and melted cheese on top and added some toasted English muffins to her plate. Nix poured a mug of black coffee, leaned back in the booth.

"My husband has a crush on you," said Tina after a while. Clive and Miles watched without moving. Meredith came running back out of the kitchen to listen.

"I know," Nix apologized. "I'm sorry. I haven't done anything to encourage it. Do you believe me when I say that?"

"I do . . . I think." Tina hesitated. "But are you maybe sending him signals that give him hope?"

Nix picked up her English muffin, bit into it, and melted cheese pulled away like a thread. Everyone in the restaurant, including the dog out front, waited while she swallowed.

"When I think about it now," she said, "Ed's a definite Barney Rubble. He's nice. He's nice to me. But I don't want to sleep with him, and I definitely wouldn't want to get between him and that gorgeous Betty." She rolled her eyes heavenward at the mention of Bedrock's siren.

Tina smiled. Meredith went back and got a bowl of oatmeal. Little cups on the side held yogurt, raisins, and brown sugar, and Tina looked down at it.

"I think I'll have the buffet," she said. "I'm a brand-new Betty." She sounded amazed, but Nix held the palm of her hand up and they high-fived.

The rest of the band came in one by one. They stamped the snow off their feet before opening the door and blew on their bare hands once they were inside. Earl walked over to the booth, greeted them with, "They're not out of the crab, are they?"

They weren't.

Miles took his pot of tea over to the counter where Bonnie was sitting on a stool, hunched over a menu.

"We really only look at the menu when we don't want to talk to folks, but since you are relatively new here, I could be misinterpreting the signals," Miles said to the side of her face.

"Huh?" Bonnie looked up. "I'm sorry, Miles, I was just thinking."

He sat down. Billy billowed through the

door, nodded over to Bonnie, and then walked to the back of the café.

"Billy's got a whole new look now." Miles turned to watch the jeans and black tuxedo jacket, the unshaven face, and the new haircut stride over to the horn section. "It's that half-shaven, magazine model, 'Oops! I didn't realize I was so sexy' look."

"Tell me about it." Bonnie didn't look up.

"Let me buy you breakfast." His good mood was holding up rather well, probably would until the southerly weather blew up in a couple of days. The wind that would come and make a grey, sloppy mess of the whole town.

"No, that's okay, Miles." She smiled weakly at him. "I'm just going to have some toast and coffee. I'll save up your offer for the time I can really soak you."

"You look like you're thinking about heading out of here."

Bonnie kept her eyes on his. "No . . . not really . . . well, I don't know. I like this place, Miles." She looked at the plate of toast that Meredith set in front of her as if it held some answers. "You know, my life has been screwy for the last few months. I took some right turns when everyone expected me to go straight ahead."

"But now the glamorous rock and roll life

has jaded you?"

"No, that's not it. I don't regret coming to Cold Storage, it's been great . . ." Her voice drifted off.

"But?"

Bonnie looked out the steamed up window, out past Little Brother waiting on the cold table. The snow was falling past the rigging on the boats in the harbor; the water was a flat slate-green, and the snow fell into it without a ripple. A crow was standing on the handrail of the boardwalk, snow gathering on its back.

"I don't know what I'm doing here." It sounded as though the thought had just occurred to her. "It's dumb, I know, but I'm still not sure if I'm in the right place, doing the right thing." She put down her mug and turned toward him; opened her mouth; stopped and looked down into the swirl of her coffee; didn't notice the sound of the door opening, one person coming in, another one leaving.

Miles spoke finally. "Heck, Bonnie, I don't think anybody ever really knows." He played with the damp string on the tea bag.

The crow on the handrail strutted back and forth for a moment, jabbing the air with his pointy beak until a kid with a sled came barreling down the boardwalk.

"You know what I thought your big question was?" asked Miles.

"No . . ." Bonnie drew the word out. She looked as if she were expecting a scolding.

"I thought you were wondering if you should have bothered rescuing Billy."

"Ah, no, that's not it." She looked at Miles. "That was a good thing. The weird part is, as incredibly romantic as this all sounds, pulling him out of the ocean and all, I just don't love him."

"That's the weird part?" His eyebrows arched.

"That's terrible, isn't it?"

"Heck, no. It's not terrible. Jumping in and grabbing him was a choice you made at the time. It wasn't a contract," said Miles clearly.

Bonnie shook her head. She looked him straight in the eye. "I know *that,* Miles, but . . . you know . . . sleeping with him for a few months could give him an impression that I was in love with him."

"People make that mistake all the time." Miles smiled at her.

"I don't."

"Well, do you want to stick this out with Billy because you rescued him?"

"No."

"So, where do you want to go? What do

305

you want to do?" Miles picked up a triangle of her buttered toast.

"Maybe I just need to go some place warm for a while." She sighed, hunched up her shoulders.

Miles stood up and pulled on his gloves. "You want to come up with me to the tubs?"

Bonnie looked down again and slowly took a sip of her coffee. Outside on the rail, the crow lifted into the air and shook off the snow like a spray of water. Cold Storage, Alaska, was too small, she thought to herself, but then the crow flapped off into the same sky that covered the Pacific Ocean, the same sky that covered Hawaii and the Sea of Japan. The crow was either gone forever or just around the corner.

"Yes." She stood up, walked directly out the door without fanfare.

Clive turned and watched from his booth. "Come by the bar later?" he asked. "I need a signature on the last of the forms. I promised to mail them. Can you do that?"

"Uh . . . yeah . . ." Miles tried to look out the door and over at his brother all at the same time. "Yeah . . ."

"Well, don't worry about it now. You better get going."

"Uh . . . yeah . . ."

"Go!" said Clive, and Miles went.

In its heyday, Cold Storage had been the summer headquarters of the salmon fleet. There had been a well-stocked store with fishing and mechanical supplies, three shipwrights, a welder, a portable sawmill, and a fair selection of lumber. There had also been a snack bar on the docks and three fully professional whores who lived above the two bars. When one of the whore-houses featured a short wave radio and a tall antenna to pick up late night radio signals in distant towns, the old timers complained about the encroachment of civilization.

Use of the bathhouse had been divided into men's and women's hours, but in the summertime at the height of the season, it was generally acknowledged that any time after eleven o'clock at night the tubs might be used by both sexes. By eleven o'clock in late June, the sky was a purple bruise of twilight; if you were walking down the boardwalk on such an evening, you would likely see the impossibly white skin of Norsky fishermen's backsides as they stood naked and steaming by the railing outside the bathhouse. They would be drinking from a can of cheap beer and talking about fish prices. They would nod to you with their chins as you passed, without an ounce of shame at their startling white nakedness. It had not become so civilized that a man couldn't stand naked in the middle of town.

On Sunday afternoons now, the bathhouse was closed for cleaning. Different volunteers signed up for duty but it was hit or miss if any of them ever showed up, so even though it was noon on the dot by the time Miles and Bonnie showed up with towels and cleaning brushes, the place was empty. Weasel, looking more than slightly hungover, had just arrived, but he wasn't overwhelmed with enthusiasm at the prospect of draining the tub, scouring the rock sides, and scrubbing the concrete decking. When Miles suggested that he and Bonnie take care of the cleaning, Weasel handed his buckets to them with a smile and walked away without saying a word.

Miles swung the sign on the door over to the CLOSED FOR CLEANING — DON'T BOTHER KNOCKING BECAUSE WE WON'T LET YOU IN side and locked the door.

"What do we have to do?" asked Bonnie.

"We warm up in the tub. Then we drain it, scrub it, mop around the sides with some

308

cleanser, and then sweep out the dressing room on the way out." Miles started to unbutton his shirt. "There are some extra bathing suits in the lost and found, or you can work in your underwear. I usually just take my clothes off, if that's okay." He stopped and looked at her, trying to look completely impassive about working in the nude.

"That's fine. I'd rather not wear someone else's old suit anyway," she said, and slipped off her parka, sat down to untie her snow boots.

The oil stove didn't throw out enough heat to keep the air much above freezing; they took their clothes off, went into the next room and down the concrete steps to where the tub lay sunken into the floor. Miles filled one of the plastic dipper jugs. He carried it over to stand by one of the drains and poured the water over his head, and Bonnie followed suit. The sound of the water hitting the concrete clattered in Bonnie's ears like marbles. Then they walked back and eased themselves into the warm water.

The skylight above them was covered with snow that melted around the edges, and the only sound in the cavernous room was the fat plonking of drops falling into the hot water where they leaned back across from each other, their white skin flushed red, their heads resting on the upper lip, and their legs spread out. The tub was large enough that their legs overlapped but their toes didn't touch the sides.

"Are you in love with anyone here, Miles?" Bonnie's voice echoed.

"No." They listened to the drops hitting the water.

Bonnie turned away, rolled into the water, dunked her head, embarrassed. Sputtering, she came up next to Miles's outstretched legs. He noticed that her hair was very thick and more red than it had first appeared.

"I'm sorry. I didn't mean to pry," she said. "Just forget I asked that."

Miles sat in the hot water, felt the heat easing into his bones, and fanned the water with his hands, held up one red leg to let a fat drop of snowmelt land on it. He didn't say anything. He lowered his leg back into the water and watched drops falling through the gloom and plopping into the water near Bonnie's face.

"All right, tough guy. Enough out of you." She smiled. "I don't want to know anymore." She cupped his bare foot in her hand for a moment and sat up on the ledge. She had small breasts and broad shoulders, like a good swimmer, Miles thought, and his mind flashed on a picture of her pulling through the waves to snatch Billy out of the sea.

"You pretty warm?" he asked her.

"Yeah, I'm hot." She waved her hand in front of her face.

"Come on," he said, and walked over to the darkest corner of the concrete bunker, to a door of thick planking with mildewed canvas stuffed around the edges to keep out the cold air. He wrenched it open.

Outside at the base of the hillside was a small fenced yard, smooth as a blanket, with fifteen inches of undisturbed snow. Fence posts wore white caps, and trees were laden with pillows of snow. Wind blew near the ridge up on the mountain, and snow sizzled off the trees like goose down. The woods were a tangle of dark green, and Miles stepped out into the yard, lifted his feet like a crane and punched holes through the snow.

"This used to be where they stored coal for the dressing room furnace. They used up all the coal and switched to oil," Miles explained and turned toward her, spread his arms wide and looked straight up into the falling snow. Flakes clung to his hair, melting as they touched his flushed skin, and he fell backward, landing with out-stretched arms to make a snow angel.

Bonnie jumped in, too, swung her arms and legs, shrieked as the cold crept back into her bones. She was ready to run and jump into the hot water until she looked over at Miles. Snow lay on his chest, around his groin, and his penis had retreated; she reached over and put her hand on his chest.

"Holy cow, Miles," she asked. "How much cold can you take?" She rubbed her cold hands up and down his chest.

"I don't know," Miles kept staring up into a maelstrom of flakes, "but I've just decided something."

"What's that?" She rolled over, her belly and breasts against his chest, and started to shiver, but he could feel her warm breath on his face.

"I've decided I don't want to find out." And he jumped up, rolled Bonnie off into the snow.

"Good," she said, "because I'm not up to saving another man."

Miles looked down at her pale heat-pink body curled into the outline of the snow angel, steam rising from every inch of her. He pulled her up with both hands, and as he did, he kissed her. He had meant it to be a quick kiss, a sort of introductory offer, but she held him hard and her slick mouth stayed against his mouth. Her skin was warm underneath the melting snow clinging to her back, and as they kissed, he moved his hands up and down her back, wiped the ice off her body. She wiped the ice off the back of his arms, then leaned away from his face, wiped the snow from his hair and put her cold fingers to his cheeks.

"Let's go get warm," she said, and put the flat of her cheek against his chest.

Getting back in to the hot water, their bodies ached at first; their hands and feet stung where the cold had taken hold. Miles sucked in his breath and eased into the water and felt as if his bones were bending out of place, but then the warmth came on like the blush of morphine and his body relaxed into the thermal water. Bonnie's eyes closed and she pushed the water with her hands, floated over to the ledge and put an arm around Miles's waist.

He got up to get the bucket and the stiff-bristled deck brushes from the dressing room and, as the water level went down, he showed her how to clean the sides of the pool. They spent an hour scrubbing the walls while hot water continued pouring in through cracks in the rocks, and if they began to cool, they poured water over their heads. Miles finished his side of the tub; he sat near a small stream of hot water at the bottom of the rocks, sluiced water over his head, and watched Bonnie.

She had her back to him, and against the sharp angles of grey-green rocks, her body seemed a miracle of smooth edges and pliable strength. She poured water over her head; Miles watched it slide down her throat to the groove along her spine, between her shoulders, up over the curve of her hips, then spread over her bottom, flowing to her legs. Miles had never looked at a woman like this before. Her arms were strong and, as she worked the rock with the brush, the wings of her shoulder blades widened and her muscles pushed against her reddening skin; she occasionally reached behind her back and scratched the skin above her waist or on her upper thigh, and in the heat-soaked atmosphere, her fingers left faint red tracks.

He felt almost dizzy watching her. He wanted to say something about how beautiful she was, but he didn't know if he could say anything clearly; he had become too thickheaded. But they talked about their lives, about the different wars they had fought and the journeys they had made. They talked about people they had lost and books they had read and music they loved. The talk was easy as they were working in the nude, and their minds were unhinged with the strangeness of it all.

They finished scouring the rocks, put the plug back in, and scrubbed the decking around the tub as it filled with fresh water, then sat in the clean water on the freshly scrubbed rocks and enjoyed the product of their labor for a few moments.

Miles swept the floor of the dressing room and Bonnie got dressed, then she folded some towels for the lost and found as Miles got dressed. The job was done, and they looked around. A silence overtook them as if the door to the dressing room opened up onto a busy city street, and they didn't want to walk out there just yet. Bonnie reached up on a shelf where someone had left some hair bands wrapped around a pair of reading glasses. She stretched the hair bands between Miles's fingers and plucked them with her thumb.

"Come by the club tonight. They are going to be working on some new material," she said. "It's good. Some really wild arrangements of Stan Rogers songs, kind of sea shanty swing." She nudged his shoulder with hers and smiled. "Don't be glum."

"I'm not glum," said Miles. "I'm just not ready to go outside, you know, to work and everything."

"What would you rather do?" she asked.

"I would rather watch you clean those rocks," he said seriously.

"You were watching me?" She laughed. "My God, Miles, I thought you were a professional."

Miles started to lean away from her, embarrassed, but she stepped forward and kissed him and he could feel the heat of the earth through her clothes as they held on to each other in a long kiss, until they heard footsteps coming toward the door. It was time to open the bathhouse for men's hours. There was a knock on the door, but Bonnie and Miles kept hugging each other in their damp clothes, each of them wanting just one more second.

The knocking came again, and Miles said, "I better get that, or they just might break it down." He went over and unlocked the door, and there was Lester, standing in sweatpants and slippers with a towel slung over his shoulder. He stared at them, and they picked up their towels, got ready to go. His eyes scanned them: Miles, then Bonnie, then back to Miles.

"I'm glad you two finally got together," he said. "Is it like official now, or do you want me to keep it on the QT?" Lester smiled. It might have been the most perfect smile of irony that Miles had ever seen.

They walked the boardwalk down to the Love Nest through snowflakes floating like dust motes. Bonnie slipped her warm hand into Miles's, and he squeezed softly but let go.

The bar was dark, a CLOSED sign hanging in the door. Miles rapped against the glass, tried the handle and they walked in, flipped on the one set of lights behind the bar. Little Brother raised his head from his bed and growled but only halfheartedly.

"I think this dog trusts women," Miles said. He looked around the bar. Where was Clive?

"I'm not saying a thing about this dog and who he trusts or does not trust." Bonnie eased around the other side of the bar away from the dog, but his eyes followed her and his chest heaved gently like a bellows with the fire banked down.

"Clive?" his brother said, and shined a beam of light around the room. He spoke to Bonnie. "He said he needed me to sign some papers." The beam of light landed on

317

a missing ceiling panel with a ladder standing underneath. They stopped to listen.

No sound.

And then a bump in the attic. Little Brother was up off his pad, standing beside the ladder, and growling up into the mouth of the hole in the ceiling. Miles started to climb but he heard scuffling along the rafters; he held the flashlight high above his head and away from his body in case it attracted the wrong kind of attention . . . or he had to use it as a club. The ugly dog roared, and Miles jumped up the ladder, two rungs at a time, shining the light toward the rustling.

There was nothing to see at first, just a series of forms stacked along the rafters. Then he saw the top of Weasel's head, poking out from between a dozen or so bales of marijuana.

"Some fucking lookout you are!" yelled Weasel.

Little Brother barked and lay back down on his pad by the door.

CHAPTER SIXTEEN

The next morning, Tina wrote a letter to the school board asking for an extended period of unpaid leave to last for an indefinite period of time. She walked up the boardwalk, dropped the letter on the counter of the city office, and asked Betty to give it to the school board. She walked down the ramp to the floatplane dock, swung her small daypack up to the pilot, climbed into the back seat, and flew away.

Ed was at the clinic within half an hour. Miles was there waiting for a kid who had phoned ahead to tell him, very loudly, that he had a peanut stuck in his ear.

"Jesus, Miles, you could at least have told me you were sleeping with my wife!"

Miles sat at his desk, stared out the window overlooking the harbor. The southerly weather had come in overnight and rain was falling on the snow, turning the ramps and floats of the harbor into rutted runways of slush.

"Ed, I've got someone coming to see me in five minutes. I don't have time to get into this with you."

"So you are not denying it?" His face was flushed, his leather boots were soaked, and he looked like he was hot and cold at the same time.

"I'm saying I can't get into this right now. Come back at five. We'll go have a cup of coffee and you can yell at me all you want, and I'll tell you everything I know about this situation."

"Shit!" Ed blurted. "You know that Trooper Brown? He called me. He's coming out here tomorrow. I'm going to fucking tell him everything. You know, I'm going to tell him everything about Weasel and the marijuana." He stormed out and slammed the door.

Miles felt the echo as he watched rainwater streaming off the icicles hanging from the eaves. Maybe he should have told Ed that he had never slept with Tina, but it wouldn't have helped. Ed would have blustered and fought, and he would have still been arguing when Mark White walked through the door to have Miles take a look in his right ear.

When Mark was four years old, he'd had

a raisin lodged up his nasal passage for "an unspecified number of weeks," according to his old medical records. Miles was curious to see what might be lodged down Mark's ear now and didn't want the kid scared off by the sight of an angry teacher screaming at the only health care provider in sixty miles.

Ed could wait. In fact, Miles thought it might be a good idea all round if Ed thought he had been sleeping with Tina. If word was out that Miles was sleeping with Tina, the local judgment against him would be harsh, but if it were followed by the rumor that he was actually sleeping with Bonnie, then he would be redeemed and brought back into the fold without ever having done a thing. This was the backfire theory of gossip, and Miles had seen it successfully applied on a number of occasions.

But the idea of Ray Brown coming back to Cold Storage was worrying him. There were bails of marijuana in the rafters of the bar, and it wouldn't take much of a drug dog to sniff it out; there were probably patrons of the Love Nest who were coming in there just for the contact high.

Fine, Miles thought, *let him come.* Search warrants and evidence teams, lawyers and plenty of gossip, his only brother being flown out of town in handcuffs — there was nothing Miles was going to try and do about it. He had to get a peanut out of a kid's head.

Mark claimed to have no idea how a cocktail peanut had wedged itself into his ear, and Miles didn't press him for a confession; he just flushed it out with baby oil and a soft plastic probe, got the papery peanut skin out with warm water, and sent Mark scrambling out the door to meet his sledding buddies. In Cold Storage, the snow season was so short that kids were willing to put up with the regional challenge of snowboarding through slush.

Miles was in his office when Jake arrived.

"Where's your receptionist, for God's sake?" he called down the hall.

"She's on vacation."

"Really?" His voice was headed for Miles's office. "How long has she been gone?"

"I don't know." Miles didn't look up from his desk. "I think she went to Disneyland sometime in the winter of 1979. No one has heard from her since."

"I can see why. They've added a lot of good stuff in Disneyland." Jake pulled up a chair and sat down, his blue sling visible under a wool coat of Lester's.

Miles finished up his report on Mark.

"Are you getting tired of our idyllic little corner of the world?"

"I've lived in worse spots."

"You aren't interested in getting back to your old life?"

"Which old life you talking about?"

"Your glamorous life of crime."

"You know, Miles, I don't care how good Quentin Tarantino makes it look. Crime sucks." Jake had refused to go into Sitka for treatment. He'd cut his cast off months ago. He and Lester had fashioned a unique type of binding/sling arrangement that still bedeviled him with itching and periodic rashes. He flopped down in the clinic chair and started poking a knitting needle he had brought with him down into his binding.

"How so?" Miles set the notepad down and looked at Jake, watched him scratch his arm.

"Too much stress. And you have to deal with too many assholes." Jake closed his eyes and moaned slightly as he scratched under the calico fabric he had bought from Tina.

"Isn't the money good?"

"You know how much you can make on one of those friggin' spaceship movies?"

"Which spaceship movie?" asked Miles.

"Christ, pick one!" Jake kept scratching.

"A ton of fucking money. Even a bad space-ship movie is better money than cocaine, and the best part is people love you. They point you out to their kids. Waiters are genuinely nice and ask for your autograph. That kind of shit doesn't happen to Pablo Escobar." Jake withdrew the knitting needle and inspected it as if expecting to find some strange organism stuck on the end of it. "At least not in America, and who the fuck wants to be famous in Colombia, no matter how much money you've got?"

Miles wheeled over on his chair and started inspecting Jake's arm and gently unwinding the packaging.

"That is true," Jake continued. "Trust me. Not many people make it. But that's the same in crime. Shit, crime is a lot more competitive, and of course the competition is a lot rougher." Jake pantomimed a pistol to his head. "But this script. I can feel it, Miles. This script Lester and I have got going. It's bankable. I'm telling you it has what people are looking for: humor, social comment, great characters, and fresh action."

"You got an ending that is satisfying? That's my big problem with most movies." Miles watched Jake's face as he rotated his shoulder.

"Fucking endings. Ouch! Christ, that still

hurts!" Jake tried to get his damaged limb back from the PA.

"That's because you have a torn rotator cuff. You are going to have to have that looked at when you get somewhere with a good hospital. You can tell them you did it playing softball."

"Yeah, softball . . . Let me ask you something: do you think Lester is stubborn?"

"Lester?" Miles looked amazed. "I don't know quite how to answer that. I've never heard of him apologizing or ever changing his mind, but I guess that doesn't necessarily mean he's stubborn. He may be the one person who is always right."

"This guy! He's a genius. He comes up with things that I couldn't in a million years, you know what I'm saying? Hc's like a pipeline directly into some deep fucking well or something. But he doesn't know how to piece the stuff together. I mean, if it were up to Lester this would be a six-hour picture. I'm begging him to cut, and then I go on and he forgets about what he wanted. But this ending, he won't cut it and he won't forget it. I'm telling you, this ending is just not going to work, and I can't get him to budge."

"What's the problem?" Miles started wiping down the pale white and discolored yellow skin of Jake's arm with an antiseptic lotion and a disposable wipe.

"In the last shot he wants everybody, all the characters, every single one, to turn into animals." Jake stared straight into Miles's eyes.

"And there is a problem with that?"

"This is an action picture. Can you imagine the look on the face of some studio big shot when I try to pitch the ending? Christ, I mean, we do something like that, we might as well make a movie about trees or something. I don't know. I might have to go back into crime." Jake raised his good hand to his forehead.

"You say Lester is good at his script ideas?"

"He's the best I've ever come across. I mean it." Jake reached out and touched Miles's elbow as he made his point.

"Then do the ending his way, wait a bit, and read it back to him. If it's stupid, he'll know how to finish it. But my advice is not to try to fight him. It's a no-win proposition."

"I believe you are right." Jake stood up. "But I've got too much time invested here to come up empty. You know what I'm saying?"

"Yes, I do," Miles ushered Jake out the

door. "There's a cop coming to town tomorrow. He's an Alaskan state trooper. I just thought I'd tell you in case you've got something you might be worried about."

In the waiting room, Jake stood by the window, looking at the boats in the harbor. "I'm not in on that action. Shit . . . all that pot, having it dumped in the ocean side and bringing it back here to dry out. What's he going to do with it now? He needs a better business model. But I ain't giving it to him."

"Why don't I ever hear about this important stuff? I hear all the bullshit, but when a member of my own family is committing multiple felonies no one says a word. Didn't you ever think of telling me?"

"No," replied Jake.

"What do you think I should do? About Clive and all this pot?"

Jake still stared out the window. "I don't know. Maybe we'll smoke some and all just turn into animals," he said, and his breath made an ovoid circle of fog on the windowpane.

Miles gave him some ointment for the itching and started saying something about obstructing justice and the possibility of going to jail, but Jake was lost in thought. "Yeah," he said absently, "we just need a good ending."

■ ■ ■ ■

Gloria Ballister came to see Miles every other week because she felt terrible. She weighed 285 pounds, smoked two packs of cigarettes a day, and easily drank a fifth of vodka every two days. Her husband was a heavy drinker, and she had stopped trying to get him to cut back. They lived out past the end of the boardwalk in a damp cabin with broken fishing gear piled in front: nets with holes and rusty haulers moldering into the moss.

Gloria was sick. Miles had given her everything he could think of in the way of practical health advice. She had boxes of books and pamphlets on everything from weight loss to sobriety. She had an oxygen bottle to help her breathe even though it was not strictly necessary, and she had gotten this on her own; she said the oxygen made her feel better, and Miles didn't dispute it.

Gloria wouldn't get up on the scales anymore. She came to the clinic to talk about her aches and pains; she came to ask questions about getting her stomach stapled; but mostly, Miles was convinced, she came just to get out of her cabin, have some human contact.

"Your color looks better this week, Gloria," Miles said. "Have you tried to walk a little more each day, like we talked about?"

She overflowed the small chair in the exam room, her arms folded awkwardly high up on her chest as if her body was trying to pinch them off. Her red eyes sank back into the folds of her face. She slurred her words, she was drunk, and everything about her spoke of unhappiness.

Miles had tried to be stern with her. He threatened not to see her at the clinic unless she flew in to Sitka and had a full screening, started taking responsibility for her health. She missed a few scheduled visits after that, and Miles got a call from a neighbor up the trail that Gloria hadn't been seen outside. He went and found her, lying on a filthy pad on the floor, her ankle badly sprained, blood and vomit smeared across her face; her husband sprawled unconscious on the bed in the middle of the room, his white belly extended like a corpse. Miles got a wheelchair, stopped her nose from bleeding, and made sure her ankle was propped up. She'd cried as they bumped down the trail to the boardwalk and as they'd trundled along to the clinic; Miles had let her spend the night there.

"You've just got to be ready, Doc," she said to Miles. "You've got to be ready before any change will come."

"What can we do, Gloria?" He spoke in a soft voice and patted her on the shoulder. "What will it take to get you ready for that change?"

"I don't know, Doc." She wheezed, touched his fingers. "Maybe I am as ready as I'll ever be."

So Miles let her visit the clinic every other week, and he tried to say something to inspire her to fly to Sitka. Every week he talked about a new diet plan or told her stories of people who had turned their lives around. She picked apart every suggestion, waved them away as if they were flies.

But Miles knew she was ready for change, ready for the most substantial kind of change. Nothing was going to shake her off her course. She was not going to stop drinking or start exercising, no matter how possible or even easy Miles made it look, and one day he would get a call from a neighbor or her husband might be sober enough to make it down to the clinic. Miles would grab some volunteers and a stretcher and lug Gloria's empty and unhappy body to the plane for Sitka where they would do a postmortem examination and ship her to the mortuary to be cremated.

Both Miles and Gloria knew that the day was coming soon, and after acknowledging it with gestures and subtle shifts in the tone they used with each other, they both relaxed. Miles still pestered her, but gently, and she still came to see him; she'd been the first to tell Miles the joke about a patient with only a few minutes to live.

Now she heaved herself up and said, "Well, Doc, you boiled me up another couple of eggs. I'll see ya." And she put on her rain slicker, picked up the two bent ski poles she used as walking sticks, and lumbered out the door onto the slushy boardwalk.

"I'll see ya, Gloria," Miles called, but she was already poking her shoulder back into the clinic.

"Hey, I heard that cop is coming to town to arrest your brother," she said.

"I hadn't heard that. I don't think that's true. Clive's broken no law I know of," assured Miles.

"Oh yeah. Okay." Gloria smiled weakly. "We've been talking about it, Doc. That cop can shove it up his ass as far as we're concerned. We're no snitches."

"That's good to know, Gloria." Miles unenthusiastically patted her shoulder, and she was gone.

By four thirty, it seemed dark as midnight. The rain had let up, but the air that rode in through the door with Billy seemed as wet as seawater.

He walked straight into Miles's chest. "Whoa! I'm sorry there, Miles." He peered up at Miles's nose.

"You okay, Billy? Something you need?"

"Naw, not really. I just came by, you know, just came by to talk." He looked around the room as if expecting someone else to be there; followed Miles as he walked back to get the fat folder of notes on Gloria; stood in the doorway and watched him write in the file.

"What you need, Billy?"

"I don't know really, Miles. I just kind of wanted to talk to you about something . . ." Billy eyes roamed around the room, not stopping to rest anywhere.

"I've got some time," said Miles. "Is this about Trooper Brown's visit tomorrow?"

"Huh? Oh, no, that's under control. I wanted to talk to you about something else."

"Good, because I think Ed is going to come by in about half an hour to shoot me, but I've got some time before that."

Billy laughed nervously. "Well, you know, Miles. I was kind of wanting to talk to you about Bonnie." He scratched the knuckles of his right hand and made a strange kind of grimace.

"Just spit it out, Billy."

"I'm just kind of screwed up is all, Miles. You know she saved my life and you know we were really close on board the ship, but now I don't know. She's nice and everything, but I don't know. It's different here. It's not like it was on the ship."

"Why are you telling me this, Billy?"

"I don't know, man. I know she likes you. I thought maybe you had some advice for me. Or maybe . . ."

"You want me to talk with her?" Miles tried to dampen the incredulity in his voice.

"Yeah . . . that would be great. Maybe you could talk to her like my doctor. You could tell her I've been unbalanced all my life. I've got some personality disorder or something. It's kind of true, you know, it wouldn't be like . . . lying or anything."

Miles stared at him. "So you are telling me you'd rather have me tell her you are crazy than talk to her yourself about your own completely understandable feelings?"

"Well, yeah, I guess so." Billy looked like he, too, couldn't believe how dense he was. "Yeah, I do . . . I mean, it's not all that strange. She saved my life. How can I just dump her right here in this little dinky town with nowhere for her to go?"

"Shit, Billy, there is always somewhere to go."

Miles had been prepared to fend off an accusation, so this strange request came as kind of a letdown. He had been prepared to justify his own feelings for Bonnie, so this suggestion that she was helpless and not worth fighting for was making him grumpy.

"And you want to dump her because of what?" He frowned at Billy. "Because she saved your life? Because there are so many other gorgeous women for you to choose from around here? I don't get it."

"Listen, Miles, what if . . . say . . . Ed McMahon came to your door and gave you a million bucks? You'd be happy, right?"

"Ed McMahon? You mean the guy from Johnny Carson?"

"Yeah, him. So say he shows up at your house and tells you you won a million dollars. You'd be so happy you might even invite him in and have a drink. You'd feed him a meal and maybe go out and get drunk with him. But hell, you wouldn't want him to be your best friend, would you? I mean it would be hard. You'd be hanging out with your friends and you would be like, 'Oh yeah, this is Ed, he's my new friend because he gave me a million bucks,' and they'd all look at you and all they'd think about was how this guy had saved your ass and then pretty soon that would be the only thing you could think about and pretty soon you wouldn't know what the fuck to say to Ed McMahon and you'd kick his sorry drunken-sidekick ass out on the street. You know what I'm saying?"

"The scary thing is," nodded Miles, "I think I do."

"So you'll talk to her for me?"

"Sure. Sure, Billy," he agreed and smiled weakly. "I won't even bill you."

Billy said something else, but Miles didn't hear him. He listened to Billy's footsteps fade out past the door and disappear, looked at his notes and didn't read them; he wanted to go home.

He wanted to avoid Ed. Something about the combination of Gloria and Billy had put him in a bad mood. He looked at his watch; he could close up shop and be gone before Ed could show up if he hurried.

He had unplugged the coffee pot and turned out his office light when Liz came in with her cat.

"Miles, I don't mean to trouble you, but can you help me? I don't know who else to ask." Her voice was shaking, her face was pale.

"Come on in, Liz." He hid his irritation. "What's wrong?"

She held out Louise, a delicate tabby with a white chest, two white paws, and a three-inch cut on top of her head. There wasn't a lot of blood, but the cut gaped through the grey fur. The cat was calmer than Liz.

"Let me take a look," said Miles.

Everyone knew that he wasn't supposed to work on pets, but it was too expensive to fly to Sitka. Before he'd agreed to the "no complaints, no returns" policy, most sick animals had been slung into a sack and buried at sea; now they lived. And even though it was against his policy, Miles started allowing "follow-up" exams for which he generally got paid with food: fish, berries or venison. Since he had terrible luck with his hunter-gatherer skills, this was not a bad thing.

Liz held Louise while Miles gently stitched up the wound.

"Does this have anything to do with my brother's dog?"

"No, I don't think so. We'd be looking at something worse than this. No, I think she got tangled up with a tomcat down at the cold storage. I try to keep her in the house, but with Bob and Matt running in and out all day long, she slips out."

Miles gently put one of her fingers on the thread to maintain the tension while he reached for scissors. She kept her gaze elsewhere, and they talked about new books in the library and the decline in the number of kids in school and whether the school would be able to stay open much longer.

"I hear we might be having a decline in the number of teachers, too." Liz looked at him for the first time since he'd started patching up Louise.

"I heard Tina flew out this morning," he countered. "You know anything about that, Liz?"

"No . . . nothing." Her eyes swept through the office. "Just what I've heard . . ." Liz's words drifted out on the still silence between them.

"And we all know how reliable boardwalk gossip is," said Miles, sounding cheerful but carefully changing direction. He snipped the thread and said, "There! You can bring her back in a couple of days. Don't tell my bosses back in Sitka, though."

"I won't, Miles." She picked up the cat, held it in her arms and thanked him, but she looked sad, sheepish.

"Don't worry about it, Liz." Miles said it

again. "Really, don't worry about it," and they understood each other.

Tears welled up in her eyes. "I don't know what we'd do without you, Miles."

He did not look directly at her. He was touched by her words particularly because he knew that she was sober. He tried to remember. Was she a drinker? He didn't think so.

"Take good care of Louise, and I'll see you both in a couple of days." Tears ran down her cheeks.

Miles was grateful that Ed was late. He rushed around, turning off all the lights and grabbing his coat off the rack in his office. But Billy tapped him on the back as he was locking the door, and Miles jumped back as if he'd been shot with a dart.

"Christ, you scared me." Miles put his hand over his chest, leaned against the door.

"Here she is, Miles."

Bonnie stood there, perplexed, as if waking up from a vivid dream into unfamiliar surroundings.

"Here she is," Billy said again. "I told her you wanted to talk with her." He scratched the top of his head, shifted from one foot to the other. "Okay, I'll see you back at the bar," he said, and hunched his shoulders, rushed away through the rain that gleamed like pins under the few houselights along the boardwalk.

Bonnie had thought about Miles ever since they'd cleaned the tubs. She'd wondered what he was doing at odd times during the day. She'd tried to remember the smallest thing they had talked about, and this irritated her because she didn't want to be in love, not with anyone. Miles was good looking; he appeared to know who he was and what he was doing with his life, and while he didn't want to talk about his service in the war, he didn't seemed damaged in any way. He just seemed sensitive, as if he recognized some great beauty in her that he was perfectly willing to let slip away, or perhaps possess forever. This made her want him all the more, and it was driving her crazy.

"Did you want to talk to me, Miles?" she asked.

"Well, not really. I don't know how I got into this really, but Billy wanted me to talk to you."

"About what?" She took a half step toward him, her forehead furrowed.

"Well," he said, "it's kind of hard to explain, but he wants to break up with you because you saved his life and you remind him of Ed McMahon."

"Ed McMahon . . . you mean Johnny Carson's announcer?"

"Yep."

"And that's why he wants to break up with me?"

"Yep."

"Well . . ." She drew out the syllable and followed Miles's gaze down the boardwalk. "I'm relieved. I thought he was going to make some kind of lame excuse about commitment or something."

"Exactly." Miles took her arm, and they walked toward Lester's house. "I mean, reminding someone of Ed McMahon is pretty serious. It's something that I think would be hard to overcome. No matter how much therapy you put yourself through. I'd say it's one of those insurmountable differences."

Bonnie stopped walking. "Do I remind *you* of Ed McMahon?"

"No. Not a bit."

"Good." And she leaned forward to kiss him lightly on the lips.

"For the love of God, Miles, what is it with you?" Ed stood ten feet behind them, yelling loud enough that gulls in the harbor lifted away from the water and started hee-hawing, laughing into the dark. "Weren't you happy enough fucking my wife? Tina's gone a day, and you're on to your next woman!" Ed clenched his teeth.

Miles's voice came louder than he'd intended: "I HAVE NEVER HAD SEX WITH YOUR WIFE!"

The gulls whirled in a chorus above the town. Miles looked up, and in the darkness they looked like bits of white paper caught in an updraft. Stragglers rose up in the lights of the fish plant and glowed like miniature space ships.

"It's true, Ed," said Miles. "I have never had sexual relations with that woman. I'm sorry, I mean Tina, you know. I have never had romantic relations with your wife. I have never kissed her or seen her naked." His voice must have been louder than he thought, for he looked over Ed's shoulder and saw the women's movie club standing in front of the café. Clive and Nix stood beside them, and Nix was holding a magazine up to protect herself from the rain. Everyone's eyes were fixed on Miles.

"I didn't catch the first part of that, Miles," said Clive. "I got the part where you said you hadn't fucked Ed's wife, but what were you talking about before that?"

Rain made little splashes on either side of Ed's shoes.

"I was telling Bonnie that she didn't remind me anything of Ed McMahon." Miles's voice hung in the air like one of the gulls.

"Well, thank goodness for that," said Colleen Sheehan. "I thought you were talking about running for president," and everyone chuckled, then walked back into the café.

"Say goodbye to your brother, asshole," Ed said to Miles over his shoulder and stormed down the boardwalk.

CHAPTER SEVENTEEN

The community center's barrel stove burned a lot of firewood during the coldest part of winter. So every year a work party went across the inlet to fell some dead spruce trees. They bucked them up into logs small enough to roll out on the beach, floated them off at high tide, towed them back across to town and cut them into stove wood. The job took two days, and there were two crews: the logging crew and the splitting crew. This year, Billy wasn't signed up for any job, but Ed was on the splitting crew.

Thinking to keep himself out of town for most of the day and his brother as far as possible from Mouse Miller's Love Nest, Miles decided to join the logging crew and take Clive along. He had slept a little later than he'd planned; by the time he called his brother's house and Nix answered the phone, she told him to meet Clive after church, which was both odd and irritating because the longer they stayed in town, the greater the opportunity for Trooper Brown to find them. Miles had an uneasy feeling that he'd been left out of the loop on something.

He was walking to the bar, striding through the slushy tracks left by the slick-soled, leather-heeled shoes of people going to church, when he heard the blare of a floatplane taking off. That meant the trooper had already landed, and Miles doubled his pace, hurrying to get to the church service in the bar with a ceiling full of marijuana bales.

Before the second preacher had left town and Mouse Miller's Love Nest had become a place of worship, the only church building had been shared by three congregations. Every Sunday the Catholics had mass, then the Lutherans celebrated communion, and finally a small group of Unitarians gathered to eat and tell stories from their membership. The Catholics were workmanlike in their devotions and were in and out pretty quickly; the Lutherans lingered only somewhat longer; the Unitarians, however, could soak up the rest of the day if the spirit moved them, so they were always scheduled last.

Miles didn't belong to any of the congregations. He occasionally made it in time to hear part of a sermon, but mostly he enjoyed sitting outside on a bench under the eaves, leaning his head against the wall, listening to the singing, and drinking the coffee he'd brought along with him.

The church building was uphill from the fish plant on a little flat of muskeg surrounded by trees. It was high enough that you could see out almost to the mouth of the inlet, and fishermen often came up to check the weather out on the fishing grounds. To get the best view, they'd sometimes climb the stairs into the modest bell tower. On Sundays, they'd come tiptoeing along the back wall and clamber up the stairs while the ten or so people in the congregation kept going at their meditations, hammer, and tongs.

But this Sunday, the biggest congregation was meeting in a bar. From fifty feet away, Miles could recognize the voice booming through walls and windows, and he winced at what was awaiting him inside. He had never heard his brother, his convicted felon of a brother, deliver a sermon, and he couldn't imagine what the text would be. In this area of his brother's redemption, what little faith Miles ever had was squandered.

Dressed in his warmest coveralls, he stood outside the bar and listened to the sermon. The scent of the yellow cedar trees blended with the aroma rising from his cup of coffee and he should have felt optimistic, but he was impatient, every moment thinking he could hear the trooper's footsteps coming along the boardwalk.

The bar was surprisingly full. A board had been placed over the pool table and covered with a white cloth to serve as an altar, and on chairs lined up especially for the service sat the parishioners: Gloria in a flowered blouse with an oxygen tank beside her; Liz and her cat Louise a row behind; Bonnie in a broad-brimmed white hat over by the bar; Weasel and Billy in clean blue jeans and Hawaiian shirts; Jake in black jeans, a white shirt, and his sore arm still hanging to his side. On the far side of the pool table sat Rick and the rest of the band with their instruments. Clive stood in his dark suit and skinny black tie beside the makeshift altar.

Clive saw his brother enter the room, and he launched into the scripture reading for the day. Romans, chapter thirteen. His voice was a bit shaky but it built as he read and was without irony or sarcasm; it had the

346

quaver of humility.

"Owe no one anything," Clive began, "except to love one another; for he who loves his neighbor has fulfilled the law. The commandments — 'you shall not commit adultery, you shall not kill, you shall not steal, you shall not covet,' and all the other commandments — are summed up in this sentence: 'you shall love your neighbor as yourself.' Love does no wrong to a neighbor; therefore love is the fulfilling of the law.

"Besides this, you know what hour it is, how it is full time now for you to wake from sleep. For salvation is nearer to us now than when we first believed; the night is far gone, the day is at hand. Let us then cast off the works of darkness and put on the armor of light."

Out on the boardwalk, Miles felt a blue shadow fall across his face.

"I want to talk to you," mouthed Ray Brown. Miles heard his brother's voice hesitate, saw the parishioners turn to watch through the open door to the outside, but he followed the trooper down the board-walk.

"I don't know what you think you are doing here," Brown sputtered, "but I've been talking to the school teacher, and he's got an interesting story to tell."

"Before you get started, Trooper Brown," Miles interrupted, "I want you to know that I'm to blame for all this trouble." He could hear the congregation inside singing "Many Rivers to Cross." "Did Ed tell you that Clive was involved in any criminal activities?"

"He said that your brother was importing marijuana. He said he was associating with his former drug lord connection. He said your brother assaulted that old associate."

Miles spoke politely. "Well, Trooper, first of all, if you have reason to believe that anyone has broken the law, then you should make an arrest. I think you'll find all the parties here." He held out his hands toward the congregation as if inviting Ray Brown into the church and continued in the same low voice. "But you have to understand the motives behind Ed's statements to you, Ray. You see, he is very, very angry with me." Miles spoke softly, as if not wanting to disturb the devotions going on inside.

"Does he have good reason to be angry with you?" Brown asked with some interest.

"Actually, yes." Miles lowered his voice further. "You see, I've been having sex with his wife for several months now," he lied.

The trooper nodded nervously. Inside the church, a chorus of cracked voices swooned up to the high notes. Brown looked over the top of Miles's head through the dirty front window into the church where Clive stood with his arms wide and his voice raised in song while the musicians of Blind Donkey churned out the rhythm. The trooper watched dumbfounded, until Rick took a step forward to take his saxophone solo; then he swung back to speak fiercely to Miles. "I don't know what you think you've got going here, but I'm going to keep an eye on all this," he said, and stalked down the boardwalk, out of his face, but certainly not gone for good.

A murder of crows rose in a chorus and whirled out over the boardwalk. Miles wondered where Bonnie had got the hat she was wearing; he wondered if he would be able to see her after he got back from cutting trees and, if he did see her, what her expression would be. He looked at the sunlight slanting down through the wet cedar boughs and smiled at the thought of donning the armor of light.

"The day is at hand," Miles said out loud. He stood up, poured cold coffee over the edge of the boardwalk, and walked toward the harbor. He could hear the floorboards of the bar creaking as people got to their feet; he could hear them chatting as Clive stood in the doorway shaking hands, thanking everyone for coming, while this new sunlight slanted all around him through the clouds. It was almost ridiculously serene.

Miles was the first one down to the boat. He sat and sharpened an axe for a few minutes until he heard footsteps banging down the dock.

"Christ, it's cold in here." Jake jumped onto the boat, still wearing his church clothes but with a canvas jacket thrown over his shoulders. "Let's get this thing going. Don't we have some wood to cut?"

More boots clomped down the dock, and the boat tilted with the weight of the men getting on board. Clive thudded onto the deck and started putting coveralls on over his black suit. "Brother!" he shouted to Miles with a fine smile on his face. "Good to see you in church this morning."

For the rest of the morning and on into the early afternoon, the logging crew was busy in the woods on the other side of the inlet. It took them half an hour to fell two spruce snags just off the beach. Their tips just reached the beach and the six men limbed them, bucked them into manageable lengths, and rigged the hand winches to pull them to the tide line. Clive and Miles used a heavy axe; the others whined and rattled

350

with the saws. Lester worked on the rigging to pull the logs down onto the beach, and Jake tended the fire and sharpened a couple more axes. For a man with a torn up arm, he looked remarkably happy.

They took a lunch break at one thirty. The silence as the saws stopped seemed to rise from the ground. They'd worked up a fair sweat, so they put on dry jackets and gathered around the fire, spread their life jackets against the hillside and leaned against them to eat sandwiches and drink coffee.

The day held clear and cold. The slush from the previous day's rains had frozen on this side of the inlet. The sun slanted through the canopy, created pools of light on the forest floor, and icy snow lay in patches beneath the bare bushes. Everything seemed frozen and brittle.

Jake came over and sat down next to Miles and Clive. He put his head back and raised his face to the sunlight; he took a deep breath, smelled the wood chips and the earth they'd disturbed on the forest floor, smelled the wood smoke and felt the heat from the fire warming his legs. "Hey, boys, chow!" he said, and bit into his sandwich. He swallowed and turned to Miles. "So," he asked, "is the trooper happy?"

"I don't think he'll ever be happy until

351

one or the other of us are in jail."

"I'm a little disappointed that he didn't search the place."

Miles swallowed his hot coffee too quickly. "Why's that?" he choked.

"It would make Weasel feel a lot better about what he has to do."

"What are you talking about?"

Clive whistled into the woods and a forlorn Weasel came down the bank dragging a tarp behind him. The cutters had been building up the warming fire with slash and had split up rounds of an old hemlock which had long ago bleached silver on the beach. They were smiling broadly.

"Jesus, you're not really going to make me do this, are you?" Weasel pleaded as he used two hands to drag the bundle down the street.

"I paid you the money you fronted, and I'm giving you a job at the bar. That pot is my product, and I know what I want to do with it."

"But my God, Clive." Weasel was desolate.

"Come on now. I know you have some personal use put away. This is a good deal for you now, Weaz. You shouldn't have put that stuff in my place. You know that. It was a mean thing to do, and you are not cut out to be a mean guy."

"No . . . I suppose not." And with that Weasel pulled back the edges of the tarp and exposed three very chunky bricks of compressed marijuana, each one about the size of a five gallon can. Miles was surprised at how much bigger they had looked under the rafters of the Love Nest.

"Go on now," Clive said, and Miles noticed just the hint of threat in his voice. As soon as he recognized the tone, he noticed that Weasel had a rather prominent black eye. Clive shook his head as if he had been bitten by a wasp. "Go on now."

"Ah . . . I just can't, Clive. You do it." Weasel slumped down on one of the slick beach rocks.

With that, Clive got up and put the three chunky bricks of pot on the beach fire. All the cutters shifted around to stand downwind.

The afternoon passed at a fine, lugubrious pace. The men ate their peanut butter sandwiches slowly, chewing each morsel, and those lucky enough to have salmon-berry jam licked it off their fingers.

The sweet smelling smoke shimmied around the cove like a belly dancer, and no one worried about the tide or the time but took simple pleasure in their work of rolling the firewood to the beach.

"Why in the hell did Weasel put his pot in your attic?" Miles finally asked.

"Who the hell knows?" Clive smiled. "He probably thought that if anyone found it he could always blame me. But I also suspect he had some half-assed idea of selling the stuff out of the bar. Like I wouldn't notice him going in and out of the attic all the time?"

They both laughed too long. Then stopped. Then laughed again, embarrassed. Then they let the silence fall around them like tropical rain.

"Seems like kind of a waste," Miles said finally.

"I suppose so." Clive sighed.

"Why are you doing this?" his younger brother said as if the rashness of the act had just occurred to him.

"I guess I didn't want Weasel going to jail," he said, and took a deep breath as the trees sighed softly with a damp breeze blowing down the inlet. "And I guess there has to be some obedience if you want the love."

The brothers sat in silence again, the words churning over in Miles's fogged and tingling mind.

"Do you think Ed is going to kill me?" Miles finally said.

Clive watched his brother chew his peanut butter sandwich. "No," he said. "I don't think so. I don't think he's as pissed at you as he used to be."

Miles stared down at the toe of his boot as he spoke. "He was fairly pissed at me last night. Lord knows what he's going to think after this morning." He stopped for a moment. "I'm sure the trooper will tell Ed I confessed to sleeping with his Tina."

"Yeah, but I'm pretty certain Ed's mad at me now."

"You? How come?"

Clive stood up; he turned his back to the fire and held his hands behind him, palms to the heat. The other men were already down on the beach re-anchoring the boat. "He's mad because he heard that I'm in love with Nix."

Miles rocked back and forth gently, unwittingly. "Whoa . . ." was all he managed.

"After that little drama he had with you on the boardwalk, Ed asked Nix if she would move in with him, and she told him that she was moved in with me."

"Is that true? I mean . . . is that true?" Jake squinted and moved his head to be more directly in the smoke.

"Which?" asked Clive. "That she told him, or that she's moved in with me?"

Miles wore a twisted grin. "Is it true that you are in love with her?"

Clive rocked his head up and down slowly as he watched the smoke from the burning weed curl into the sky. "Yes," he said finally. "The best part is she feels the same way about me."

"Has she really moved in with you?"

"Yeah." Clive blew on his hands, taking a new pleasure in everything about the gesture, the warmth of his breath, the smell of wood chips, even the look of the dirt under his fingernails. "Imagine a love that isn't unrequited," his voice drifted off. "But of course Ed didn't take it well."

"I don't imagine." Miles started putting on his work gloves.

"You know what her name is?"

"Who, Nix?"

"Yeah, her name is Maya. Really. It's Maya Kendricks. She's from Madison, Wisconsin." Clive said the name of the city as if it were one of the moons of Jupiter.

The brothers were silent. The fire popped, and Mayan dancers far off in Madison, Wisconsin, were dancing in the streets.

"No kidding," Clive said eventually. "Her father teaches anthropology, and her mother's a freelance photographer. Maya Kendricks, can you believe it?"

The fire crackled, the sparks swirling upward in twisty courses toward the green boughs above, and Jake shook his head. "Yes," he said. "I think I can believe it." He pushed himself upright, steadied his legs, and walked toward the mountain.

By two o'clock, the sun was behind the ridgeline, and the cold began to bite down through their work clothes. The fire had burned down, and Weasel kept standing over the ashes, stirring them with a stick.

The rest of the crew wrestled logs down to the beach and rolled them with Peaveys over the rocks and onto the beds of eel grass; they set an anchor in the mud and tied a line to staples they'd driven into the logs. Someone would come back after dark when the tide was higher and pull the anchor and tow the logs across the inlet. They would tie the logs to the pilings of the community center, and then the splitting crew would take over, would buck and split and carry the stove wood up the hill to the woodshed to be stacked for the winter. Those fat columns of spruce were as satisfying as rolls of coins waiting to be unwrapped.

The day darkened until there was only a violet glimmer on the water. Miles's muscles were sore. His contact high from sitting near the fire was wearing off, leaving him feeling a little prickly, but he was content sitting in the cabin of the boat as it ran across the water to town.

When they got back to the dock, it was four o'clock and stars were starting to blink in the lavender sky. Miles and Clive helped put away the tools and headed along the boardwalk toward the Love Nest. Across the inlet, killer whales broke the surface, headed back out to sea. They stood and watched a moment and tried to count the animals. A mile to the north, an unscheduled floatplane was easing down for a landing.

That evening they built a big fire in the community hall and planned to watch Jake's movie. Weasel was still sulking, but he thought that watching a movie might make up for the loss of his capital investment in marijuana.

Jake hadn't seen the final cut of *Stealing Candy.* He'd told himself he wasn't going to see it at all, but when Weasel showed him the tape box with the title of the film in some secretary's handwritten lettering, an icicle of envy ran down his back. He had to see it, after all. Call it pride, vanity, or morbid curiosity, but he wanted to see what they had done with his original story.

Weasel had carried over a big video monitor from the school and propped it on a coffee table; had hooked up the cables, plugged in the machine, and pushed PLAY. The film buffs settled into their chairs; Jake felt nauseated. But as the credits started to roll and the film began, he lost himself in the dream of a man staring at a fire. Images flared and flickered: a blonde woman with red lips holding a revolver close to her face as she walked down a deserted hall with no pictures on the wall, a man in a leather coat crawling through the heating duct of a building. Then there was the blur and rattle of gunfire, the squealing of car tires with fat yellow California sunlight in the background of every exterior shot. Jake watched the movie, felt the images pushing him back further into his head, and he had the sinking feeling that he was watching dated pictures from his old life, a life before Cold Storage, a life of machines and concrete. He might have been watching jerky black-and-white images from a documentary about the French Crimean War.

He got up just as the blonde woman with big lips was putting her pistol in a holster strapped to her upper thigh. He walked out and stood on the porch and watched wet snow slice down to the ground. He could hear the wood stove rumbling and the characters' voices limping through their dialogue; their faces seemed like emissaries from another country, a nation of which Jake had once been a citizen. He didn't want to answer questions about *Stealing Candy.* He wanted to go for a walk, so he curled up his collar and stepped out into the sleet.

But there was a hand on his elbow.

"You wrote that?" asked Lester.

"Well, I wrote something like that. I'd like to tell you it was a lot better in my version . . ." Jake looked at Lester. ". . . but I'd be lying."

"It got made, though." Together they walked back toward the café and the clinic. "You've got a track record."

"I got nothing really. I didn't get a cent. I didn't get a credit."

"So, what you are trying to tell me is you are not really a Hollywood big shot?" Lester's voice was grave.

"No. I am not a big shot. I'm a small-time crook. Actually," he added to save a bit of face, "I'm a medium-size crook."

"That was never really a secret." Lester spoke more seriously to his friend than he ever had before.

"I guess I knew that too," Jake said. "I was just hoping we didn't have to deal with it."

"Well, from what you're telling me, there is nothing to deal with. If we're talking about your reputation, that is." Lester smiled. "It's no big deal. I don't care about any of that. I never did. We got a movie. We play it in our minds. It will be here." Lester tapped on his forehead with his index finger. "And if we finish it, we can watch it anytime we want."

"Great," Jake said, but he sounded like he was stepping into a dentist's office.

The sleet was gradually turning to snow, the grey slashes of ice floating, curling into balls, and rolling down the inlet on the westerly wind. Jake started to shiver.

"You are going to have to go back and talk to those folks." Lester nodded over his shoulder.

"I don't want to." Jake jammed his good hand into his pocket and hunched his shoulders; he'd stretched a wool sock over the end of his sleeve to keep his other hand warm. "Let's talk about our movie. We need an ending."

"He can't die."

"Why not?"

"I'm sick of movies where the Indian dies.

That's just no fucking story at all." Lester was resolved.

"What?" Jake asked. "Indians are immortal? Would it be better if he were white and then he could die?"

"Yes."

"I can't fucking believe this."

"Listen, I just don't want him to die. I don't want him to be some kind of mystic or some kind of wild spiritual guru. He's just as fucked up as anybody else alive in this century. Maybe a little more."

"Now wait a minute." Jake stopped. "You don't want him to be some kind of mystic, but you want him and everybody else to turn into animals in the last scene of the movie. What in the fuck is that about anyway?"

"It would be cool," said Lester.

"Cool," Jake grunted. A young heron flapped through the curtain of snow and landed on the hand railing of the ramp to the dock; it sat and stared at the men walking along the slick boardwalk, rubbed its beak against the metal rail and looked up again as they drew nearer; stood perfectly still for several heartbeats, then unspooled its body back up into the air.

"So what do you want for an ending?"

"I think we've got him set up to become a

martyr. He has done some terrible things in the movie, things that were understandable given the context, things that were heroic from a certain point of view, but hell, he's spent, he's alone, and besides we've got no sequel. Why not just kill him off?"

"Nope." Lester wasn't changing his mind.

Rinds of ice began to build along the toes of Jake's shoes. "So you are going to stick with your animal ending? Everybody simply transforms into wild creatures at the end of the movie?" Jake said, as if pleading.

"Unless you think of a better ending."

They walked in silence for a little ways until they reached the café. Lester decided to go in and have a cup of soup, said he'd meet Jake back at the community center later after the movie was over, and the question-and-answer session began. Jake grimaced.

"I'm going to get a warmer jacket and maybe a hat," he said, and pointed toward Lester's house. "I'll be back over there in a few minutes."

As Jake stepped inside and turned to switch on the light, someone grabbed his bad arm, spun him around, and crushed his face against the wall. His shoulder flared with pain so intense it numbed his face. He saw blue sparkles, as vivid as if someone had smashed him on the skull. Slowly the pain subsided, and he felt the barrel of a gun jutting into the base of his skull.

"Weren't expecting me?" asked a voice behind him. "That's perfect."

CHAPTER EIGHTEEN

Oscar pressed all of his weight into the barrel of the gun. His good leg was planted firmly on the floor. His crippled leg hung between them.

"Hi, Jake," he spat. "You don't look so good. I'm kind of disappointed." And surprisingly, Oscar did feel disappointed. He had been thinking — almost obsessing — about the sweetness of this moment ever since Ann Peel had put the idea into his mind, after she had told him how they had both been hung out to dry by their ungrateful employer who had deserted them. But now here he was in Alaska, the moment had come and Jake looked a little shriveled, an old man with a busted-up arm. Not the object of Oscar's revenge fantasies.

"I got chewed up by that ugly dog you gave to Clive," said Jake as casually as he could, considering his nose was mashed against the wall.

"I see Clive's still around," Oscar grunted. "He looks good. Looks like he's been spending a lot of money. Why didn't you shoot *his* knee off? Or was that something you reserved just for me?" Oscar was painfully aware of sounding whinier than he should have for his big moment.

"Listen," Jake huffed, "if it would make you any happier, I'd be glad to go blow his knee off. Just give me the gun and I'll go take care of it right now." He waved his good hand behind his back.

The old warehouseman tried to get back on script. "You have any hobbies where you use your head, Jake? I mean, it wouldn't inconvenience you too much if I blew out the back of your skull, would it?" Oscar leaned, and Jake could feel his bone twisting under the strain; his vision was beginning to go dim.

"Actually, I'm working on a writing project right now and maybe for a couple more months. I don't have much money left, unless of course we sign a development deal. But I'm sure we can work something out."

"Yeah." Oscar suddenly let go, stepped back. "Like how about giving me back my leg?"

Jake rubbed his shoulder. "That's better," he said, and smiled. "Listen, I know it's a bad deal about your leg. We can work something out."

He was still smiling as Oscar stepped backward, leveled the pistol at Jake's right knee, and fired one round, shattered his kneecap and the underlying musculature. Then Jake was rolling on the floor, holding his knee, and Oscar was pulling back the hammer for another shot.

"Bullshit." Jake started to cry. "Not the other one. I didn't take both."

Oscar watched the blood flowing down Jake's leg. He watched him roll back and forth in pain, watched him painting the floor red with his own blood, and he uncocked the revolver. The truth was he was getting sick to his stomach remembering his own pain, remembering the long months of boredom and surgery.

"Maybe you're right," he said, tucked the gun back into the top of his pants, stepped over him, and strolled out the door.

Miles had not been at the screening of Jake's movie; he'd been wrapping a bandage around Mary Baker's ankle when the boom of the handgun rolled down the boardwalk. Mary hadn't heard the shot; she'd been talking about her sprain. So Miles finished up, lent her a pair of crutches, patted her on the back, and told her to come back in three days; he'd take another look at her ankle then.

Gunshots in the middle of the day weren't that unusual. There were celebratory shots; there were accidental misfires. What troubled Miles was that those shots were usually accompanied by other sounds: the laughing and whooping of celebrations, the loud apologies and urgent walks to the clinic after accidents. This shot was followed by silence.

He put on his coat and went to take a look. A heavyset man with hunched shoulders was limping along the boardwalk. Had he been shot? Was he looking for the clinic? Miles called after him but the stranger didn't respond, and there was no one else to be seen. So he went home, was putting his hand on the knob of his own door, when he heard a streak of curses coming from Lester's house and he ran toward it.

Jake was on the floor. Miles stopped the bleeding and treated him for shock; told him to lie still and ran back to the clinic to grab his medical kit. He didn't ask any questions. He tried to call the state troopers; the phones were dead. He tried the marine radio, but there was no response.

Miles might be able to connect with boats

fishing at the front of the inlet, but the way the weather was now, most of the fleet would be tucked back inside and out of radio range. He'd try again later. First he'd take care of Jake and then maybe look for the gimpy man who'd been running down the boardwalk.

Lester was home when Miles returned with his medical kit. He had Jake's leg elevated and had put a blanket over him. Lester's .30-.30 was leaning against his carving stool.

"You guys have some artistic differences?" Miles bent quickly, lifted the blanket, and started immobilizing Jake's knee and trimming away his pants.

"I wouldn't have shot him in the knee."

"Fuck, this hurts!" Jake kept saying it over and over. "This really, really hurts!"

"Of course it does, buddy," Lester said with more tenderness than Miles had heard in his voice before.

Weasel poked his head through the door to say, "Hey, Jake, it's done. Everybody wants to ask you . . . Whoa, shit!" He came into the house. "What happened to you?" he said in amazement.

"Go get Clive!" Jake's voice was tight. "Tell him Oscar is here, and he wants his dog back."

"He shot you because of that dog?"

"Listen," Miles interrupted, "could you just find Clive and ask him to come down here?"

Weasel kept standing there, blinking as if trying to focus. "I knew we shouldn't have burned all that pot," he said with conviction.

"Jesus Christ," said Lester, "can you go get Clive?"

"Yeah, sure," Weasel mumbled, then added, "Does this mean you won't be talking to the movie group?"

"Go!" All three men shouted at the same time.

The rest of the evening was a blur of crises and crazy rumors. Meanwhile, snow was falling heavily, and there was no hope of getting a plane in. Miles talked to Billy. Would he take his boat out to the head of the inlet and radio the Coast Guard air base in Sitka? Tell them that they had an emergency patient who needed a transfer to the hospital? Tell the dispatcher that the patient was stable and could wait until better weather, that there was no need to risk their life for a patient in Jake's condition? Billy understood. He went to warm the engine of his boat.

Kids peeked in the clinic windows; the

young Lutheran minister came to offer his services, and Jake told him he'd call if he needed the last rites. And down at the bar, at a table in the back, Lester saw Clive talking with a man no one recognized. The stranger was angry, rapping his beer glass down on the table and reaching out to jab Clive in the chest with a finger. Lester heard the words "money" and "bust," or maybe "Goddamn money" and "trust." He couldn't be sure but by the time the vigilante gang was rousted from their temporary headquarters in the café, both Clive and the strange man were no longer in the bar; sadly for the vigilantes, the bar was locked up tight.

The movie club members still wanted to ask Jake questions about *Stealing Candy,* but Miles refused admittance to the clinic. He said Jake was resting, couldn't be disturbed, but by four o'clock that afternoon people started sliding get well cards under the door; most of them had taken the opportunity to slip in questions along with the well wishes. *We hope you get well soon. P.S. Have you ever met Jack Nicholson? Just wondering.*

Jake just nodded, turned to Miles and asked for more painkillers.

Billy returned with news that the Coast

Guard would send a helicopter as soon as the weather cleared, and Bonnie came by in the evening with a basket of food: warm venison pie, coleslaw, baked potatoes. Slowly, the tracks of the day were smoothed away by the white curtain outside the clinic windows; all the wild rumors and frantic activities were erased by the snow. The boats in the harbor turned into frosted vanilla cakes, and everyone's tracks along the boardwalk were vanishing as if the snow could wipe out the past.

Lester came to offer food and stayed to share the meal Bonnie had brought. They sat around listening for Jake and watching the miraculous snow until Lester finally got up and went home, telling them not to wake him unless there was another shooting and the victim was somebody he really liked.

It was after midnight when Bonnie spread out camping pads on the floor of Miles's office. She unfolded some quilts and un-zipped an old felt sleeping bag and spread it out, making a bed wide enough for two people; she took off her shoes and lay down in her clothes.

"I just want to be here with you," she said, and patted the pillow next to her head.

Miles took off his shoes, too. He lay down beside her and she draped her arm across his chest and he smelled the soap on her skin; he cupped her hand in his. He lay there, looked up at the bottom of his desk, and watched the shadows of snowflakes ripple down the walls; everything seemed strange to him from this angle.

He looked at her, and he wanted to love her more than he had ever wanted anything. He looked out the window and saw snow sloughing off the roof. He wanted to love her but wasn't sure exactly how to begin.

He fell asleep, and he dreamed of being out in the inlet. He was in his boat, and he was fishing. Bonnie was swimming behind his boat, and he was panicked that she might accidentally get snagged on his line. He took a hammer and beat on the side of his metal skiff, he was trying to scare her off, but of course he didn't want her to go. He kept hammering and waving, and Bonnie kept swimming closer, each stroke of her legs stronger than the last, her swimming easily able to outpace his boat.

The noise grew louder and louder until it was a banging, and Bonnie was shaking his shoulder and telling him that someone was at the door.

Billy stood outside. He was wearing a T-shirt and a pair of sweatpants; Miles could see his feet sunk down into the fresh snow.

A strange, warm light played on the side of his face.

"The bar is on fire, Miles. I can't find Clive, Nix, or Bonnie." It was four o'clock in the morning.

"Bonnie?" Miles was confused. "Bonnie is here." She stood at his shoulder, and Billy reached out to hug her.

"Good. Good. Good," he said.

Orange light lashed up and down the snowy houses on the boardwalk as Miles pulled on his boots. People were yelling, and a low rumble traveled through the air.

Awake now, Miles barked, "Have you checked Clive's house?"

"Sure. He's not there." Billy's face contorted. "Miles . . ."

"What?"

"The doors to the bar are chained shut from the outside."

CHAPTER NINETEEN

A crew from the cold storage tried to roll
hoses from a hydrant off the main water
line, but all the junctions were frozen.
Moisture in the line had frozen in the
unheated shed, and now they sat like coiled
springs. The hydrant itself was buried in the
snow, and men were running around in
nothing but their long underwear and rain
gear, poking shovels into the snow and trying to locate the main line.

Weasel walked back and forth, wringing
his hands and calling out for Clive. Miles
ran along the boardwalk toward the bar
where great orange flames burst through
the windows and waved frantic arms in the
air.

The heat blossomed out onto the night.
Every surface within fifty feet was either dry
or shedding snow. The faces of bystanders
glowed orange and red as the fire reached
toward them; men in their bathrobes

stepped back as if being scolded; some called suggestions to each other on how to get water to the site; others hugged their children close and told them to stay put; others simply stared, dulled with worry.

Anthony Cera, his finger still in a splint from his wrestling injury that cost him his spot on the championship team, had a coat thrown over his shoulders and was chopping against the front door of the bar with an axe. Flames howled through the broken windows. The two front doors were held shut by a length of shiny chain looped through the handles, and Anthony was chopping against the hinges. Between strokes Miles saw that someone was pushing hard from inside. Little Brother was standing next to Anthony and barking. He'd bark, charge to nip at the flames, retreat and bark some more.

"We can't find Clive or Nix." Lester came up beside Miles. "Someone said they were in the bar, cleaning up."

"What about the other guy? Oscar?"

"I have no idea. Someone said they saw a stranger stealing gas from the gas dock. He was filling up two five-gallon cans. But nobody has seen him since the fire started."

Miles put a scarf around his face and reached for Lester's coat, never taking his eyes off the door. The pounding from the inside had stopped.

"What about the back door on the mountain side?" he asked.

"It's chained shut. It might be easier to break down, but the fire is way worse back there. I'm betting he soaked his way out of the building, set the fire from the back door, and went up the hill in the snow. It won't be hard to find him."

"That can wait," Miles said. "We've got to get in there."

Anthony took a final stroke with the axe, and the fire pushed one side of the door away from the front wall; a smoky hole appeared and Little Brother squatted down; he jumped high into the air, straight through the opening. Lester and Anthony shielded their faces with the forearms and pulled the corner of the door to one side.

The bar was a pyre of burning timbers; a gas tank had exploded inside and broken glass spattered the snow up on the hill. "I don't know, Miles . . ." Lester said, but Miles had disappeared into the burning building.

Fire pumped through cracks in the walls; it seemed that the flames were hysterical to exit the building. Anthony's hair, his coat, and his shirt caught fire. Lester pulled him back to the boardwalk, and his friends led him away. Then Lester ran back and rammed his shoulder against the burning door. From a distance, Billy could see that Lester's hair was burning and flames danced on his jacket. Billy took a step forward, and Lester turned away from the fire.

Lester had years to consider what had made him stop; what made him stand there and call out for help from the edge of the blaze. All he knew at the moment, standing in the fire, was that if he didn't pull his neighbors out he would bear the shame of it for the rest of his life.

And the fire concurred, for before Lester had any chance to reconsider, the floor gave and Mouse Miller's Love Nest collapsed in a shower of sparks, flames, and blackened mats of char-encrusted timbers.

Everyone in town was facing the fire as the building fell. They all put their hands up in front of them as if trying to hold the image upright in the air; if they had been able to turn around and look toward the inlet, they would have seen the light from the fire pushing out into the darkness, lighting the paddling gulls as if they were Christmas toys. The wind was calm, and the snow, which no one noticed now, was falling silently without a ripple into the black water. And if they had strained their eyes they might have seen Oscar getting into Miles's red skiff, starting the engine and moving slowly out into the darkness.

Lester walked back toward the shadowy boardwalk where Bonnie put her arms around his neck. "Thank you for coming back," she said.

"I don't know where Miles went." Lester's tears trickled from ravaged eyes.

"He's in there," Bonnie said softly, holding Lester's head in her hands.

Crews got water flowing that night around the same time Nix showed up on the scene. She'd fallen asleep during Jake's movie and stayed asleep next to the stove in the community center for the entire evening. There were books on the shelves, and when she had woken up around eleven thirty, she lit a candle and started reading *Pilgrim's Progress* until she fell asleep again. What woke her the second time was the sound of the bar collapsing.

The tide was high at the moment it had collapsed, so there had been several feet of water underneath the front, but the back of the building nearest the hillside burned fiercely and a couple of volunteer fire fighters sprayed two feeble streams of water onto the flames. Meanwhile, tired men and women in sooty rain gear climbed under the boardwalk and waded into the frigid water, tried to pull pieces of the blackened wreckage away in their efforts to find the bodies. No one saw any sign of Clive, Miles, or the dog, but they called out their names. As the fire slowly quieted, their voices sounded thin, tired, like the bleating of goats.

Billy was down under the boardwalk when he saw the stainless steel ice machine that had been the cooler for beer bottles. The six-foot-long machine lay upside down, beneath several beams, on a piece of flooring that had broken away. It was rocking back and forth.

He heaved a shoulder against one of the timbers. The heat seared his shirt to flames, and he winced but pushed the beam off. Lester came, and they threw the next timber out into the inlet, and their hands were burned. But they rolled the chest over, and Miles fell out in a slurry of slushy ice cubes, beer, and broken glass.

He choked and Billy and Lester rolled him over, but he was clinging to something raw and red: a man whose clothes had burned away. Miles was holding his brother in his arms.

"Watch it!" someone yelled, and a section of wall plummeted onto the rocks below them; soot and sparks flew up.

"We have to go." Lester and Billy pulled the two brothers out from under the pier. Eight others were running down the beach with two stretchers from the clinic.

The next morning the snow stopped and the weather cleared; smoke drifted from the site of the bar and curled around town like a wandering cat. Trooper Brown and a crime scene team landed at first light, and the pilot flew Miles and Clive to the hospital in Sitka. Jake, whose injury had been forgotten in all the excitement, had accessed Miles's pharmacopoeia; he chomped down on painkillers in the privacy of Lester's home and said nothing. While out-of-town investigators scoured Cold Storage, the white gangster and the Indian artist quietly tended their wounds and stayed away from the police.

Nix had seen Clive before he'd been flown out unconscious. He hadn't looked human; his skin was too tight and blood frothed around the edges of his peeling flesh; burned meat, still breathing. She hadn't watched as they'd carried him away on a stretcher; she stayed in Clive's house and waited for news.

She couldn't read, couldn't concentrate, and there was no one to call so she found one of Annabelle's Peggy Lee records and played it over and over on the old portable record player. One by one, the other members of the band came by and someone made scrambled eggs and someone else made toast, but they left it on the stove too long and Nix started to cry.

Trooper Brown started looking for the stranger who'd purchased gas; he went door to door, asking questions, but he soon lost interest. He'd come to the conclusion that this had been a well-planned drug hit, and the perpetrator was already long gone and frankly, he wasn't concerned about drug people killing each other. "Saves on court costs," he'd told one of the lab technicians.

The real truth was that he didn't have the patience to wade through statements from the people of Cold Storage. He couldn't bear to memorialize the wild, almost mythic accounting of events: love triangles and drugs, mysterious boats waiting offshore to offload teams of assassins, Satanic cults, a dangerous dog who was probably responsible for the whole thing.

Very late in the day, someone discovered Miles's skiff was missing. Billy informed the trooper and a day later Brown requested that a helicopter fly the inlet, but no trace of the skiff was ever found. By the evening of the second day, troopers had secured the scene and an arson team had arrived to finish the investigation.

Smoke washed up and down the boardwalk, and all the houses were covered in a film of soot. People flung open their doors, fed the policemen at any time of the day or night, and drank whiskey from the bottle. They ate more sweets than usual, and their clothes carried the smell of fried food. They let their children stay up as late as they wanted, which wasn't that far from their usual routine, but now they felt good about it. Happy to be alive for one more day. No one had heard if Miles and Clive were going to live.

Bonnie tried to help. She talked to people at the clinic; sorted out the ones who genuinely needed attention from those who didn't; sent the former to the temporary EMT flown in from Sitka and listened to the others talk off their nervous energy; gave them simple chores to do: sweeping the already clean floors, sorting through the waiting room magazines, or checking the paper in the fax machine.

Lester came dressed in his sooty clothes,

his hands wrapped in soft strips torn from someone's thrift store T-shirts, and Bonnie gently said, "You should see somebody about your burns."

"I got it covered. Got some stuff from my auntie. It's just what I need."

"All right," she said, and smiled up at her friend.

"Anybody heard from the hospital?" he asked.

"No . . ." Her voice barely cleared her lungs.

"Let's go to his house. I bet Nix is there. Maybe she's heard something." Lester's voice was beginning to crack, and that concerned her.

"Yes," she said, and stood up slowly. She let her hand rest on his arm for a moment, and he patted it. The adrenaline of the fire fading away into the soot and smoke, they walked out of the clinic. They walked down the boardwalk, past the café and the library, past the trail to the community hall, past the house with the parakeets in the window; they walked past the house with the tea kettle collection in the front yard and past the burning hole that had once been Mouse Miller's Love Nest.

The arson team was in a little shelter they'd made, hooking up flood lamps and kerosene heaters so they could work through the night, photographing and sorting through evidence, trying to piece together the char pattern and the type of accelerant that had been used to feed the fire.

Lester and Bonnie looked over the edge. A charred storage cabinet sat at the tide line; melted records oozed out of blackened jackets; pool balls lodged like Easter eggs in the rocks; the broken neck of a bass guitar lay tangled in its own strings. Ravens were hopping in and out of the ashes, poking their beaks into soot near the blackened freezer. And even though Lester wasn't a drinker and was an outsider in his own land, his chest sank between his shoulders for he missed the bar already.

Ever since he'd been a kid, Lester had hated getting sick to his stomach. He'd choke back the urge to vomit with even the most violent stomach flu; he would gulp air and stand up straight and let the cramps rumble through his body. Now he looked at Bonnie and said nothing.

She rubbed her hands between his shoulder blades. "They will be okay. You did the right thing," she said, and reached over, put her arms around him.

Someone had left a frozen hose, still connected to a faucet, lying in snow that was melting away in the heat radiating from the scorched ground. The hose, thawing, started hissing and leaping like a fish as bits of ice chunked and rumbled down its length; broken cylinders of ice jumped out; clear water washed away; and the old canvas lay flat again.

Lester looked down at the wreckage of the bar. "I hope so," he said, and they made their way to Clive's house.

The members of the band were all there. Rick sat on a chair by the oil stove and played an acoustic guitar; the others drank beer and ate soda crackers they'd found in the cupboards. Nix lay on the couch, and Billy rubbed her feet; her hands were folded under her face like a sleeping child, her eyes red and her pale skin blotchy from crying; she said nothing and noticed no one in the somber crowd of friends.

Bonnie went over and kissed her face; Nix started to cry. Earl gave Lester a beer and clumsily hugged him; Lester tried to give the beer to someone else and wished Rick would stop strumming his guitar. The music sounded thin, like hearing a car horn from the top of a skyscraper.

They perched in their seats as if half expecting to be called away until Earl heard thumping on the porch and went outside.

Lester heard his voice: "Oh my Lord." He was punctuating each word with an extra beat: "Oh . . . My . . . Lord."

Little Brother walked into the kitchen, past Lester and into the living room, dragging his right hind leg behind him. His brindled hide was smeared black, and his paws left smudges of blood on the floor. He smelled like a fire pit full of burning dog carcasses and looked even uglier than he had before.

But Nix sat up, let him up on the couch and onto her lap, rubbed her hands over his head and body, kissed his ears and jowls. Little Brother looked into space with his eyes half shut, savoring every caress.

"Well," said Nix, "there you are."

Clive was being prepared for a charter jet flight to a burn clinic in Seattle and down on the first floor, under the eaves of the emergency entrance, an ambulance sat idling.

Miles walked down the long hall toward the ICU pushing an IV pole. He should have been in a wheelchair; his chest ached from damaged lungs; his hands and legs were scoured by second degree burns. He turned the corner and stood in a doorway, watched his brother's chest rise and fall.

Even though Clive was unconscious, he had a smile on his face and his breathing was steady and strong. Miles wasn't certain, but he could feel the promise of its continued rhythm like the coming of spring and summer.

AND THIS IS HOW THINGS WORKED OUT IN THE MONTHS AND YEARS AFTER

Following the fire, the smoke hung in the air for weeks on end. The future lay behind the membrane of each moment and remained hidden as Miles went on living and sitting by his brother's bed.

A few months after his return to Cold Storage, Miles put a note on his desk for the woman who was temporarily replacing him at the clinic. "Gone salmon fishing. Will monitor radio for emergencies." Perfectly acceptable to anyone who'd spent a winter in Cold Storage, but it kind of irritated the young woman since she was earnest about her duties and wanted to do a good job.

Miles felt old now. He had served his country, he'd served his community, and he was proud. Now he wanted to serve his family. And he wanted to catch a king salmon.

Miles bought a brand-new skiff and motor from a shop in Juneau. The first thing he'd done was read the engine's repair manual. He took the powerhead apart, down to its largest constituent pieces, for the newer engines seemed to be made of several bricks of electronic gear bolted onto a sleek-looking aluminum block; he used every ounce of his intellect to understand this engine; he invested in the best fuel filters and fuel additives; he gapped the plugs himself and checked the automatic oil injector by inspecting the plugs for dark spots. He was determined not to be bullied.

He gathered all his new gear together and walked resolutely to the boat, stowed the gear, went through a quick checklist on the engine, and pushed the electric starter button. The engine sputtered and hummed without entreaty.

He steered his new skiff standing up, holding onto a steering wheel, not like his old skiff where he'd had to sit, reaching back for the tiller arm. A VHF communication radio was mounted on the console, as well as a GPS unit, a depth sounder, and a compass for navigation; he had a separate, small engine that he'd lower once he arrived on the fishing grounds. Miles was better outfitted than he'd ever been on this, his first fishing trip of the new year.

The engine easily pushed the new skiff over the light chop in front of the town, and as he drove down the inlet, he noticed that for the first time in a long time he didn't smell smoke in the air. He pushed the throttle forward; his skiff lifted up onto a gliding plane, and the grey-green water turned silver in his wake and this silver matched the curve and color of the mountains mirrored on the surface of the inlet. Something rose up in Miles's chest. It was as if the speed of the boat pressed against the boundary that confined each moment, and he pushed the throttle forward as if there was a chance he could break through that membrane and into the happiness that must surely lie ahead.

Miles's injuries had healed well enough. He still wore protective gloves and his doctors didn't want him exposing his burns to fish bites, or to gasoline or dirt, or much of anything, but Miles wanted to catch a fish today. All he wanted at this point was to be open to good luck. He would prepare himself for any eventuality and try to be ready for whatever good fortune came. Clive would be weeks more in the burn unit; his good luck would come in smaller and slower increments. With not one feeling of disloyalty to his brother, Miles was ready for some good luck that very day.

He got to the grounds at the opening of

the inlet and set his gear. He put on the brightest herring he could find from the one packet of bait he'd brought along. He threaded the line through the belly and set the hooks perfectly. He attached the leader behind a brand new flasher, snapped the line into the downrigger, and sent the line down to where his depth sounder was showing a ball of feed. His new engine ran perfectly, and he watched his GPS to judge his trolling speed.

The sun sparkled on the water, the distant horizon gleamed robin's egg blue, thin clouds blew like banners to the north, and an easy swell lifted the boat in a rhythm that loped along the seas.

Miles settled into his chair and steered the engine with a foot on the wheel, watched the end of his line.

"Let us cast off the works of darkness," said Miles and laughed at himself for remembering the scripture.

On the end of his downrigger not four feet from where he sat, a raven landed, cocked its head back and forth, watched him carefully.

"And put on the armor of light," he added, nodding to the bird.

"Miles!" said the raven.

Miles's feet turned cold, his hands turned

cold, and he felt like puking. Had it said his name?

"Miles!" said the bird again, poking its head back and forth as if to indicate he should come closer.

He stood up, frightened, startled, and leaned closer to the glittering bird.

"Yes?"

The raven fluttered, jumped into the bait cooler, and grabbed the entire packet of herring. It lumbered into the air and flew down the inlet carrying the small cellophane packet, little silver fish spilling out into the sea.

Miles watched the fat black bird fly to the southern shore, drop the packet on the beach and land on top of it with a kind of open-winged victory jig; he watched it eat the remaining silvery fish; listened to it laugh; began to be angry but then started to laugh, too, at the absurdity of it all. And he cried.

He cried as if something in his chest had broken. His nose ran, his eyes were blinded, and he cried as if he'd become unfrozen, great heaving sobs so powerful he felt like everything inside was going to spill out of him into the water and into the air.

When he slowly hiccuped to a stop, he was light-headed. He looked back at the distant beach; the raven was gone. He looked toward Cold Storage; a great cloud of birds circled the town. He thought he saw large, brown, four-legged forms walking on the beach, and he thought he saw two deer walking into the fringe of the beach. And he thought that it might be possible that everyone in the village, maybe everyone in the world, had turned into animals.

He reached for his radio to call someone, to hear the comfort of a human voice, but just then the tip of his fishing rod jerked down and line screamed off the reel. Twenty yards behind the skiff, a massive salmon rose from the water, shaking itself against the hooks set deeply into its jaw.

Of course the world changed, and the past both was and remains a hallucination that intrudes into our day-to-day life. Buildings fall and rise again, elections are won and lost, armies parade into the field and then find their way home. In Cold Storage, Alaska, stories came into currency concerning the whereabouts — or even the existence of — the person who had shot Jake in the leg and burned down the bar. The safe money said it was the man with the limp who had flown into town that same afternoon. There were some who speculated that

Ed had torched the bar in revenge for Clive sleeping with Nix, although this rumor never gained much purchase; for one thing Ed both denied it and had an alibi, and for another he didn't fit the gossip machine's requirements for an arsonist. Ed was too pale a personality to be a firebug.

Of course the man with the limp had disappeared, and most people speculated that he had taken the skiff on the outside coast in a snow squall, dumped it over, and died in the frigid waters. This story had a ring of poetic justice to it, but early that next spring a doctor from Juneau opened up his fishing cabin on the coast and found that it had been broken into sometime during the winter; all of his emergency food was gone, and Miles's old cranky skiff was hauled up into the trees near the beach fringe where it appeared someone had put a bullet through the engine's power head. The doctor also reported that the kayak he kept stored at the cabin was missing.

Jake finally went in to the hospital in Sitka for surgery on his leg. Each day when he woke up he thought it would be the day a police officer with a warrant from Seattle would come take him into custody, but it didn't happen. Miss Peel called from her rented house in Arizona. She was sounding a little sheepish and did not tell Jake how she got the hospital's number or knew how he was there but *asked* if Jake had gotten the news about the IPO that the kid in Seattle and a couple of his friends had gone ahead and held. He had never taken Jake off the corporate papers and now, instead of owning stock in a company that never produced anything, he owned fifteen million dollars' worth of stock in a company that never really produced anything. Miss Peel giggled when she told him this, and all Jake could do was shake his head and wonder at the strangeness of it all.

Miss Peel had stood up to the DA in Seattle, had gotten out of the grand jury proceedings without perjuring herself or snitching off Jake. As a result, the grand jury "no true billed" the proposed indictment against him, so that there would be no federal charges coming. When she asked so sweetly for the numbers to take care of the IPO account transfer money, of course Jake gave it to her, and when Jake asked if she had heard anything from Oscar, she answered in a very sing-song voice that she had and that he was safe and sound after his trip to Cold Storage this winter and that in fact he was renting a house right there in Sitka. This was the moment that Jake Shoemaker realized that he was not an independent business man but just the beard for Miss Peel's own business dealings. He had been working for her unwittingly all along.

He put down the phone, shivered once, then smiled broadly.

It was in this atmosphere of the miraculous that Lester wheeled Jake out of the hospital and into a cab for the airport where they picked up their tickets and flew to Seattle to meet the glorious Miss Peel and start discussing how to liquidate all of Jake's business holdings.

After he got his money together, Jake gave Miss Peel five hundred thousand dollars in cash and three quarters of all of his investment assets, and he moved to California. He and Lester spent a month at the ranch in the Santa Barbara hills where they finished the final draft of their script, and Jake made appointments to pitch the project to several studios. Jake never spoke to the police about Oscar, figuring that at best they were even and at worst, it would piss Oscar off; even so, Jake kept a nine millimeter under the seat of his car and in the drawer beside his bed in case Oscar ever wanted to come by for another chat.

Jake's injuries from his season in Alaska continued to nag him for the rest of his life.

He would never throw a ball overhand and would always have a hard time swimming the crawl, which hurt his vanity more than having to carry a silver-tipped cane wherever he went. The cane became his trademark, made a nice stylish statement, but not being able to swim in the ranch's marble-lined infinity pool out on the bluff made him feel old.

Lester enjoyed Hollywood but came home by early summer saying that, while he liked the restaurants, he couldn't take the traffic. He came back just in time to help with the rebuilding that had started on the site of the old bar.

Clive spent months living near the burn center in Seattle. The troopers made noise about charging him with something, but Miss Peel's lawyers helped dissuade them. And sitting on a bench outside of a court-room in Seattle one uncomfortable day, Clive came up with a new plan for the Love Nest.

Nix's parents flew to Cold Storage, pre-sumably to bring their daughter home, but ended up staying the spring and summer. Once they arrived, Nix began going by her given name, and after that she was called Maya by newcomers to the village. Miles went back and forth with the names, but

Bonnie always called her Nix.

Nix's parents gave her the money they'd saved against the day she'd want a formal wedding. That money combined with the fire insurance Clive had purchased became the working capital for the new building. Nix, Bonnie, and Miles all became partners in Clive's property. They built a new business: a bakery, a coffee shop, a bar with a dance floor, and up on the hillside a fifty-seat theater that had a small stage, a twenty by thirty screen, and a real sloping floor with theater seats. The new place was called "Little Brother's," and the ugly dog presided over every aspect of its financing and construction. The older citizens worried and fussed that it spelled the end of the town and the final acceptance of decadent urban life, but this was to be expected. Once the joint opened, people defended it or complained, but gradually it worked its way into the story of a town that kept bumping along from one tragedy to the next.

Clive oversaw the project like a family patriarch. His skin was too painful for him to move quickly, too prone to infection to get dirty. He sat with a broad brimmed hat, drinking lemonade and gin with Weasel as others swung hammers. On the first day of framing up the walls, he hung a sign on the center beam. It was hand painted on rough plywood and read:

How can I curse whom God has not
  cursed?
How can I denounce whom the Lord has
  not denounced?
For from the top of the crags I see him,
From the hills I behold him;
Behold a people dwelling alone,
And not counting itself among the nations.

The framers didn't know why it was there, but they didn't mind. They liked the parts about the mountains.

Bonnie took to the construction with a vigor people had not seen in Cold Storage since the long-dead founders cribbed together the first storefront. She loved shoveling debris and setting pilings in that blackened spot on the boardwalk; she loved the wild country that came in and out of focus from the building site. When she wore her tool belt and worked framing in a wall, she knew exactly where she was and what she was doing. She loved measuring and making a clean cut; she loved setting up the wall and feeling the future of that interior space; and she loved to look through the studs to see the wind lifting snow off the mountains. Fashioning a new building on the site of the fire felt as good as saving lives.

It took three years for the partnership to complete the project, but the inaugural party was well worth any wait, for the first event was the premiere of *Circling the Wagons.* The movie became the hot center of gossip in the film industry for years to come, particularly because of its controversial ending.

Robbie Robertson had done the music, and he was there. Sherman Alexie was listed as a producer, and he came to the party. Harvey Keitel, even though he wasn't in the cast, had been invited, and everyone expected him to come solely on the strength of Weasel's five-page invitation. On the weekend of the party, Weasel met almost every plane that came to the dock and smiled at everyone who wandered up the boardwalk, but he finally had to make do with Gary Farmer, who was the star of the film, and Clint Eastwood, who was the executive producer along with Miss Peel. Jake had an associate producer and screenwriter credit and a berth on Eastwood's yacht. Clint had sailed his own boat from over the horizon to the docks of Cold Storage, Alaska, and had impressed the locals by helping his crew tie off the docking lines while keeping a cold beer in his pocket.

Members of the international press stayed in the newly refurbished cold storage bunkhouse. Mrs. Cera served smoked black cod collars at the pre-screening reception, and that season, smoked black cod started turning up in many of the more expensive restaurants in Los Angeles. Blind Donkey played at the post-screening party, and Robbie Robertson came on stage and did a set that ended in a terrific version of "Love Is the Answer, But What Was the Question?" Weasel became so drunk that he missed the set; he complained about it for years to come.

Jake appeared wearing a Spanish designer's suit that looked like it was made from a kind of weather balloon, but he was laughing, joking, calling everyone by their first names, and generally acting more local than any of the locals.

Lester wore his regular work clothes, held his own open house for his friends and family back at the studio, and refused to take a back seat at any of the proceedings. He'd been getting out more in the last few years, had spent time in Hoonah with his aunties and nephews, had fished with them, and gathered herring eggs in Sitka to take to them in spring. He was no longer a student of other people.

At the opening of his movie, Lester strolled through the crowd like the host of the evening. He kept mixing up the seating so that his friends and family could be together, and he would not be shunted to one side. He teased Jake every chance he got but let his collaborator enjoy the Hollywood spotlight and later admitted that he'd enjoyed the evening more than he'd expected. For several seasons, his jewelry became one of the required accessories for both men and women in Hollywood, but Lester never wrote another film script.

Bonnie, Miles, and Nix served the food and, together with Clive, tended the bar. Ed and Tina watched Miles and Bonnie's little girl, who was almost the same age as their son. Ed would come to the party and then go back and stay with the kids, while Tina came and listened to the music and to the celebrities. Neither of them watched the movie. They were afraid to spoil their hopes for it, but later when they were alone together, they watched it in the new little theater; they laughed and clapped until their hands were sore.

While the party raged on, Miles continued to serve food. As he came out of the kitchen with a plate of black cod, he watched his brother Clive gingerly holding an LP between the palms of his hands, a smile dazzling out from his broken face. He'd been turned inside out by the fire and spoke very little now; but he still had the soul of a great liar, a trickster, which reassured Miles. Clive turned toward him and the brothers looked at each other for perhaps one beat longer than usual, and in that one second acknowledged all of their good luck. And then Miles turned and quietly offered a black cod collar to Mr. Alexie, who was joking with Lester and Chris Eyre, the director; he smiled at all of them and offered the fish all around.

Clive motioned to the door, and the big dog hobbled into the room and with a surprising show of strength jumped up onto the bar. Clive cleared his throat, and the guests settled down. He thanked Lester and thanked Jake, who he called the "Angel of Cold Storage, Alaska," then he thanked all the assembled luminaries. He paused and turned to Little Brother and asked him to say a few words. The crowd tittered, expecting a parlor trick. A pretty woman in a silk skirt and dull gold jewelry laughed aloud and asked for another drink. None of the locals smiled but leaned forward. As some people shuffled their feet and waited for something to break the tension, Clive just looked at the battered dog, expectant — and, as always, patient.

AUTHOR'S NOTE

Cold Storage, Alaska was the first book in the Cold Storage series. That it is the second one to be published (after *The Big Both Ways*) is an accident. *Cold Storage* was written as a tribute to one of my favorite genres: the screwball comedy. I'm drawn to comedy because it reminds me that all chaos does not resolve in tragedy, but sometimes chaos produces delightful connection. I also believe this is what both the Bible and Dharma teach as a possibility. I have long recognized that I am an oddball in the crime writing world in that I do not recognize revenge as the lifeblood of a great plot. Instead, after almost thirty years as a criminal investigator as well as a writer, I still believe that love and compassion are what move through the hearts of *all* characters.

I am deeply indebted to a wonderful reader, Sophie Rosen, from Abbotsford, British Columbia, who gave me intelligent feedback and insight into this story early on. Also to my editor, Juliet Grames, from New York, New York, who showed courage and patience by taking me back into the fold. My heartfelt appreciation and thanks go to both women.

ABOUT THE AUTHOR

John Straley, a criminal investigator for the state of Alaska, lives in Sitka with his son and wife, a marine biologist who studies whales. He is the Shamus Award–winning author of *The Woman Who Married a Bear, The Curious Eat Themselves,* and *The Big Both Ways.* In 2006, he was appointed the Writer Laureate of Alaska.